THE SOUTH BEND DART FROG MURDERS

D1713333

ROBERT CANTER

outskirts
press

Woe is me, I am doomed! For I am a man of unclean lips, living among a people of unclean lips; yet my eyes have seen the King, the Lord of hosts! -Isaiah 6:5

Catholici sunt fideles unius veri Dei sectatores. Non habemus locum in mundo superborum peccatorum. In exilium acti, in oratione miraculi expectantes, cito perimus.

Libera nos Domine.

There's a lover in the story
But the story's still the same
There's a lullaby for suffering
And a paradox to blame
But it's written in the scriptures
And it's not some idle claim
You want it darker
We kill the flame.
They're lining up the prisoners
And the guards are taking aim
I struggled with some demons
They were middle class and tame
I didn't know I had permission
To murder and to maim.

-Leonard Cohen

As Catholics, we are called to imitate Christ.

Being a follower of Christ means telling people things they don't want to hear.

Christ did not care who he was offending when he stood before the Sanhedrin and said, "I AM."

There once was a blind knave,
Who stumbled into a bear cave.
He could not see the bear,
But that did not mean it wasn't there,
Or that it couldn't send him to his grave.

I have endeavored in this ghastly little book to open people's eyes to the existence of the evil that thrives in this period of history that I have come to call *The Twilight of the Church*. I'm sad to say that in this dark age of moral relativism and moral insanity, too many people would rather turn a blind eye to evil and pretend it isn't there. Some people deny the existence of evil altogether. Others simply acknowledge evil and choose to tolerate it. But neither of these courses gets rid of the evil. It only festers, grows, and takes deep root.

Evil cannot be tolerated or ignored; it must be destroyed.

WHAT DOES IT MEAN TO BE A CATHOLIC?

Christ came into this world with only one message.
That message was not, morality is relative and not objective.
That message was not, I abolish the law.
That message was not, the law doesn't need to be followed
if it's inconvenient for you.
That message was not,
men and women are free to live as they please.
That message was not, rationalize and justify your sins.
That message was not, enable, encourage,
and give license to the sinner.
That message was not, actions don't have consequences.
That message was not, men and women's actions
are justified by their feelings.
That message was not, all points of view are equally valid.
That message was not, everyone gets a free pass into heaven regard-
less of what they choose to believe and how they choose to live.

Christ's message was, "Repent and believe."

CONCERNING SOUTH BEND

South Bend, Indiana, is famous for the University of Notre Dame
and the defunct Studebaker company.
If you're not a sports fan, there isn't much to do.
You wouldn't expect South Bend to be the kind of place
with a serial killer on the loose.
But as the Bible and Agatha Christie so eloquently put it,
there is evil everywhere under the sun.

CONCERNING MURDER

God inscribed in the Ten Commandments, "Thou shall not kill."

The Catechism of the Catholic Church describes murder as one of the four sins that cries out to heaven for vengeance.

In the Book of Genesis, original sin entered the world when Adam and Eve disobeyed God. In the story of Cain and Abel, we see sin progress from simple disobedience to deliberate murder. God condemns Cain to wander the Earth, saying that all his toils will come to nothing. He also brands Cain, saying that anyone who kills him will receive vengeance sevenfold. God does this not to protect Cain, but to ensure his suffering.

Every once in a while, we hear about some gruesome or senseless loss of life and wonder why and how someone could do such a thing. While motives for taking another person's life may vary, the ugly truth is that anyone is capable. Evil is like billiard balls; all it takes is a little push.

CHAPTER 1

Eighteen-year-old Thomas "Tom" Lime stood staring at himself in the mirror. He had gone to bed early and had gotten up early to get ready for his first day as a senior at Saint Thomas More High School, and now he was thoroughly scrutinizing the final product. There wasn't anything particularly special about his short brown hair, apart from the fact that it had been cut recently. Thankfully, there wasn't a trace of acne anywhere on him, he had spent the weeks leading up to today carefully avoiding anything that might cause a breakout. His usually white skin had a healthy tan about it, and it looked like he had gotten his money's worth from the teeth whitening mouthwash he had been using all summer.

Tom was dressed in his best casual clothes. Despite his surname, there wasn't a single trace of green on him. He was wearing a thin light blue shirt with tan pants and brown shoes. He would've preferred to wear something red or black, because his research on the internet told him that's what the situation called for, but his mother had insisted. He was also wearing some tropical cologne, which immediately made him feel like he was at the beach. The only piece of jewelry he wore was a golden Miraculous Medal that was around his neck. It had been given to him by his grandmother, and he was told that those who wore it would be showered with graces. Tom prayed that the Blessed Mother was smiling on him today.

For Tom, today wasn't just the first day of his last year at Saint Thomas More High School. Over the summer, he had resolved that he would finally ask Kiania Martins on a date. Tom had never had a serious relationship with a girl in his life, but when he first laid eyes on Kiania during freshman year, he knew then and there that this was the girl he wanted to take to senior prom. Unfortunately, he had never once worked up the courage to speak to her in the past three years, and with good reason. Kiania was one of the core members of the girl's swimming team. She was also one of the most beautiful girls on campus, but if you had asked Tom, he would've told you there was no contest. Despite her position in the school's social hierarchy, Kiania had a reputation for being an ice queen, having rejected the advances of some of the most well-known boys in school, including the current football team captain and big man on campus, Fred Smith. As a result, Kiania had been nicknamed the "Icy Mermaid."

Tom had spent the whole summer preparing for today. He had been working out, toning his muscles, getting a healthy tan, and buying new clothes, but it didn't change the fact that he was little more than the eldest child of two bakers. Granted, *Crazy Caroline's Cakes and Confectionaries* was regarded as the best bakery in South Bend and maybe the entire state of Indiana. However, Tom had still passed through his high school years largely unnoticed by the higher-ranking members of the school's social hierarchy. Tom didn't have any particular reason to believe he would fare any better than any of the other boys that had asked Kiania on a date. But he knew that if he didn't at least try, he'd regret it for the rest of his life.

After convincing himself that there was nothing more to be done about his appearance, Tom finally went downstairs, where his mother, Crazy Caroline, had his favorite breakfast waiting for him. Tom dove right into the bacon, sausage, and cheese omelet, and pretended to listen to his mother go on about how she couldn't believe her baby boy was already a senior in high school. When breakfast was done, his father pulled him aside.

"You look like total girl bait, Son. Take it from me, you've just got to go out there and do it. All you need is a little confidence, and I have just the thing for that."

Tom's father took him into the trophy room, where he kept all his keepsakes from his days as a college basketball star. This was also where Tom's father kept his most prized possession, a basketball that had been signed by the entire Chicago Bulls 1991 team, the year of Michael Jordan's first NBA championship.

"You're going to let me touch the ball?" asked Tom.

"With a glove on."

The basketball was in an airtight display case. Tom's father never let anyone touch it. He must've somehow known that asking this girl out was REALLY important to him. Tom pulled on a latex glove and very gently pressed his right hand against the ball. It was probably just his imagination, but he felt like he had been struck by a bolt of lightning.

"Feeling the power?" asked his dad.

"Oh yeah, I can feel it."

"Excellent, now go get her."

Tom wanted to get going before his younger sisters, Jennifer and Britney, woke up and told him he was doomed. He grabbed his backpack, allowed his mother to take her obligatory pictures, leapt into his used black sedan, and was off. The whole time he was driving, he cycled through his favorite motivational songs.

Nothing but positive vibes, nothing but positive vibes.

Tom didn't have any trouble talking to women, not as long as he wasn't romantically interested in them. But whenever he was attracted to the girl he was trying to speak to, he had all the wit, charm, and grace of an inebriated dinosaur after a lobotomy.

I've just got to smile, walk up to her, and ask her if she'd be interested in seeing a movie with me.

Tom already had the digital tickets on his phone. He may have gotten the proverbial cart before the horse, but the movie would've been sold out if he hadn't gotten the tickets early. If successful, he would be taking Kiania to see the highly anticipated blockbuster, *Sherlock Holmes vs. Jack the Ripper*. Now, maybe this wasn't an ideal movie for a first date, but the only other movie out right now was a romantic comedy about a man that had a midlife crisis before he had a first date. Tom's research told him that romantic comedies weren't Kiania's cup of tea. Kiania seemed to enjoy the mystery stories that they had to read in school, so the blockbuster thriller seemed the obvious choice when buying the tickets. But Tom still needed to ask the girl out. Eventually, he arrived at school and felt a quick rush of pride as he parked in a vacant space in the senior lot. He waited until the song he was currently listening to was over before he stopped the engine.

I can do this. What's the worst that could happen?

Tom had a sudden recollection of what happened last year when Mark Xeg asked Juno Simpson on a date. While Tom had his eyes on Kiania, most other men on campus would say that Juno Simpson was the girl they wanted to be with, and not just because of Kiania's reputation as an ice queen. Juno was the queen bee on campus and captain of the cheerleaders. Her father was the current mayor of South Bend, and she was a blonde bombshell that loved to flaunt it. Mark Xeg, on the other hand, was the president of the school's gaming club. Mark was one of the favorites to be class valedictorian; he was also a tall scarecrow of a man with glasses and messy red hair that looked like a used wad of steel wool. But last year, Mark led the gaming club to victory in the national tournament for the hit sci-fi action MMORPG, *Star Warrior*. Mark had thought that winning a substantial amount of prize money and earning celebrity status in the gaming community would've been enough to impress Juno. Tom had no idea what Juno said to Mark when he asked her out, but she didn't just reject him; she must've blown him out of the sky with a tactical nuke. Mark had looked like a sad, sick, and dying animal for the rest of the semester. It made Tom think of all the boys Kiania had rejected.

Your father just let you touch the basketball; you have to try.

Tom touched his Miraculous Medal, said a quick Hail Mary, and went inside.

The seniors were all assembling in the gym for their class photo. Tom didn't see Kiania anywhere, so he took an open seat in the bleachers that wasn't too close to the front or too far in the back. He was presently joined by his friends Rick Stuart and Samantha Brandy.

Rick was another member of the gaming club. He wasn't unattractive, but was the kind of person who spent too much time trying to make himself appear more attractive than he really was, as evidenced by the amount of gel in his blonde hair. After the gaming club won the national *Star Warrior* tournament, he really let it go to his head. He was wearing blue jeans, tacky sunglasses, and a t-shirt with his gamertag and avatar displayed on it.

Samantha was a member of the women's basketball team and something of a gossip in certain circles of the social hierarchy. Even with her wavy long golden-brown hair, she couldn't hold a candle to some of the other girls on campus; but no one would dare say it to her face.

"Hey, buddy!" said Rick. "We've made it! We're all senior Paladins now! And they said I wouldn't make it past freshman year!"

"I'm sure it will be a very eventful year for all of us," said Tom.

Samantha studied Tom's appearance for a moment before speaking.

"Who is she?"

Tom never had any trouble talking to Samantha, but he hadn't told his friends that he was planning to ask Kiania Martins on a date. If he had, it would be all over the school by now, and he didn't want that.

"I don't know what you mean."

"Boys like you only groom themselves to the degree you have for one reason," said Samantha. "I want to know her name."

Tom didn't know what to say, so he pretended not to have heard Samantha. It didn't work.

"Old Tommy's planning to put the moves on someone?" asked Rick. "Tell me it isn't Juno Simpson."

"I wouldn't dream of it."

Tom didn't want this conversation to go any further. Fortunately, he was saved by some less than savory hoots and whistles from some of the other boys in the bleachers.

"Speak of the devil," said Samantha.

Juno Simpson walked gracefully into the room looking like she owned the place. She tossed her majestic long golden hair, which was the envy of nearly every girl in school. Then there was her trademark cat-like smile. She was like a beautiful lioness ready to pounce. Once in front of the bleachers, she stood to face the class, and then leapt up and span in the air like an Olympic figure skater.

"Go Paladins!" she cheered.

"Go Paladins!" returned the rest of the class.

Juno gave a big hug to her best friend and fellow blonde bombshell, Kareen Fabbrie, the captain of the girl's swimming team. When Juno took her seat at the front of the bleachers on the left side with the other cheerleaders, Tom looked around for Mark Xeg. He found him sitting isolated at the top of the bleachers. It had been months since Juno rejected him, but he still looked like someone he knew had just died.

"He's still not over it?" asked Tom.

"He doesn't talk about it," said Rick. "It's really affected his performance in *Star Warrior*. Most days he doesn't even log in. When he does, you wouldn't know he led us to victory in the national tournament."

"Having a girl tell you that you're a hideous waste of oxygen that she wouldn't be seen dead with in a plague pit will do that," said Samantha. "She even dumped a specimen like Isaiah James, what chance did a lanky gamer like Mark have?"

Isaiah James was the football team's running back. He had competed fiercely with Fred Smith for the position of team captain, but had come up short. At that moment, Fred, Isaiah, and all the other members of the football team came into the gym and were greeted like rock stars.

"Let's go Paladins! All the way to state!"

As Fred and the other football players basked in their glory, Tom wondered how they all got so ripped. He had been working out all summer, preparing for today, and hadn't come close to looking like them. Not that it would've helped. At one point or another, Kiania had turned down just about everyone on the football team.

After bringing up the incident where Juno had dumped Isaiah, Rick asked Samantha for the full details of the resulting drama. Tom wasn't listening, because Kiania had entered the gym at that moment. Tom immediately felt both his temperature and his heart rate skyrocket.

I don't believe it. Did she get even more beautiful over the summer?

Kiania had a flawless diamond-shaped face that made her look like a princess. She didn't use much makeup, but Tom didn't think she needed it. The natural beauty of her tan skin was one of the reasons he found her so attractive. The other thing that made her so irresistible was her waist-length raven hair, which was decorated with light blue stripes. She always wore it down. As she took her place on the bleachers with the rest of the girl's swimming team, Tom tried his best not to look at her so it wouldn't tip off Samantha. But now that Tom could actually see her, the confidence he had spent his summer vacation building up was starting to evaporate.

You must be joking; she's going to laugh in your face!

She could say yes, stranger things have happened.

She's rejected the best-looking boys on campus, men that play sports and earn college scholarships. You're a nobody that wants to write comic books. She'll never go to the movies with someone like you.

I don't know that until I try!

After the class picture was taken, Casey Rosewood, a petite girl with glasses and two braided pigtails, revealed that she had made cookies for the whole class. Casey was a hopeless romantic and far from being the best-looking girl in school, but her cooking skills had earned her a certain degree of popularity. Several students had started to swarm over the cookies, but Casey exclaimed that she had only made one for every senior. It was Isaiah that came to the rescue.

"You heard the lady," he said making his deep voice audible for the entire gymnasium. "Everybody gets one!"

Tom and all the other seniors went to their assigned lockers before heading to their first classes. If Tom and Kiania didn't happen to be in the same class at any point during the day, then his plan was to approach her either during lunch or before she left for home. He probably wouldn't have time to intercept her between classes. When Tom's lunch finally came, he was disappointed to find out that Kiania went to lunch at a different period.

That's probably for the best. She would have likely been sitting with her friends from the swim team.

During his next class, Tom got permission to use the bathroom, but instead went upstairs. Saint Thomas More High School was a Catholic school, so naturally, there was a small chapel on the second floor. Students could go there to pray, and the school's resident priest would hear confessions on certain days. Tom went in and knelt before the altar.

"God, please let me have just one date with this girl. It means a lot to me. I'm not asking for the moon."

The day was almost over when Tom made his way to his obligatory religious class for the semester. The school offered a special Church History class that highlighted the various persecutions the Catholic Church had endured over the past two thousand years and how they pertained to the persecutions it faced in the modern world. The class was being taught by Sister Joan, a nun who, despite being a rigid disciplinarian, was very pleasant to be around outside the classroom, but God help you if you pushed the wrong buttons. When Tom entered the room, he saw that Kiania was in the front row.

Why did it have to be in Sister Joan's class? Never mind, just make yourself appealing and don't stare!

Tom did his best to smile casually, but Kiania's attention was fixed on the open book in front of her. Tom took the vacant desk on Kiania's right. Sister Joan and everyone else would be able to see him plainly throughout the entire period, but he would just have to work with it. Kiania wouldn't notice him if he took a seat in the back. When the bell finally sounded for the period to start, Sister Joan entered the room and immediately commanded everyone's undivided attention.

"Let me make one thing perfectly clear. I don't care if you are seniors; the days of Batty Bergoglio are a thing of the past," said Sister Joan, speaking in her rich French accent. "I will not tolerate evil in any way, shape, or form in my class. If I catch you messing around on your phones, you get the yardstick! If I catch you sticking gum under your desk, you get the yardstick! If you fall asleep in my class, you get the yardstick! If I catch you cheating, you go to hell! Do I make myself clear?"

The entire class responded with a resounding affirmative.

She could give lessons to Coach Matthews, and he used to be in the Marines.

Being in such close proximity to Kiania made Tom's heart race, but he knew he needed to display confidence and somehow attract her attention.

Confidence?! She's turned down all the best-looking boys in school, and I'm just some nobody!

Tom stole a quick look at Kiania out of the corner of his eye. He almost wished she wasn't so gorgeous. Whenever he saw that beautiful black and blue hair and that angelic face, his brain turned into jelly. He never had this problem when he talked to girls like Samantha. When the opportunity presented itself for Tom to steal another look at Kiania, he suddenly realized that he forgot what he was going to say to her when the time came.

Calm down! Calm down! You've just got to smile, walk up to her, and start with a simple hello. But how should I say it? What did grandma always say? Just smile and ask her name, but I already know her name! Does she know I exist? Should I introduce myself?

Tom's train of thought was interrupted by the sound of a yard stick smacking down on his desk.

"Mr. Lime!"

Tom was immediately aware that all the eyes in the room were upon him, including Kiania's.

CRAP! CRAP! CRAP!

"Would you mind explaining the heresy of adoptionism to us?

Fortunately, Tom had been going to Catholic schools since pre-school, so he knew the answer.

"Adoptionism falsely claims that Christ was born a mortal man and that later in his life he was figuratively adopted as the Son of God," he said calmly.

"And how is heresy relevant today?"

"The Catholic Church cannot effectively deal with outside threats to our beliefs, values, and our continued existence when we're too busy fighting among ourselves. It doesn't matter what opinions some people have, there is only one true path."

"That is correct," said Sister Joan.

Tom breathed a sigh of relief. As soon as it was safe, he looked in Kiania's direction, and felt his face turn pink. She was looking right at him.

Oh crap! Smile, you dumb-dumb!

Tom forced himself to smile and make eye contact, praying that his smile didn't look goofy.

My god, her eyes are like two pools of chocolate syrup.

Tom's brain was melting, but he knew he had to do something. He mouthed hello, and Kiania returned the gesture.

SHE ACKNOWLEDGED ME!!!

Tom couldn't remember if he was supposed to break eye contact first or not, but was saved by Sister Joan, who brought her yard stick down on another student who attempted to pass a note along. When the bell finally rang, signaling the end of the period, Tom knew it was now or never.

Tom had been practicing martial arts since he was in grade school. He knew how to tackle armed opponents, even if he never had to put that knowledge into practice. From the way his heart was beating, he felt like he was facing a dozen men armed with assault rifles. At least in this situation there might be a happy outcome, but Tom couldn't see it.

She smiled at me! That mean's she's interested.

No, she didn't. You're just imagining things!

Tom battled with his thoughts for a moment, but as he clasped the Miraculous Medal around his neck, something his father had once said when he received the sacrament of Confession for the first time came to him.

"Fear is a survival instinct that helps you stay alive. Fear of God is also the first step toward wisdom. Just don't let it make you a coward. God hates a coward."

Tom stuck a breath mint in his mouth and beelined for Kiania's locker. If she rejected him, he would just have to live with it.

As Tom approached Kiania's locker, he waited for her to turn around and see him coming and establish eye contact. His research told him that his chances would be a lot worse if Kiania thought he snuck up on her. Of course, the moment his eyes met hers, his courage started evaporating again.

"Excuse me, Kiania," he managed to say.

"Yes, what is it, Tom?"

SHE KNOWS MY NAME!!!

You've gone to the same school as her for the past three years. She probably picked up on it.

Kiania had referred to Tom by name. Her expression wasn't hostile either. If anything, she seemed amused. Both were good signs. Accounts of other students dictated that if Kiania had taken offense to Tom, she would've responded by speaking in Portuguese and would've pretended not to understand English. Unfortunately, as a result of being this close to Kiania and actually speaking with her, Tom's brain stopped working again.

What's wrong with you?! Don't stare! Say something!

"You probably hear this a lot, but you have very beautiful hair."

"Thank you,"

What did I just say? CRAP! CRAP! CRAP!

Tom told Kiania to wait, but she never made any indication that she was leaving.

"Was there something you wanted to ask me?"

Tom took a deep breath.

"I know you don't know me very well, but we've been going to the same school for years now. Would you be interested in going to the movies with me on Friday?"

By this point, Tom and Kiania had attracted the undivided attention of over half the people in the hall, but Tom wasn't paying attention to them. Kiania's face still didn't display any signs of hostility.

"Which movie?"

For the second time that day, Tom felt like he had just been struck by a bolt of lightning.

"Well, word around the school is that you don't like romantic comedies."

"*Sherlock Holmes vs. Jack the Ripper* it is then."

"Is that a yes?" asked Tom.

A very small smile formed on Kiania's amused face.

"Thomas Lime, I'd be happy to accompany you to the movies on Friday."

Kiania ripped a small piece of paper out of her notebook, wrote something on it, and handed it to Tom.

"There's my number. We can work out the details when we don't have class. And in response to your previous statement, I know you're the son of the owners of *Crazy Caroline's Cakes and Confectionaries*, an aspiring comic book writer, and something of a martial artist in your spare time, as well as an amateur gamer. Most importantly, you seem to be a man who takes his Catholic faith very seriously. You may call me at about eight o'clock. Until then, tchau."

After Kiania disappeared down the hall, Tom stood where he was, completely stunned. Several bystanders also stood there with their mouths wide open.

"Did that really just happen?"

Very slowly, Tom's brain processed everything. He wasn't sure how Kiania knew half the things she said she knew about him, but he didn't care.

"I HAVE A DATE!!!"

Tom started leaping down the hall to his next class. He was so euphoric that he wasn't paying attention to his surroundings. As he turned the corner, he collided with one of his fellow students and hit the ground with a resounding crash. Once his head stopped spinning, Tom realized there was someone dressed head to toe in black standing over him. Tom had crashed into Kalin Doyle, son of

Saint Joseph County Sheriff Sam Doyle, president of the literature club and school goth. Though not involved in any of the school's athletics, his build was as muscular and foreboding as anyone on the football team.

Kalin was accompanied by his girlfriend, Lilian Andersen. Lilian was a voluptuous beauty with long dark hair and skin as white as fresh snow, but like Kalin, she was always dressed head to toe in black. She held the class record for most violations of the school's dress code. This was because many of her outfits exposed too much. It was assumed that Kalin and Lilian were together because of their mutual love of horror stories, whether they were literature or film. Tom suspected it went a little deeper than that.

Kalin glared down at Tom like a big venomous snake. Lilian looked slightly amused.

"Watch where you're walking, bub," growled Kalin.

"I'm sorry."

Not wanting to start something, Tom promptly got up and ran to his next class.

When the last bell of the day finally rang, Tom was intercepted by Samantha and Rick as he made his way to the parking lot.

"It's all over the school that you asked the Icy Mermaid on a date, and she didn't reject you!" exclaimed Samantha. "Is it true?!"

Tom just smiled.

"Tommy, what did you do, make a deal with the devil or something?!" asked Rick.

"Absolutely not," replied Tom. "All I did was tell her that she had beautiful hair."

"And that worked?"

They talked all the way to their cars. Tom drove home blasting his favorite songs at full volume. After months of preparation, despite a few slip-ups, he had successfully asked Kiania Martins on a date. He felt like he had just hit it big in the lottery. This was the happiest day of his life so far. Tom and the other students never suspected the danger that was present that day.

So many happy faces. It's going to be a very fun year...

CHAPTER 2

When Tom came home that afternoon, his mother had prepared his favorite ice cream cake with the words "Congratulations on taking the first step" written on it. It was almost impossible for him to think about homework for the rest of the week because he was too busy thinking about the date and making preparations. In school, he was constantly badgered by other boys inquiring how he had done the impossible and successfully asked Kiania Martins out. The worst came from Randolph "Randy" Parker.

Randy was a reporter for the school's digital newspaper and an aspiring investigative journalist. He had transferred to Saint Thomas More High School during his sophomore year. The way he went about his extracurricular activities made him very unpopular with the rest of the school. It didn't help that it was conjectured that he had been expelled from his old school because he had been caught peeping in the girl's locker room.

Tom was approached by Randy first thing on Tuesday morning. He had his phone out and was recording the entire conversation.

"Thomas Lime, how long have you been practicing witchcraft?" asked Randy.

"What?!"

"You've successfully asked Kiania Martins on a date. You and I both know that the Icy Mermaid has turned down men that are worth a hell of a lot more than you. The only logical explanation is that you seduced her using the black arts."

Randy hadn't been polite in his approach, and this conversation was getting more disrespectful by the second.

"If I practiced the black arts, I wouldn't be attending a Catholic school."

Tom started walking away, but Randy followed him.

"People say they believe in God, but they always look to the devil when they receive no help from him."

Tom turned to face Randy.

"If you aren't out of my sight within ten seconds, I will shove that phone so far down your throat; whoever pulls it out will be crowned the king!"

Randy ran off like a rabbit on steroids.

Despite both Tom and Kiania's refusal to offer any comment, the impending date was all anyone was talking about, and it was bound to be an eventful day right from the moment Tom walked into school that morning.

"I'M GONNA KILL YOU!"

The exclamation was not directed at Tom. It was coming from further down the senior hall. Tom cautiously poked his head around the corner to see what was happening.

Well, that explains it.

Kalin was apparently having a very heated discussion with Jasmine Diya, the girls' basketball team captain.

"YOU THINK THIS IS FUNNY!?!"

Kalin showed Jasmine an image on his phone. Jasmine was wearing her best poker face.

"What's that got to do with me?"

"DON'T PLAY STUPID; YOU CANCEL CULTURE FEMINAZI!"

By this point, Kalin's outbursts had attracted the attention of the faculty. Tom hastily made his way to his locker and then to class. He was sure he would hear all about it later, but he had a pretty good idea of what it was all about.

Kalin was the president of the literature club, a position he took very seriously. It was no mystery that his favorite works of fiction were the existential and cosmic horror stories penned by Howard Philips Lovecraft. Lovecraft was the most enduring horror writer in history whose name wasn't Edgar Allan Poe. Lovecraft was also an overt xenophobe. During sophomore year, Jasmine, an African American, had spearheaded a movement to have all Lovecraft's stories banned from the school. Naturally, there was a lot of bad blood between her and Kalin. The conflict was never resolved, and Tom stayed out of it. Tom was not a racist, he had asked Kiania Martins on a date, and she was Latin American. But Tom wasn't the kind of person to take a cinematic masterpiece like *The Godfather* and chuck it on the fire because of a few slurs exchanged between the characters.

Between classes, Tom caught wind that Kalin had been so furious because someone had covered his car with raw bacon during the night. He had obviously drawn his own conclusions as to the perpetrator's identity.

Well, that's enough to make anyone mad. Can't be good for the car, and a waste of good bacon.

It wasn't until lunch that Tom got his nasty surprise. Every Friday, the school released a new issue of its digital newspaper. When Tom sat down at his usual table and pulled out his phone, he saw that both he and Kiania made the front page.

What the @&$%!?! The Icy Mermaid & The Teddy Bear

"Teddy bear?!" exclaimed Tom. "Teddy bear?! In what way do I resemble a teddy bear?!"

"Well, you've got that brown hair and that little nose," said Samantha, smiling.

Tom had managed to pass through his high school education

largely unnoticed by the social hierarchy. Now, for the rest of his final year, and whenever his fellow students pulled out their yearbooks to reminisce, he would be remembered as the Teddy Bear. He reminded himself that he was going on a date with Kiania Martins, and if he played his cards right, this could be the first of many. That was all that mattered.

"What makes you think she meant it?" asked Rick. "Let's be honest; the Mermaid has turned down men that any other girl on campus would kill to be with. Who's to say this isn't all just a cruel prank, and she's just setting you up to crush you?"

The thought never occurred to Tom. He honestly had no idea why a girl as breathtakingly beautiful and intelligent as Kiania Martins would agree to go on a date with him. As much as he didn't want to admit it, this all seemed too good to be true.

"Relax, Tom," said Samantha. "Ricky here is just jealous, like nearly every other boy on campus. Kiania isn't going to prank or jilt you."

"How would you know?" asked Rick. "You don't know her."

"No, but I do know members of the swim team that do," replied Samantha. "If Kiania had no interest in going on a date with Tom, she would've just rejected him then and there. Leaving someone hanging, or getting the football team to hang him from the goal post is more like something Juno Simpson would do."

Everything was arranged. Tom would pick Kiania up at 6:45 and take her to the movie theater. The movie was supposed to start at 7:20, but Tom knew that they would only start showing previews at that time. Their seats were reserved, and allowing five to ten minutes to buy snacks, they'd be fine. When the movie was over, he'd take Kiania to get some frozen yogurt.

"Remember, you're the first person to successfully ask Kiania Martins on a date," said Samantha. "Don't ruin it by pushing your luck."

"I wouldn't dream of it."

Tom may have had his eyes on Kiania throughout their high school education, but he was embarrassed to admit that he didn't know much about her. If their conversation the other day was any indication, she somehow knew a lot more about him than he knew about her. Of course, this was partially because Kiania wasn't known for socializing outside the swim team, and even then, she wasn't the most open of individuals. It was because of Kiania's cold nature that Kareen Fabbrie was the captain of the team instead of her. In any event, Tom wouldn't dare to try kissing Kiania on the first date.

When the bell signaled the end of lunch, Tom was approached by Adam Jones, the school's mascot and resident film geek. Adam wasn't an unattractive young man, but was nowhere near as well-built and appealing as men like Fred or Isaiah. There weren't many immortal names of African American descent in the history of film directors, and it was Adam's ambition to rectify that.

"Teddy Bear, word around the school is that you're taking the Mermaid to see *Sherlock Holmes vs. Jack the Ripper*," said Adam.

"One, my name isn't Teddy Bear. Two, her name is Kiania. Three, what of it?" asked Tom.

"I already went to the midnight showing last night. Don't worry, I won't spoil it for you. But, if it's not too much trouble, I'd like your opinions on the movie for the video I'm planning to put on my UBox channel."

Adam's UBox channel was full of videos about specific movies and filmmaking in general. While he hadn't achieved internet celebrity status, he had amassed a small following.

"I'll see what I can do."

When school was finally over, Tom went home, said his daily Rosary, and immediately started preparing for the date. He showered, brushed his teeth, and applied some more of his tropical cologne. He knew it might get a little cold in the theater, so he picked out a simple black t-shirt, his best jeans, a red jacket, and his best shoes. Once again, the only piece of jewelry that he wore was his Miraculous Medal. Just like on the first day of school, he thoroughly scrutinized his appearance in the mirror until he was absolutely sure there was nothing else to be done. When the time came, he texted Kiania to let her know he was on his way. As he jumped into his car, which he had made sure to thoroughly clean, his parents and his sisters came out onto the porch to wish him good luck.

"He's doomed," said Jennifer as Tom drove off.

It wasn't dark yet. There was something about daylight savings time in Indiana which meant that the sun wouldn't set until about nine o'clock during the summer months. Tom was driving with the windows down to avoid expending gas on the air conditioner. The air seemed unseasonably cold for late summer. For some reason, Tom felt very uneasy. He had been nervous for weeks about asking Kiania out, and now he was understandably anxious about the date, but this was something different. An unknown fear filled his heart, and he had no idea why. He turned on the stereo, but something still didn't feel right. Instinctively, he reached for the Miraculous Medal around his neck. It didn't immediately expel the unknown fear from his mind, but he felt comforted knowing that the sacred icon was there.

Blessed Mother, please watch over me and mine tonight.

Finally, Tom pulled up to Kiania's house. It was a very nice house, but that was to be expected. Kiania's mother, Patricia Martins, was the Prosecuting Attorney for Saint Joseph County. Kiania's father, César, was a semi-retired male model with lucrative endorsements. If Tom and Kiania's relationship survived their first date, he'd have to remember to ask her how her parents met.

You know the rules. If you honk the horn, you better be delivering pizza. Park the car, walk up, ring the bell, escort her to the car, open the door for her, shut it, and we're off.

Tom walked up to the door and rang the bell. He had hoped it would be answered by Kiania herself, but it was her father. César Martins was a tall imposing man who had managed to stay in shape. His most distinguishing feature was his well-groomed facial hair.

"Good evening, Mr. Martins," said Tom as politely as he could without sounding intimidated. "I'm Thomas Lime."

For a long moment, Mr. Martins sized Tom up like a piece of meat, and then he let out a long and very hearty laugh. When he spoke, he did so with a rich Latin American accent. At school, Kiania only spoke with an accent when she spoke in Portuguese, and that was usually only when she was angry or rejecting someone's advances. Mr. Martins had the accent hardwired into his voice.

"The school newspapers don't exaggerate; he really does look like a little urso!"

Tom didn't need to be able to speak Portuguese to know what that word meant. All he could do was facepalm himself.

That's not going away anytime soon, is it?

"Papai, you're embarrassing him."

Tom's embarrassment quickly subsided and he remembered why he was there. Kiania was dressed in a white halter top, a jacket, and denim jeans. Whenever she was at school, her clothes always carried the air of being casual but professional. Tom had never seen her dressed like this. Not that it mattered. With her hair and figure, she looked good in anything. Right now, Tom felt like he was standing in the presence of royalty.

"Good evening, Kiania."

"Evening, Thomas."

Without warning, Kiania's father pulled his phone on them.

"My wife wants pictures. She'd do it herself, but she's detained this evening."

With the ways Tom and Kiania were told to pose, you would have thought it was time for the prom already. During this little photoshoot, Tom got so close to Kiania that he could smell her hair. His brain instantly turned to mush.

I want to stay like this forever.

"Tom, we're going to be late," said Kiania.

"Oh, sorry! Don't worry, Mr. Martins, I'll take good care of your daughter."

Mr. Martins smiled.

"My daughter can take care of herself. It's you I'm worried about, boy."

Having Kiania in his car made Tom forget all about the unknown dread he had experienced earlier, now he was anxious about the date again. He had closed the windows, and the car became filled with the intoxicating smell of Kiania's perfume.

Eyes on the road.

"You've been really quiet for five minutes," said Kiania.

"I'm sorry. In the interest of full disclosure, this is the first time I've ever taken a girl on a date."

"That's okay, this is my first time going on one."

During their time at Saint Thomas More High School, Tom had seen Kiania reject the advances of more boys than he cared to keep track of, and he still couldn't believe it.

"So, why did you agree to come on a date with me?"

Tom's brain still wasn't working. He had spoken before he considered the wisdom of the question.

"Out of all the boys that have ever asked me on a date, you, Thomas Lime, are the least objectionable."

Tom wasn't sure if that was a compliment, an insult, or both.

"You also seem to take your Catholic faith seriously," said Kiania. "Tell me, was it your First Communion or your Confirmation?"

"I'm sorry?"

"When your grandmother gave you that necklace," said Kiania.

"How did you know it was my grandmother?"

A faint smile cracked on Kiania's lips. She loved it when she was right. She spoke rapidly and fluidly.

"I didn't, it was a roll of the dice, but I called it right. Despite the fact that we go to a Catholic school, you're the first boy that I've ever seen wearing a Miraculous Medal. In my experience, women tend to take their faith more seriously than men, but not always. Further evidence that you didn't buy that medal yourself is the age of it. That medal isn't new, it's been carefully cleaned and treated numerous times. Young men don't spend money on antique jewelry, that necklace is a gift. The fact that the jewelry is a religious icon suggests it came from an older woman, so it was either your mother or your grandmother. I didn't rule out the possibility of it being an aunt, but I didn't think you'd wear a religious icon given to you by an extended family member, unless you were close to them. Most young men aren't close with their aunts, so the dice roll becomes a coin flip."

Tom tried to process everything that Kiania had just said.

She was able to determine all that just by glancing at my necklace?

"It was a Confirmation present."

"But do you take your faith seriously?" asked Kiania.

When Tom didn't answer, Kiania resumed speaking.

"You said that the necklace was a Confirmation present. Catholics that are baptized as infants by their parents receive the sacrament of Confirmation later in life to give them an opportunity to make the decision for themselves. I received the sacrament of Confirmation about the same time I graduated from middle school, so I can assume you did too. Curious then that during the time we've been students of Saint Thomas More High School, I never once saw you wear it until Monday when you asked me out."

Tom's face had turned pink, but he kept his eyes on the road.

"How could you possibly know I haven't worn this necklace once over the course of three years?"

"I see everything, Thomas Lime," said Kiania, still smiling. "Just like I noticed that your hair had been freshly cut, your skin tanned, your teeth are whiter, and your body is better toned than it has ever been. You've been carefully working on your appearance."

Tom's face went from pink to red.

She has always noticed me!

"Also, I've noticed that you've had a habit of looking in my general direction with the same faraway expression that most of the male student body makes when they look at Juno Simpson. It wasn't hard to work out what your intentions were."

Tom's brain still wasn't working.

"Are you planning to become a detective after graduation?" he asked.

"I'm planning to join the FBI."

"Any particular reason?" asked Tom.

Kiania's smile vanished.

"I don't know you well enough to answer that question."

Tom was smart enough to drop it.

You'll just have to get to know me better.

"You still haven't answered my question," said Kiania. "Do you take your faith seriously?"

Since Kiania was smart enough to put two and two together, Tom figured he should lay his cards on the table.

"Every Catholic who knows the story of the Miraculous Medal knows that it isn't a good luck charm. But I wanted to feel like there was someone looking out for me on Monday. As for my faith, I really do feel a lot better about it now than I have in years... You really do have beautiful hair, Kiania."

Kiania smiled again.

"That's sweet."

Tom asked Kiania how she knew he practiced martial arts, and she told him that she was able to deduce it from the faint bruises on his hands, though she admitted that she couldn't pin down his fighting style. Since Kiania's mother was the county prosecutor, and since it was her ambition to join the FBI, she was more than capable of defending herself if the occasion called for it. Kiania also explained that she knew Tom was an amateur gamer because of his friendship with Rick, but the fact that Tom wasn't a member of the gaming club meant that he didn't go about it as passionately as Rick. Next, Tom asked her how she knew he wanted to make comic books. She told him it was an educated guess based on his performance in language arts and that he always seemed to be drawing something outside of class.

But I know almost nothing about you. I'm really going to have to work on that.

Upon arriving at the theater, Tom got out of the car first and opened the passenger door for Kiania.

"And they say chivalry is dead," she remarked.

Tom saw that there was a bit of a line at the snack bar, but they still had a few minutes. Besides, he wouldn't mind missing a few previews. He noticed that he and Kiania weren't the only students from Saint Thomas More High School attending the theater. At the front of the line, he saw Casey Rosewood.

She must be here for the romantic comedy. I can't see her sitting through a movie about some of history's most infamous unsolved murders.

Casey had gotten her snacks and was heading to her designated theater when Tom and Kiania were ambushed by another girl from school.

"Good evening, Kiania."

Juno Simpson wore a black tube top, tattered skinny jeans, and her school jacket, which proudly displayed her cheerleading captain badge. She was also wearing a necklace and rings that probably cost more than Tom made in a year by assisting at his mother's bakery. As usual, she tossed her long and elegant golden hair like she didn't have a care in the world. Even Tom had to admit she looked like a pop star.

Whatever you do, DO NOT look at her cleavage! Look at the movie posters!

"Good evening, Juno," said Kiania, as politely as she could. "What brings you here?"

"Well, the whole school will be talking about this movie on Monday. I figured I'd see what all the fuss was about. And... I just had to see *this* for myself."

Juno came dangerously close to Tom. She never stopped smiling; her cat-like eyes looked at him hungrily.

"And this must be your cute teddy bear!"

This is getting really old really fast.

"Juno, we've been going to the same school for almost four years, how do you not know my name?" said Tom aloud.

"Really?" said Juno, still smiling. "I've known many boys, but I don't recall seeing you before."

Bitch.

"I think it's great that you've finally got yourself a date, Kiania," said Juno. "Kareen's been really worried about you, and people were starting to talk."

"Some people like to talk about how they think the grass is pink," replied Kiania. "It doesn't mean they're right."

Juno laughed at that. It was the gentle and aristocratic laugh of a young woman who was well used to privilege and the finer things in life.

"I must confess, I am curious. Out of all the so-called men on campus, why did you choose this one?"

Once again Juno came dangerously close to Tom, only this time she gently, almost affectionately, touched his face.

"Does this little bear have some... hidden talent?"

EYES ABOVE THE NECK LINE! OH GOD, SHE'S UNDRESSING ME WITH HER EYES!

Tom was saved by Kiania's timely intervention.

"If you want a date, get your own."

Juno was still smiling.

"Sorry, I got a little carried away. Well, you two lovebirds enjoy yourselves."

Juno walked gracefully off towards the ticket taker, immediately drawing the attention of every person that she passed. She showed the digital ticket on her phone to the ticket taker and disappeared down the hall.

"Why do I suddenly feel like a canary?" asked Tom.

"It's not your fault," said Kiania. "She has that effect on people."

"She talks like she knew you personally," observed Tom.

"Our relationship has never developed beyond acquaintance. I only know her because she's best friends with my team captain."

Tom thought of that time Juno shot down Mark Xeg, and then he thought of all the men she had been with. She had been seeing Fred over the summer, but he was just the latest in a long line of tools and saps. Tom doubted that Juno knew how to make a serious connection with anyone.

"That woman goes through boyfriends like toilet paper, and she's worried about you?"

"Juno Simpson is a woman who does whatever she wants whenever she wants," said Kiania. "She's had the world handed to her on a silver platter since birth. Hopefully, before graduation comes along, reality will give her a much-needed kick in the butt."

Tom bought a large popcorn to split with Kiania and one drink for each of them. As they walked into the theater, they saw Juno sitting in one of the front rows. She smiled and waved at them like they were old friends. As Tom expected, Casey was nowhere to be seen. Thanks to Tom's foresight, he and Kiania had some of the best seats in the theater. Their row was not too close to the screen but not too far away, and their seats were right in the middle. As far as Tom could see, the only problem was that the previews still weren't finished.

Where do they come up with this stuff?

After an agonizing fifteen minutes, the lights finally dimmed.

Now that the previews were over, Tom reached for his first handful of popcorn. His hand found Kiania's. It was so warm. Tom's face turned red, but Kiania just smiled at him. The previews had almost made Tom forget that he was on a date with the girl of his dreams. He pinched himself hard, but this was no dream.

Sometimes life is good.

The movie started with shots of Victorian London by night while eerie and foreboding music played in the background. Each shot faded into another, illustrating the sharp contrast between the British aristocracy and the underprivileged and destitute that lived in the East End. Eventually, the screen faded into a shot of 221B Baker Street. Holmes was sitting in his armchair playing furiously on his violin, bored out of his mind.

Tom paid careful attention to everything that happened in the movie. It was too dark in the theater to appreciate Kiania's beauty anyway. There would be time for that later when they went to get some frozen yogurt. For now, he was looking for things within the movie that he could discuss with Kiania. Like many adaptations, this movie tried to expand on the character of Mrs. Hudson, Holmes's landlady.

After she was done scolding Holmes for making an ungodly racket, Watson tried to remind Holmes that there were people in London that had worse things to worry about than boredom.

As long as this movie doesn't turn into some woke propaganda, I don't mind how they pad the runtime.

The writers had done their homework. The first Sherlock Holmes story, *A Study in Scarlet,* was first published in the 1887 issue of *Beeton's Christmas Annual*, barely a year before the Ripper murders took place; but the events of the story took place in 1881. By the time of the Ripper murders, Dr. Watson would've known Sherlock Holmes for the better part of a decade and would've been married to Mary Morstan.

About twenty-five minutes into the movie, during the murder of Annie Chapman, two patrons ran out of the theater in terror and didn't come back in. It was at this point that Tom also saw Juno get up and gracefully walk out. He knew it was Juno because her hair and jacket were unmistakable. But unlike the other patrons, Juno returned within ten minutes with a drink in her hands.

Down in front.

Tom and Kiania were glued to their seats throughout the entirety of the movie. When it was finally over, Tom and several other patrons got up and involuntarily applauded. It was then that he realized just how badly he needed to use the restroom. Tom always made sure to do his business before he went to the movies so he wouldn't have to get up in the middle of it, but this movie had been almost three hours long. After he and Kiania had finished in the restrooms, he asked her if she still wanted some frozen yogurt, which she delightfully accepted. They both texted their parents to let them know the movie was over, where they were going, and went out.

It was past ten o'clock, and by this time it was quite dark. Tom escorted Kiania to his car and promptly drove away. They hadn't met Juno on the way out. Tom had seen her run out of the theater as soon as the credits started to roll, which was fine because neither Tom nor Kiania felt like talking to her again. As they made their way to the yogurt shop, Tom became aware that a certain red Volkswagen was following them. He didn't want to startle Kiania, but she must've noticed the unease on his face. She looked at the car in the rearview mirror.

"Calm down, it's just Randy," she said.

"Randy?"

"That's his car."

Teddy bear, that was yours wasn't it, Randy?

Tom had no doubt that Randy was following him and Kiania because they were all anyone in school would be talking about for the foreseeable future. He considered trying to lose him, but this was not the time for reckless driving.

If he's still bugging us at the yogurt shop, I'll get rid of him.

The yogurt shop was always open late during the summer; the hours wouldn't change until fall started. Tom and Kiania were likely going to be the last customers they'd have that night. They had just ordered two bowls of mint chocolate with watermelon granita when Tom noticed the familiar red Volkswagen pull into the parking lot.

"Wait here. I'll take care of this."

Tom walked so it looked like he was going to the bathroom, but instead went out the side entrance. As he crept across the parking lot, he thought he heard police sirens in the distance. Randy was sitting in his car with his phone intently fixed on where Tom and Kiania had chosen to sit. Tom made his way to the car's rear and then crept up to the driver's side, where he tapped on the window.

"SCRAM, YOU CREEP!!!"

Randy started the car and took off like a spooked deer.

Tom went back inside and talked about the movie with Kiania.

"Why are we whispering?" asked Kiania.

"Maybe someone here hasn't seen it yet," said Tom. "I don't want to spoil it for them."

"Fair enough."

Tom had to admit that his knowledge of Sherlock Holmes and Jack the Ripper was rudimentary, but he still found the movie very entertaining.

"I'm surprised the Ripper wasn't the creepy Francis Tumblety."

"Serial killers like Jack the Ripper don't stop killing until they either get caught or die," said Kiania. "The historical Tumblety fled to France and then to America, where he died in obscurity. The Ripper killings didn't follow him to Maryland."

"I see," said Tom. "I guess it doesn't make sense for Jack the Ripper to just stop killing after he had already gotten away with five or more murders."

Since Kiania seemed to be so knowledgeable about the history behind the movie, he asked if the London police really did all they could to stop the Ripper.

"Back then, forensic science was very much in its infancy. The conflicting accounts of the Ripper's appearance are a testament to the fact that eyewitness testimony is unreliable. Naturally, things have improved over time, but to this day, there are plenty of unsolved murders and kidnappings. I intend to do something about that."

Tom couldn't help but admire Kiania's enthusiasm for justice. While he did enjoy a good whodunnit, he couldn't see himself matching wits with the most depraved criminal minds the world had to offer. He wondered what had put Kiania on her chosen path, but he knew better than to pry on the first date. After they had finished their frozen yogurt and were on the way back to Kiania's house, he made his move.

"Well, as fun as this was, do you think next week we could watch something less... morbid?" asked Tom.

"That depends, what did you have in mind?"

"I have a well-loved collection of old British sitcoms at home. Say what you will about the English, they know how to make good comedy when they want to."

Tom held his breath. For weeks he had begged God for just one date with Kiania Martins. But after seeing her in informal clothes, watching a movie with her, and talking with her, one date wasn't going to be enough. He wanted more, a lot more. Fortunately, some heavenly force seemed to be smiling on him.

"You know, I've never watched a British sitcom in my life. That sounds very interesting."

YES!!!

Kiania breathed a sigh of relief as Tom drove up to the house. For some reason, her mother still wasn't home. Apparently, Kiania wanted to avoid introducing Tom to her for the time being. Tom pulled into the driveway, got out of the car, opened Kiania's door for her, and escorted her to the front door.

"Thank you for a very pleasant evening, Tom."

Tom wasn't about to try and kiss Kiania, but he could still feel his heart pounding like a rampaging kaiju. The fact that she had agreed to go on another date with him had caused his brain to stop working again.

"Kiania, I am both grateful and honored."

"I look forward to seeing what British comedy is like with you; until then, I bid you, boa noite."

Tom had never seen Kiania smile when speaking Portuguese. Usually, when she did that, she was either angry or turning down another man's advances in her favorite fashion. But the way she said it now almost made Tom forget himself. Once again, he said a silent prayer of gratitude.

"Good night."

Tom's spirit soared as he started to make his way home. He would remember today for the rest of his life. He wanted to turn on one of his favorite songs, but his car's stereo was acting up.

"Darn it, now I've got to reset this thing again."

Without the stereo, the ride home was very quiet. Tom yawned. By now, it was past eleven o'clock. Tom had never come through this part of town in the dark before. He was alone on the road, with no cars in front or behind him. Suddenly, the cold and unknown dread Tom had experienced hours ago returned to him. For some reason, he checked to make sure all the car doors were locked.

Better pick up the pace...

Tom had just taken Kiania Martins on a date, and she had agreed to go on another date with him. He should've felt happy; he had been happier than he had ever been in his life, but now something about this night felt very wrong. He couldn't shake the feeling that something of terrible consequence had either happened, was happening, or was about to happen. He wanted to get home as quickly as possible. He felt his heart rate quicken whenever he was forced to stop at a traffic light or a stop sign. He kept his eyes in front of him whenever the car was in motion and looked around nervously in all directions whenever he had to stop. Finally, the entrance to Tom's neighborhood came into view.

When Tom pulled into his family's driveway, he scanned the nearby area. The surrounding houses were illuminated by a few scattered porch lights and lamp posts, casting eerie shadows all over the place. There was faint light emanating through the windows on the first floor. Tom imagined that his father must be up late watching TV while his mother and sisters had already gone to bed. Tom didn't unlock the car until he was absolutely sure no one was waiting for him outside. As he got out of the car, the silence of the night was broken by the chirping of insects and the croaking of frogs and toads. It was a normal thing to hear at night in late summer, but the sound seemed to build upon his dread tonight. He quickly entered the house through the garage and locked all the doors behind him.

"So, how did it go?"

Sure enough, Tom's father was sitting in the family room with the TV on and nursing a nearly spent glass of iced tea.

"What?" asked Tom, sounding less than composed.

"How was your date?" asked his father.

"Oh, it went well. Next week we're going through my collection of British sitcoms."

"Are you alright?"

"I'm okay," replied Tom. "It's just, driving home late at night; I guess I have Jack the Ripper on the brain."

"I haven't seen you this jumpy since that year your uncle told you that the Mothman was coming to our neighborhood for Halloween," chuckled Tom's father. "But she agreed to go on another date with you! That's excellent news!"

Tom went upstairs to floss bits of popcorn out of his teeth. When he was done, he brushed them before finishing with some whitening mouthwash. This stuff had helped get him his date with Kiania Martins; he would use it for the rest of his life. When Tom entered his room, he looked out the windows before pulling the blinds down. There was no one outside. The house was locked up for the night, Tom should've felt safe, but he didn't.

Tom remembered how he used to think there were monsters in the hallway, in the closet, and under his bed when he was a kid. His parents took him to a child psychologist, who told him that humans weren't nocturnal creatures. At night, it was only natural that people would be uncomfortable and on edge. During this time, the human brain used imagination to try and fill in the gaps and see what a person couldn't see with their other senses. Right now, he had *Sherlock Holmes vs. Jack the Ripper* on his mind. Tom tried to tell himself that he had experienced the exact same feelings when he had to read *Dracula* for school or the time when Rick and Samantha made him binge-watch all the *Friday the 13th* movies with them. He tried to tell himself that his imagination was running wild with the anxiety he had felt about taking Kiania on a date. Tom didn't know it yet, but something unspeakable really had happened that night...

CHAPTER 3

Joe Simpson, the mayor of South Bend, was driving home from a long day at the office. It was about nine o'clock, and the sun had finally gone down.

"Whoever made daylight savings time what it is in Indiana needs to have their head examined."

Joe Simpson had won the election for mayor of South Bend not by taking a certain stance on controversial issues, but by promising to fix all the bad roads. He had spent the better part of his day trying to follow up on that promise. Now all he wanted to do was pop a few beers and maybe rekindle the old fire with his wife, Marion.

At the next stop light, Joe took the opportunity to look at his phone. The runtime for *Sherlock Holmes vs. Jack the Ripper* was two and a half hours. Juno had gone to the 7:20 showing. If Joe hurried, there would be plenty of time for him and his wife to take advantage of the empty house and its indoor pool. When Juno was younger, Joe and Marion needed to leave Juno with her aunt, grandparents, or a sitter to get some time to themselves. But now that Juno was old enough to own a car, she gave her parents all the time they needed without incentive.

Two decades into our marriage, Marion still manages to drive me wild.

Joe turned on his private playlist on the car's stereo as he drove off.

Joe was remembering a particularly special occasion where he and his wife had indulged themselves when the house finally came into view. There were no lights on in the house, at least none that he could see. Worried that his wife might be out of the house for some reason, Joe pulled out his phone and looked at the GPS tracker. According to the app, Juno was still at the movies, and Marion was home.

Don't tell me she's asleep already. I've got an itch that needs scratching.

Joe pulled his car into the garage and went inside. He fumbled for the light switch in the hall.

"Marion, I'm home!"

There was no answer. There must've been an open window somewhere, because the only thing Joe heard was the faint sound of croaking frogs and chirping insects.

"Marion?!"

Joe's phone pinged. He had just received a text message from his wife.

Hey, Hot Stuff. I want to have a little fun. Come find me.

Joe's mind lit up at the possibilities. One of the reasons his marriage had lasted as long as it had was because both he and Marion kept coming up with creative ways to keep the flame alive. He remembered one night when he dropped Juno off at a sleepover and came home to find his wife covered with luminous body paint. Joe's body temperature skyrocketed as he replayed that memory and others in his mind.

Okay, Sexy. Ready or not, here I come.

Joe's first instinct was to check the secret room in the basement that he and his wife affectionately referred to as "the play room." He quickly made his way down the stairs and felt the hinge that would open the secret door. There was no one inside, just some well-loved furniture and various paraphernalia.

I guess we don't have to do it down here, but Juno won't be at the movies all night.

As Joe came out of the basement, he heard footsteps up on the second floor.

"Alright, the game is up!"

There was still no response. Joe eagerly made his way up the stairs, tossing off his jacket, undoing his belt, and getting to work on his tie as he did so. There were still no lights on when he reached the second floor, but he saw that the door to the master bedroom was slightly ajar. Joe excitedly threw it open, turned on the light, and stopped dead. For a moment, his brain tried to process what he was seeing, then his heart felt like it leaped out of his chest, his knees grew weak, and he felt the fast food he had for dinner fighting for release. A second later, his dinner was all over the floor, and he screamed.

Marion Simpson was lying on the king-sized bed, clothed only in a violet kimono that was thrown open. Her eyes had been gouged out, her breasts had been cut off, and there was a wide gash that stretched from her abdomen to her pelvis. There was blood everywhere. On one side of the bed, there was a pile of organs that had been removed. Joe was on all fours, still screaming. He didn't hear the muffled footsteps creeping up behind him. Suddenly, his head exploded with white-hot pain. As his arms gave out under him, his vision blurred into red mist. The last thing he saw was the outline of something that looked like a human being with a frog's head, and then everything went black.

CHAPTER 4

Tom dreamt that he and Kiania were walking down a street in Victorian England late at night. They were dressed in the attire of the time period, but Kiania still had light blue streaks in her hair, and everyone noticed. It was the sort of thing that the incredibly posh people looked down upon. But Tom and Kiania didn't care what a bunch of stuck-up protestants thought.

"KILL THE CATHOLICS!"

That made Tom and Kiania break into a run. They ran through the narrow and winding streets and alleys of London's East End when out of nowhere, they were ambushed by a humongous bear. They ran down a different alley and came to a dead-end, where a man in an opera jacket and top hat was waiting for them.

The man slowly raised his head, revealing his ghost-like complexion, fiery red eyes, and fangs. Tom and Kiania turned to run back the way they came, but the bear had caught up. Both their attackers started to charge when the dream was shattered by the sound of Tom's phone ringing.

Tom woke up in a cold sweat. He had expected his imagination to run wild with his dreams after last night, but he hadn't anticipated a giant bear, an angry mob, and Dracula. He glanced over at his phone and saw that it was only 7:20, a whole hour and ten minutes before his usual rising time on Saturday morning. It obviously wasn't the alarm, so he checked to see who was calling. It looked as though Rick had tried calling him multiple times in the past twenty minutes.

This had better be good.

Tom picked up the phone and answered it.

"What?"

"Have you seen the news?!"

Tom had expected Rick to ask him how his date with Kiania had gone. He was relieved that he hadn't. Tom was far too much of a gentleman to discuss something like that, even with his best friend.

"No, I haven't," groaned Tom. "I usually sleep in on Saturday mornings."

"Juno Simpson's parents were killed last night!"

Tom's still groggy brain didn't immediately process what his friend had told him.

"And that justifies waking me up this early? Wait, what did you say?"

Tom turned on the news app on his phone in time to see an image of a screaming and hysterical Juno Simpson being escorted away from a mob of journalists by the police. It said that Juno had returned from the movies late last night to find her parents savagely murdered. The police weren't sharing any details, but it sounded awful. The cameras had caught sight of several officers being violently sick. Tom listened intently until the screen finally cut to an ad. With a shiver, he remembered what Kiania had said to him last night.

"Juno Simpson is a woman who does whatever she wants whenever she wants. She's had the world handed to her on a silver platter since birth. Hopefully, before graduation comes along, reality will give her a much-needed kick in the butt".

"I'd say her butt just got thoroughly kicked."

Tom found it very hard to focus on his homework that Saturday. In the evening, he called Kiania and asked for her thoughts on the matter. She told him it wasn't something to discuss over the phone, but she promised they could discuss it freely on Friday if the police hadn't already caught the killer. Tom did not sleep well that night.

He didn't think he would get any sleep at all, knowing that there was a killer on the loose and that his dread on Friday night had been justified. On Sunday, the only new development in the case was that someone had leaked information to the press. A thirteen-inch hunting knife, evidently the murder weapon, was left at the scene, along with a red and black-spotted frog mask. Now every media outlet was calling the killer the "South Bend Dart Frog." The fact that no arrests were made that day told Tom that there were no fingerprints on the knife or any other form of forensic evidence to be found at the crime scene.

Tom had hoped that the murders would make everyone forget about his date with Kiania. But when he opened his locker that Monday morning, he was met with an avalanche of plastic honey bottles. The whole hall was filled with the sound of laughter and people calling him "Tommy the Teddy Bear." Tom was late for his first class, but the teacher let him off since he was clearly on the receiving end of someone else's practical joke.

Be glad the honey stayed in the bottles.

When Tom went back to his locker between third and fourth period, he found himself surrounded by Marcus Johnson and half a dozen other members of the football team.

Oh shit.

"Hello, Teddy Bear," said Marcus.

"I have a name," said Tom without thinking. Marcus and the others weren't listening.

"It's been confirmed that you actually took the Mermaid on a date last Friday."

"Her name is Kiania."

Without warning, Marcus slammed his fist into the locker, a mere inches away from Tom's head.

"Now what's a hot piece of ass like that doing with a shrimp like you?"

Any intimidation Tom may have felt was suddenly replaced with white-hot anger.

"Don't you dare talk about her like that!"

"Or you'll do what?"

Marcus had the advantage in muscle mass, but Tom doubted he was anything more than a brawler. He was sure he could easily trip him and send him crashing to the floor, but Tom didn't know what he was supposed to do about Marcus's six friends.

Stinking coward.

Fortunately, Tom didn't need to get his hands dirty. At that moment, Coach Matthews came out of his classroom and saw them.

"What's going on here?!"

Marcus and the other six boys immediately fell into a line against the opposite side of the hall.

"Nothing," they all said together.

"Then get your butts to class!"

Marcus shot Tom an ugly look and left reluctantly. The rest of the boys took off like it was the Kentucky Derby.

"Are you alright?" asked Coach Matthews.

"I think I know who put all that honey in my locker this morning."

The murders and Tom's little misadventures were all anyone was talking about during lunch.

"I didn't know you had the balls," said Rick. "First you ask Kiania Martins on a date, then you stare down one of the football team's tacklers and six of his best friends!"

Samantha gave them the whole story of how Marcus had been one of the many boys that asked Kiania on a date and failed. It had happened last year. Marcus had come on way too strong and with all the charm of a sex-starved gorilla on crystal meth. He wouldn't take no for an answer, and Kiania had brought the episode to an end with a judo throw. Marcus ended up missing the rest of football season because of his injuries.

"He's a brainless and sexist pig," said Samantha. "He'll probably get a football scholarship and lose it on a drug violation."

"Be that as it may, many men feel emasculated when a girl like Kiania Martins goes out with someone like our Tommy here," said Rick. "Speaking of which, how was the date last Friday?"

"It went well."

"Is there going to be a second date?" asked Samantha beaming.

"Maybe."

Tom left it like that. If boys like Marcus Johnson and Randy Parker were going to accost him for dating Kiania, he didn't want the whole school to know when and where those dates were going to take place.

Despite Juno's bereavement and absence, things carried on very much the same at school. The murders just didn't seem real. Tom had heard about things like this on the news or when he listened to the occasional true crime podcast, but he never heard about them happening to people he knew. South Bend was supposed to be safe. In his eighteen years, he never heard of anything like a particularly brutal double murder taking place in the city.

I guess there's a first time for everything.

Tom made sure to come home immediately after school each day that week. Every night, he'd check in with Kiania and his friends to make sure they were safe. The rest of the school seemed to be comparatively unaffected by the murders. The honey in Tom's locker wasn't the only prank pulled that week. On Wednesday, seven seniors brought cats to school. The cats were given collars that were numbered 1, 2, 4, 6, 8, 9, and 10. Before the second period began, the signal was given, and the cats were released. The rest of the day was spent in abject chaos as students and faculty alike tried to round up the cats. The faculty would spend the rest of the week looking for the number 3, 5, and 7 cats that didn't exist. By Friday, the murderer of Joe and Marion Simpson still hadn't been caught. It was the day of the first football game of the season, so Tom shouldn't have been surprised when he came into school that morning and found that there were billiard balls all over the floor in every hall. The guilty parties behind the prank were never identified.

Where the heck did they get this many billiard balls?

That night, most of the school was going to the football game. Tom was having his second date with Kiania. She was coming to his house for pizza and a binge of one of his favorite British sitcoms. It fell to Tom's father to get the pizzas.

"One Big Apple Garden with a Poi Pig Pen, a Spicy Ray with Chicken Pox and Freckles, and extra French cologne on the side, got it!" said Mr. Lime.

"I didn't even know what half of that meant," said Tom's sister, Britney.

Both of Tom's younger sisters had been pessimistic about their brother's chances of actually getting a date. Now that Tom had successfully come to his second date, he wasn't sure how they would act. Britney might just leave them be, but he couldn't be sure about Jennifer. In any event, Tom's mother gave the girls strict orders not to disrupt Tom's date. If they did, there would be hell to pay.

Tom was busy scrutinizing himself in the mirror until he heard the doorbell ring. Kiania had been dropped off by her father. Once again, Tom had his breath forced out of him at the sight of Kiania in casual clothes. It may have just been a simple sleeveless purple blouse and blue jeans, but Kiania really did look amazing in anything, and the sight of her long and elegant tan arms was too much for him.

"Are you going to invite me in or what?" asked Kiania smiling.

"I'm sorry, I... you look very beautiful tonight, Kiania."

Kiania was about to reply, but Tom's mother came to the door at that moment.

"Hello! Hello! Welcome to our house!"

Mrs. Lime understood why her son had fallen for this girl, and she couldn't get enough of her. When Tom's father got home with the pizzas, it was clear that he felt the same as his wife. Tom was worried that his parents might be too welcoming, but fortunately for him, Kiania didn't seem to mind. With the pizzas laid out, Tom's parents retired to another room while he and Kiania were left alone to watch TV.

Tom laid out a variety of British sitcoms for Kiania to choose from. She picked one that sounded interesting and sat down on the couch. At first, Tom was hesitant, but he had already sat beside her at the movies a week ago. It would be okay as long as he didn't push his luck. He sat up straight beside Kiania and started the video.

In the entire course of his high school education, Tom had never once heard Kiania laugh, not even a giggle. But as they sat there watching British sitcoms, she was laughing like someone watching *National Lampoon's Christmas Vacation* for the first time. Her face turned red, and she fell to the floor at one point, laughing and banging wildly with her hands. Tom had to spend fifteen minutes trying to calm her down, and she still had the giggles afterward.

"That almost made me forget there's a murderer on the loose," said Kiania.

"Who do you think did it?"

Tom didn't know why he asked the question; it just slipped out.

"I haven't the foggiest," replied Kiania. "All I know is that the crime was very personal, and the mayor could've had any number of enemies. I can't make a theory beyond that. You can't solve a jigsaw puzzle if you don't have all the pieces, and when it comes to crime, you don't have a picture on the box to serve as a reference."

"What makes you say it was personal?" asked Tom.

Kiania eyed Tom critically.

"Can you keep a secret?"

"Yes."

Kiania looked over her shoulder to make sure Tom's parents weren't there, then her voice dropped to a whisper.

"I'm only telling you this because I know for a fact that you're not the murderer. Mayor Simpson and his wife were killed while we were at the movies."

"How do you know that?" asked Tom.

"I'd tell you, but then I'd have to kill you," replied Kiania, smiling. "I'm sure you've heard from the news about the thirteen-inch hunting knife and the frog mask. What hasn't been made public is the fact that both victims had their eyes gouged out and their reproductive organs removed post-mortem. Mrs. Simpson also had her breasts cut off."

Tom felt his stomach turn at the thought.

"That's... disturbing."

"Homicide is common, mutilation is rare," said Kiania. "The fact that the bodies were desecrated in such a way means it was personal. Whoever it was also knew how to bypass the house's security system without sounding an alarm. This combined with the fact that there was no forensic evidence at the scene suggests that this crime was premeditated and calculated. We're dealing with an organized serial killer."

"Serial killer?" said Tom. "But there's only been two people killed in one setting."

"You're forgetting about the frog mask and the knife," said Kiania. "One-time murderers don't take trophies or leave calling cards."

"Trophies?"

"I told you their reproductive organs and their eyes were removed. The police didn't find them at the crime scene."

Tom didn't want to think about what the murderer could've done with those body parts.

"The police are interviewing people who knew the mayor and his wife," said Kiania. "And we better hope they find something soon. If this is a serial killer that we're dealing with, then it's only a matter of time before he or she strikes again."

CHAPTER 5

When he came home from his first football game as a senior and team captain, Fred Smith felt like a boy who was immortal. The Saint Thomas More Paladins had crushed the other team. Fred had gone to the showers with the rest of the team when the game was over, but he had hardly broken a sweat.

Seriously, who in their right mind would name their team 'The Neanderthals?'

Fred had wanted to play football since the first time he went to a college game with his dad. From that day forward, he had worked hard to make that dream a reality. He had never been an outsider throughout his high school education. He had come to Saint Thomas More High School with a whole circle of friends from middle school and had all the right connections. He always did his best to distinguish himself as an athlete, all the while maintaining good grades. Granted, he needed a little help in the academic department every now and then, but there was no shortage of brainy students hoping to improve their social standing by helping out a member of the football team.

Now Fred was a senior and the team captain. He loved being the big man on campus. His achievements were well known, and it seemed like the entire city of South Bend was wondering where he might decide to go to college. He had his friends, his parents couldn't be prouder of him, and he could have any girl he wanted. Well, almost any girl. Earlier that week, before practice, Coach Matthews sat the entire team down for a lecture on their behavior at school. Apparently, Marcus and several other boys had been the ones who filled the Teddy Bear's locker with honey. Fred didn't even know that Thomas Lime existed until word got around the school that Kiania Martins had agreed to go on a date with him. It must've gone well, because the rumor was that the two were on another date tonight.

I still can't believe the Icy Mermaid is going out with a scrawny kid like that.

Fred had been in a serious long-term relationship with Juno Simpson for some time now, so he really shouldn't have been thinking about other girls. But it was hard not to think about a gorgeous well-built Latina like the Icy Mermaid, and Juno hadn't returned any of his calls since Friday. Understandable as it was, Fred still wished she could've been there at the game. He had actually met Juno's parents. Mayor Simpson seemed like a really nice guy and was an avid sports fan. Mrs. Simpson also seemed like a good person and had been quite attractive for her age. Fred couldn't imagine why anyone would want to kill them. Juno hadn't been at school all week. According to Kareen Fabbrie, Juno was staying with her aunt across the state line.

I hope they catch the psycho.

When they got home, Fred and his parents found their dog, a German Shepherd named Bruno, sound asleep in his dog bed. After a quick celebratory dessert, Fred went upstairs and opened a single can of beer from his secret stash. He always had one after the team won a game. When the opportunity presented itself, he would sneak the empty can out of the house and dispose of it in someone else's recycling bin. When Fred had finished his drink, he brushed his teeth and went to bed. He didn't want to sleep, but he'd need to get cracking on his homework immediately after breakfast if he wanted the afternoon off. His parents stayed up and watched their favorite game show on the DVR, just like they always did.

Fred lay in bed dreaming about becoming a pro football player, making more money than he could ever hope to spend, and winning the Super Bowl. He also dreamt about marrying Juno, provided he couldn't find an even more beautiful blonde bombshell to be his wife. He thought about using his inexhaustible income to buy a tropical island somewhere to serve as their own little Garden of Eden. He dreamt he was running down the beach hand in hand with Juno, who had developed a divine golden tan. Suddenly, she stopped to kiss him and began slipping out of her exotic one-piece bathing suit.

Fred's dream was shattered by the sound of a dog barking. He immediately recognized it as Bruno.

"Bruno! Shut up!"

But Bruno didn't stop barking. Fred tried burying his head beneath his pillows, but it didn't do any good. He angrily tossed the pillows aside and woke up completely. There wasn't a single hint of sunlight coming in through the window. As Bruno continued to bark and claw at the door, Fred felt around in the dark for his phone to see what time it was.

"IT'S 4:30 IN THE MORNING!!!"

Bruno was still barking. It was at that moment that Fred realized that his parents weren't yelling at the dog to stop.

Are they deaf?!

Fred didn't know if his parents popped open a particularly strong bottle of wine when he went to bed, but this was getting ridiculous. He got out of bed and went to the door. Bruno was sitting right in front of him, whimpering.

"What in the name of all things holy is..."

Even though it was dark, Fred saw that Bruno had left tracks on the floor. He turned on the light on his phone and saw that the tracks were red.

"What the hell?"

Bruno walked down the hall to the bedroom shared by Fred's parents and whimpered again. Fred slowly followed him.

"Mom? Dad? Are you awake in there?"

There was no answer. The entire house was filled with an eerie silence, broken only by the sound of Bruno's whimpering. Fred slowly pushed the door aside and showed his light on the room.

Fred thought he must still be asleep, only his wet dream had suddenly turned into a nightmare. He slapped himself repeatedly in the face, but the vision in front of him didn't change. The horrible reality hit him like a freight train. Fred felt as though his body had been flash frozen. He fell to the floor and screamed out in pure animal terror. For the better part of twenty minutes, that was all Fred did. His parents lay on the bed, caked in blood, their entrails tossed here and there; and in the center was a blood-stained thirteen-inch hunting knife and a yellow and black-spotted frog mask.

CHAPTER 6

It was all over the news that the Dart Frog had struck again. If the entire community had been shocked by the first murders, then this latest development was fanning the flame dangerously close to a powder keg. Not only had the victims been the parents of the local football star, but Fred's father had been a respected doctor, and his mother had taught kindergarten.

Two double murders in as many weeks?! This is nuts!

Tom didn't leave the house at all that weekend, except on Sunday when his family went to church. After church, he spent the better part of the day improving security around the house with his dad, using everything he had brought home from the hardware store. All he learned from the news was that the killer had used the same type of weapon, but the color of the frog mask was different than the first. Tom checked in with Kiania on Saturday and Sunday to ensure that she and her family were all right, but they never discussed the murders in great detail. Tom imagined that she was discretely learning everything that wasn't being revealed to the public.

I finally ask the girl of my dreams on a date, and something like this happens. I hope this doesn't become a pattern.

On Monday morning, Tom wasn't surprised that Fred wasn't in school. But he was shocked to see that Juno had returned. Or was it Juno? She didn't look anything like she did on the first day of classes, so alive and enjoying herself. There were visible mascara stains beneath her eyes, and her usually glowing skin seemed as pale as a ghost.

Her parents were just murdered, and splatter movie murdered at that; what do you expect?

Tom felt obligated to say something, but he didn't know what to say. He had never had to comfort someone who had lost loved ones in such a terrible way.

"Juno, you're here?"

Real smooth, dumb-dumb.

When Juno looked at Tom, she cracked a fake smile that wouldn't have fooled a five-year-old.

"I've already missed a full week of school, Teddy Bear. If I get too far behind, I won't graduate."

If Tom's parents had been murdered, schoolwork would've been the furthest thing from his mind. Juno was right, but the way she looked now, Tom would've thought a stiff breeze could snap her in two. He couldn't imagine sitting through one of Sister Joan's lectures under these circumstances.

"Juno, I'm not going to pretend to understand what you're going through, but I am very sorry for your loss. If you need anything..."

Juno's insincere smile now looked slightly amused.

"You're not already tired of Kiania, are you? Or did she get tired of you?"

The comment took Tom completely by surprise, and his face turned a shade of pink.

"Absolutely not! Common humanity isn't flirting."

"No, it isn't," replied Juno. "I just need to laugh..."

Tom saw that tears were beginning to form in Juno's eyes.

"Because if I don't, I'm going to cry."

They left it like that, it was time for class.

Everyone was talking about Juno's return and Fred's absence in hushed whispers, but Juno didn't last long on her first day back to school. During the brief interval between second and third period, Tom was exchanging books in his locker when suddenly he heard a loud metallic bang coming down the hall. Screams and more sounds of violence promptly followed it. He ran to see what was going on.

When Tom turned the corner, he saw Mark Xeg lying in a crumpled heap on the floor. His glasses had shattered against his face, and a small stream of blood was trickling from the back of his head. Even more alarming was the sight of Juno mercilessly kicking him in the chest and stomping on him. One student tried to restrain Juno, but she viciously swiped him across the face with her nails and immediately resumed her assault on Mark.

"I WOULDN'T TOUCH YOU IF YOU WERE THE LAST MAGGOT ON EARTH! NOW STAY AWAY FROM ME! GO BACK TO GEEK ISLAND! SCREW YOUR MOTHER! AND KILL YOURSELF!!!"

Juno didn't stop attacking Mark until Coach Matthews came into the hall and restrained her. Principal Miller came down the hall a moment later, looking very angry. The entire hall had fallen silent, the only sound that could be heard was Mark's anguished moaning. When Mrs. Miller spoke, her voice was dangerously calm and collected, but there was no mistaking her tone.

"Sister Joan, please escort Mr. Xeg to the nurse's office. Mr. Matthews, please escort Ms. Simpson to my office."

Mrs. Miller then addressed all the other students still in the hall.

"The rest of you, GET YOUR BUTTS TO CLASS!"

Tom and the others rushed off as if the devil were on their heels.

It was during lunch that Tom finally got the full details of what had transpired that morning. Rick saw the whole thing and gave a play by play

"Apparently, Mark thought now would be an excellent time to offer Juno a shoulder to cry on. She responded by punching him in the face, slamming his head into the nearest locker, and then just started wailing on him."

"For someone with a perfect GPA, that wasn't a very smart move," said Samantha.

"You don't understand men," said Rick. "When we find our dream girl, we need to have her. Unfortunately, we can't all be as lucky as Teddy Tommy here,"

"Don't you start," said Tom.

Juno was sent home and suspended for three days. Mark did not return to school the next day; his parents woke up to find him sitting in bed with his father's gun in his hands. He was promptly sent to the Saint Dymphna Mental Hospital and placed on suicide watch. On Wednesday, it was all over the news that Fred was in the hospital and had nearly died from alcohol poisoning. He was so distraught over his parents' murders that he tried to drink himself to death and was saved only by the timely arrival of his relatives. Worst of all, the Dart Frog still hadn't been caught.

On Friday, when Juno returned to school, she was ambushed by a group of Mark's friends as soon as she entered the building.

"What is your problem?!" demanded Gaming Club Vice President Haru Fukuda.

Juno wasn't intimidated at all.

"My parents are dead, my boyfriend's parents are dead, and my boyfriend almost drank himself to death. Don't you watch the news?"

"And that justifies you beating the shit out of my friend and then telling him to kill himself?!" said Rick. "He almost did just that!"

Juno's face became contorted with rage. Tom had never seen her so angry.

"Have you not been listening to a word I've said?! My parents are dead, and I'm living with my pothead aunt! And now my boyfriend is in the hospital! Do you think I care if one worthless maggot couldn't face reality?!"

There was no self-reproach in Juno's voice. There was no guilt or remorse. The air around her seemed twenty degrees colder. Tom knew in his bones that if Mark had gone through with his suicide, Juno wouldn't have shed a tear. Juno's friends rallied around her, but the bell rang before anyone could do or say anything else.

That evening, Tom had another date with Kiania. She came to his house again, but this time they ordered Japanese take-out. After dinner, Tom and Kiania sat down to watch another British sitcom. As much as Tom enjoyed Kiania's company, the incidents at school had left him rattled.

"I still can't believe Juno," said Tom. "I know Mark is no Prince Charming, but he didn't deserve that. He almost killed himself."

Tom knew that suicide was the worst sin a person could commit. If Mark had gone through with it, his soul would have been condemned to hell, all because he fell in love with someone that would never love him back.

"I guess even a particularly strong kick in the butt isn't enough to make someone like Juno Simpson grow a conscience," said Kiania.

"Does her aunt really use marijuana?"

"She lives across the state line and owns a shop. It's legal in Michigan."

"I see."

Despite the morbid nature of their conversation, the British sitcoms once again left Kiania in stitches. Tom waited until he had to change the discs before asking his next question.

"Any updates on the Dart Frog?"

"I'm sure you've heard from the news that the mask left at the Smiths' was a different color, specifically yellow. Despite this, and all the other differences, the police are confident that this is the same person who killed the Simpsons and not a copycat."

"What other differences?"

"The causes of death vary. Mrs. Simpson's throat was slashed. Mayor Simpson was killed by a blow to the head with a baseball bat. Both the Smiths died from an overdose of morphine. But all the victims were mutilated postmortem in exactly the same way."

Tom didn't need to be reminded about how the Simpsons' bodies had been mutilated. It gave him the chills just thinking about it.

"So, we're looking for someone with access to morphine?" he asked.

"Morphine wasn't the only drug used that night. According to the police report, the Smiths' dog tested positive for acepromazine, a veterinary sedative."

Tom didn't even know the Smiths had a dog, but obviously the Dart Frog did.

"The police have spent the better part of this past week interviewing the Smiths' neighbors, coworkers, and acquaintances, but no one has shown any signs of having struggled with a dog. That means the police either haven't met the killer yet or..."

It took Tom a minute to realize that Kiania was letting him finish the sentence.

"The dog knew the murderer and didn't attack."

"Exactly," said Kiania, smiling.

Kiania laid out the timetable she had made of the events that transpired the previous Friday.

"The football game between the Paladins and Neanderthals started at seven o'clock. Doctor and Mrs. Smith left home at around six-thirty. The game ended at around nine o'clock. The Dart Frog probably broke into the Smiths' house during this window. You may have heard that my friend Dasha was babysitting down the street from the Smiths' residence during that time. According to Fred, Mrs. Smith was in the habit of leaving the windows around the house open in late summer and early autumn, weather permitting. Dasha understandably had her hands full with her charge, but did not recall hearing any unusual barking fits from the dog that night. In addition, the fact that there was no forensic evidence at the scene that didn't belong to any of the victims reinforces the point that the Smiths' dog knew the murderer."

Tom was really beginning to wonder where Kiania got her information from. He was about to ask why the Dart Frog didn't just kill the Smiths' dog but stopped himself. Killing the dog would've immediately tipped the Smiths off that something was amiss when they got home. Putting the dog out for a few hours had been the smart thing to do.

"So, the Dart Frog breaks into the Smiths' house, drugs the dog, and waits for the Smiths to come home?"

"Not exactly," replied Kiania. "The effects of acepromazine vary depending on what kind of animal it is used on. On average, the effects last six to eight hours on dogs, and it takes about thirty minutes for the drug to take effect. High school football games can usually last two hours, but can sometimes take longer. The Dart Frog did not know how long the game would last, when the Smiths would get home, or how long it would take them to fall asleep. Fortunately for the killer, the game was being livestreamed on UBox."

"But unless the killer was a student or someone in their immediate family, they would've had to pay to watch it," said Tom.

"Yes, unfortunately, that means a good fraction of the people in the county would be suspects. Even if the police were given the freedom to seize every electronic device in the county, not likely, the killer probably would've found a way to cover his or her digital footprints."

"Do the police at least have any persons of interest?" asked Tom.

Kiania laughed at another gag on the TV before answering.

"At the moment there is no solid evidence, such is necessary in court. As I've said before, the mayor could've had any number of enemies. At present, they can find no definite connection between the Simpsons and the Smiths. Mrs. Smith taught kindergarten, and Dr. Smith was a reproductive endocrinologist."

"A what?" asked Tom.

"A reproductive endocrinologist is a physician who specializes in the diagnosis and treatment of endocrine disorders that are directly or indirectly related to reproduction."

Kiania saw the brief flash across Tom's face.

"I know what you're thinking, and the police have already looked into it. Dr. Smith never knew the Simpsons privately or professionally prior to Fred's courtship of Juno. She is very much their daughter."

"So, the only known link between these two crimes is that the victims were parents of seniors at Saint Thomas More High School who just happened to be dating and at the top of the social hierarchy."

CHAPTER 7

Thankfully, there were no more murders over the weekend. But the drama at Saint Thomas More High School was just beginning. On Monday, Tom arrived at school to find a mob of students clustered outside the entrance that opened directly into senior hall; they were making more noise than a swarm of angry bees. Even though classes were due to start in fifteen minutes, they seemed to be trying to leave the school. There was even more noise when Tom finally fought his way through and got inside, but the noise wasn't the first thing he noticed.

"My god! This place smells worse than a German trench after the first World War!"

The smell had been coming from Juno's locker. At some point during the night, someone had broken into the school and filled the cheerleading captain's locker with cow manure. The smell was so unbearable that classes were canceled for the day. It was the beginning of what would go down in the history of the school as *The War Between the Butterflies and the Geeks*.

The staff spent the day cleaning the manure out of Juno's locker, airing out the school, and spraying the entire building down with odor neutralizer. The perpetrators of the vandalism were never identified. The next day, Principal Miller dragged the entire senior class into the gymnasium and gave them all hell, but the war had only just begun. That very same day, students who were low on the social ladder had begun throwing dog treats at Juno and her friends whenever they passed them in the halls. Everyone was smart enough to bring only one dog treat into the school, and no one low on the social ladder would dream of ratting out their class-mates to the faculty, but Juno and her friends didn't forget. After a week of this, twelve different people who had been accused of throwing dog treats were on the receiving end of paint bombs that had been planted in their lockers.

Pranks were being pulled throughout the school on an almost daily basis. Before a big game, someone thought it would be a funny idea to use bleach to draw male reproductive organs on the football team's uniforms. On the following Monday, the computer lab was infested with ladybugs. Shortly after this, Tom was warned by an anonymous source to bring his own hand sanitizer to school and avoid the soap dispensers at all costs. He went into school that day and discovered that the soap dispensers had been filled with WD-40 and bacon grease.

Near the end of September, several students broke into the school at night and ransacked the library. Principal Miller forced the entire senior class to pay for any damaged or ruined books. They all spent the following Saturday learning the Dewey Decimal System and setting the library in order. Anyone who didn't show up wouldn't graduate. This was a large annoyance to Tom. He was supposed to meet Kiania's mother that evening and was un-derstandably exhausted after spending a large portion of the day categorizing books. He had almost completely forgotten about the murders until Kiania brought them up.

"Don't talk about the murders at all," she said. "If my parents get wise to me, I'll never forgive you."

"My lips are zipped," said Tom. "Is there anything else I need to know?"

"Don't try to impress my mother, just be yourself."

Well, it's worked so far.

Kiania's father seemed nice enough, but her mother was the county prosecutor. Naturally, Tom felt a little hot under the collar as he made his way to the Martins' residence that evening.

At least I don't have to worry about my sisters butting in.

When Tom rang the bell, the person who answered the door looked a lot like Kiania, only older and without the blue streaks in her hair. Mrs. Martins was dressed in the same casual but professional manner as Kiania when she was at school.

"Good evening, Mrs. Martins."

"So, the cute Teddy Bear finally shows himself," said Mrs. Martins, smiling.

This is getting REALLY old.

"So, tell me how you managed to ask my daughter out," said Mrs. Martins pulling Tom inside a little too enthusiastically.

"I just told her that she has beautiful hair," said Tom, flustered.

"No argument here, I taught her everything she knows."

Tom was saved by Kiania's timely descension of the stairs.

"Mãe, you're scaring him," said Kiania.

"Says the girl who has been scaring away boys throughout her entire high school experience," said Mrs. Martins, smiling too much.

Tom made a diversion.

"What smells so good?"

"That would be dinner, right this way!"

As Mrs. Martins led the way to the kitchen, Kiania pulled Tom close.

"Don't worry, she'll leave us alone after a few cocktails," she whispered.

"She's not a heavy drinker, is she?" asked Tom.

"Not in public, but her job can be very stressful at times."

Mrs. Martins was very cheerful throughout the evening. Tom had expected the county prosecutor to be much more protective of her daughter, but she seemed positively thrilled to meet him.

The main course was garlic picanha, and Tom thoroughly enjoyed it. Mrs. Martins did all the talking. Tom did his best to answer all of her questions, but once or twice an embarrassed exclamation from Kiania stopped him from speaking.

"So, what do you want to do after you graduate?" asked Mrs. Martins.

Tom was a little nervous about answering this question, but on the day that he asked Kiania out, she guessed that he wanted to make comic books. She may have already told her mother, but he still didn't want to tell her in a way that made him sound like a geek.

"Well, there's a crippling shortage of God-fearing Catholics in the entertainment industry. I'd like to do something about that."

"What did you have in mind?"

"Well, I'd like to write and draw my own comic books, but I imagine college can make me adaptable."

"Tom does have good grades in both literature and his extracurriculars," said Kiania.

Mrs. Martins was still wearing the same smile she had been wearing throughout the evening. But Tom wasn't convinced. Mrs. Martins couldn't have gotten to be county prosecutor if she didn't have a good poker face.

"Can I see your portfolio?"

By his own admittance, Tom still had a lot to learn. It was his ambition to create the definitive comic book adaptation of the Arthurian legends. He also spent his spare time writing a satirical superhero story. To his relief, Mrs. Martins laughed at some of his more farcical creations. He did however have to explain some of the basic concepts of absurdist humor to Kiania's father.

"Speaking of humor, I believe you have a British sitcom with my name on it," said Kiania.

"Yes, I certainly do."

Kiania's parents retired to the second floor to give them their privacy. The walls of the living room were lined with rock panels, giving it the appearance of a cave. The room also had a door that led out to the house's enclosed pool and hot tub. The Martins' TV dwarfed the one that Tom's family owned, and Tom and Kiania would be enjoying it from the massive leather reclining sectional sofa.

I want a living room like this when I get a house of my own.

Tom's attention was suddenly drawn to a picture on one of the end tables in the room. It showed a much younger version of the Martins family at a beach. Kiania didn't have the blue streaks in her hair yet, but the thing that caught Tom's attention was how she smiled. He had never seen her smile like that in school. She wasn't laughing like she did when they watched TV with him. In the picture, she just seemed happy and full of life. She didn't have the cold aura of seriousness that she usually carried about with her.

"Where is that?" asked Tom, still looking at the picture.

"Florida, we used to live there," replied Kiania.

"What made you move to South Bend of all places?" asked Tom.

"My father wasn't going to stay a model forever, and my mom took work where she could find it."

Tom may have only been dating Kiania for a few weeks, but he got the distinct impression that she wasn't telling the whole truth. Since she was clearly still hesitant to talk about her past with him, he didn't press the issue.

Tom and Kiania watched three whole episodes and wanted to watch more, but the next day was Sunday, and neither Tom nor Kiania had been able to get a lot of their homework done because they had been helping set the school's library in order. After Tom said goodnight to Kiania, she made her way up the stairs where she was intercepted by her beaming mother.

"I can't remember the last time I heard you laugh like that."

"And?"

Mrs. Martins wasn't sure what her daughter's intentions were, but she knew that Tom was head over heels in love with her.

"He seems very nice," said Mrs. Martins. "Promise me you'll at least try not to break his heart."

CHAPTER 8

The War Between the Butterflies and the Geeks reached its crescendo in mid-October, and Tom regretfully found himself in the middle of it. It started out as just another day at school until lunch came around. He was standing in the queue when a loud shout echoed throughout the cafeteria.

"DRINK PISS, TEDDY BEAR!"

As Tom turned around, something that looked like a water balloon exploded against his face. Marcus and his cronies immediately started laughing with unbridled hilarity. A quick sniff confirmed that the contents of the balloon were indeed human urine, and a look at the pieces of the object on the ground told him that it hadn't been a water balloon at all.

At that moment, any sense of logic and reason Tom possessed was immediately consumed in a white-hot explosion of pure rage.

"YOU FILTHY WASTE OF BRAIN MATTER!!!"

Tom picked up the nearest food product, a slice of chocolate cream pie, and chucked it across the room into Marcus's face. Several more students started laughing, but they immediately stopped when they saw the expression on Marcus's face.

"YOU ARE DEAD!!"

Marcus charged like an angry bull, but Tom effortlessly side-stepped him, and Marcus crashed head first into the nearest counter.

"THAT'S IT! FOOD FIGHT!!!"

The cafeteria descended into utter chaos. Students threw food and chairs at each other, pulled each other's hair, poked each other in the eyes, and trampled anyone on the floor. All the while, Marcus chased Tom like a wild animal. Tom almost made it out, but was intercepted at the door by two of Marcus's fellow football players. Tom tried to kick his way out, but Marcus was promptly on him. There was an explosion of pain in Tom's groin, and he collapsed before he knew what hit him. Marcus then proceeded to pummel him with extreme prejudice.

"A WORTHLESS LITTLE SHIT LIKE YOU DOESN'T DESERVE THE MERMAID! THOSE TITS ARE MINE!"

That was enough to snap Tom out of it. As soon as Marcus came in for another punch, Tom bit with all his might. Marcus screamed as he drew his hand away, blood spurting everywhere.

"I'LL KILL YOU! I'LL KILL YOU!!!"

Coach Matthews and one other teacher appeared and restrained Marcus. It was then that Tom became aware that all activity in the cafeteria had ceased. He looked up and saw Principal Miller, looking angrier than God on the day he destroyed Sodom and Gomorrah. The students that weren't writhing in pain were all pointing fingers at him and Marcus.

My Lord, I'm dead!!!

When Principal Miller spoke, it was like the hissing of a venomous snake before it struck.

"Mr. Matthews, Mr. Watson, escort that orangutan to my office. Assistant Principal Hammett, you will escort Mr. Lime."

Principal Miller then turned to face everyone else in the cafeteria and immediately raised her voice.

"I don't care how long it takes, anyone not seriously injured is to remain in here cleaning up this mess!"

Tom was helped to his feet by Mr. Hammett, who then escorted him to the office. He was shown to a chair while he waited for

Principal Miller to finish up with Marcus. Seeing that Tom's face was swelling from the beating that Marcus and his cronies had given him, Mr. Hammett went to the nurse's office to get him an ice pack.

"Good luck, kid."

One phrase kept repeating itself over and over in Tom's head.

I'm dead.

Tom had seen it in Principal Miller's eyes. The pranks perpetuated throughout the school had pushed her to the edge, and this had been the straw that broke the camel's back. His only saving grace was that Kiania hadn't seen it because she had a different lunch period, but the whole school would've heard about it by now.

I'm dead.

Tom started replaying the entire fight in his mind, trying to think of what he'd say to Principal Miller, assuming she even gave him a chance to speak. Now that he had time to reflect on it, he really wished that he hadn't taken a bite out of Marcus's hand. They had extensively covered bloodborne pathogens in health class.

He better not have syphilis; I REALLY don't want syphilis.

Tom lost track of how long he had been sitting there, but Marcus was eventually dragged out of the office by Coach Matthews and Mr. Watson, kicking and screaming bloody murder all the while.

"I'LL KILL YOU! YOU ARE DEAD, TEDDY BEAR! YOU ARE DEAD!!!"

"Mr. Lime, get in here!"

Time to face the music.

Tom closed the office door behind him and took the empty seat. For three whole minutes, the principal just stared at him angrily, and Tom was too scared to say a word. Tom noticed she was fiddling with a black die in her hand.

The Black Die of Death!

When Mrs. Miller finally spoke, her voice started low and gradually increased in volume.

"It's got to be a record. Ten weeks into the school year, and already the student body has managed to overclock my I've-Had-Enough-Of-This-Bullshit-Meter. The football team is now down four players, we've had to buy them new uniforms, we had to close the school for a day to fumigate, we spent three days looking for three cats that didn't exist, the janitor spent a day cleaning up billiard balls, the bathrooms still smell like bacon grease and someone's garage, and now the cafeteria has been destroyed!"

Tom flinched; he couldn't help it.

"It wasn't my…"

"DID I SAY YOU COULD SPEAK!?!"

Tom immediately fell silent.

"Now, tell me the truth!"

Tom recounted the entire episode as briefly as possible, making sure to emphasize the fact that it had all started because Marcus threw a urine-filled condom at him.

"And was throwing a slice of pie at him really the best way to resolve the issue?"

"No, it was a stupid thing to do."

Mrs. Miller sat perfectly still for about fifteen seconds and then rolled her black die across her desk. It made Tom flinch again.

"You will go to the cafeteria and help your classmates clean up what's left of your mess. Scratch that. Go down to Home-Ec first, clean yourself up, then clean up your mess. You will then receive detention, starting today and all of next week. And if you or anyone else pulls any more funny business, then you can all join Mr. Comedian at the High School Dropout Club. Is that clear?"

"Crystal, ma'am."

"Good, you're dismissed."

Tom took off like Curly Howard after consuming an entire pot of coffee.

A week and a half of detention. Not the best news, but it could've been worse.

After washing his face and being provided with a clean shirt, Tom made his way back to the cafeteria to help with the cleanup.

"So, you're not going to be expelled?" asked Samantha.

"Not yet. For now, I've just been given detention for a week and a half," replied Tom. "Where's Rick?"

"The Butterflies broke his arm."

"Why isn't there a single trace of food on you?"

"You must have me confused with someone who doesn't want a scholarship," replied Samantha. "I got the hell out of here before things got crazy. You can't throw a urine-filled condom at someone without opening the gates of hell."

"Thanks for the help," said Tom, making no effort to hide his sarcasm.

"Still, it didn't stop them from forcing everyone in this lunch period to clean up the mess. So, you snaked your way out of getting expelled by Miller. Have you figured out what you're going to say to your girlfriend?"

Tom got down on his hands and knees and vehemently apologized to Kiania as soon as he saw her. Thankfully, she seemed to think Tom getting pummeled by Marcus in a fight he didn't even start was punishment enough. His parents weren't too hard on him either. His father went as far as to say that he would've done a lot more than throw a piece of pie and bite someone's hand if he were in the exact same situation. But Tom's rollercoaster of a week wasn't over yet.

It was Friday afternoon, and Tom was finishing up in detention. With winter fast approaching, practice had officially begun for the girl's swim team, which meant Kiania was getting busy. They were supposed to have another date tonight before things got too hectic. Tom had just been dismissed and was making his way down the hall to the senior lot to wait for Kiania, when suddenly a loud crash echoed throughout the school, followed by a loud bang. Tom had seen enough movies to know a gunshot when he heard one. His first instinct was to take off running in the opposite direction, but then his brain processed the direction the gunshot had come from.

THE LOCKER ROOMS! NO! NO! NO!!!

Tom looked around for anything he could use as a weapon. He caught sight of the glass case containing a fire extinguisher and axe.

Won't do much good against a gun, but it will serve you better than nothing.

Tom smashed the case open with his backpack, grabbed the axe and extinguisher, and made his way down the hall.

Tom peeked around the corner and saw that no one was there, but he heard shouting and screaming. The girl's locker room was along the hall.

DAMN!!!

Tom forced himself to think of Kiania. He hugged the wall as he quickly made his way to the locker room door.

If it's anything like the boy's locker room, there should be a con-crete wall along the stairs. I can use that for cover.

Tom crouched down and crept inside.

"GET BACK! GET BACK AND SHUT UP! THE FIRST ONE TO MAKE A MOVE GETS ONE BETWEEN THE EYES!"

Tom peeked over the wall that lined the stairs. A tall person in a ski mask was holding the entire girl's swim team at gunpoint. It didn't look like anyone had been shot yet; the assailant must've just fired off a warning shot.

For a moment, Tom wondered what the hell he was doing there, and then he caught sight of Kiania, lined up with the rest of the girls. The gunman seemed to be struggling to make up his mind. Tom took the opportunity to try and figure out what he was supposed to do, armed with only a fire extinguisher and an axe. The moment he charged down the stairs, the gunman would turn and open fire.

Blessed Mother, please protect me...

Tom didn't have time to finish his prayer. The gunman had made up his mind and turned the gun on Kiania.

"YOU! STRIP!"

At that moment, Tom wasn't a scared teenager with a fire extinguisher and axe. He was one of the main characters in his comics, and it was up to him to save the day.

"HEY, ASSHOLE!!!"

Tom chucked the fire extinguisher over the stair wall. The gunman instinctively opened fire, and the fire extinguisher exploded, filling the room with smoke. The girls screamed and the gunman roared with anger. Tom took advantage of the momentary cover to charge down the stairs. As the smoke started to clear, Tom swung the blunt end of the axe and smacked the gun out of the assailant's hand.

"I'LL KILL YOU!"

Tom drove the handle of the fire axe hard into the gunman's face. The gunman's hands immediately went to his jaw, and Tom saw blood leaking from the mask. Wasting no time, Tom followed up with a series of blows with the blunt end of the axe, starting with the head and working his way down. He didn't stop even after the gunman hit the floor.

"YOU THINK YOU CAN THREATEN MY GIRLFRIEND!?!"

When Tom finally stopped swinging with the blunt end of the axe, he pulled off the gunman's mask. Despite the blood and damage to his jaw, it was easy for him to tell it was Marcus.

Demented son of a prostitute!

Tom was so angry he didn't notice that someone walked up to him until he felt their fist connect with his face. He looked up and saw that it was Kiania.

"What was that for?!"

"You idiot!" exclaimed Kiania. "You could've been killed, why did you do that?!"

Tom was hurt by this. He hadn't tackled an armed gunman just to get punched in the face.

"Isn't it obvious?" asked Tom, tears starting to form in his eyes. "Because I love you."

Kiania's face turned a bright shade of red. There was a chorus of light-hearted and amused exclamations from the rest of the swim team, who seemed to have completely forgotten that they had just been held at gunpoint. Kareen, the team captain, was the first to speak.

"You really know how to pick 'em, Kiania."

It didn't take long for word of the incident at Saint Thomas More High School to spread throughout all of South Bend, and it would be all over the country before midnight. After thanking Tom for saving the swim team, Principal Miller gave him a strict warning to never set foot in the girl's locker room again. After this, they needed to go through the formalities with the police. Then everyone had to dodge the press and go home and face their respective parents. Needless to say, Tom and Kiania didn't get to have their date that night. Much to Tom's surprise, Kiania got to come over the next evening. He had been sure Kiania's parents wouldn't even let her out of the house after what had happened the previous day.

"Tonight's pizza comes courtesy of the girl's swimming team," said Kiania.

Tom's mother unleashed a long line of shocked exclamations and questions at Kiania. Eventually, Tom's father reminded her that the young couple had already had enough of that and probably just wanted to watch their movie. Tom and Kiania were taking a break from British sitcoms to watch *Casablanca*, which Tom had never seen before.

"Level five intimidation, possession of an unregistered handgun, burglary, possession of methamphetamines, and attempted forcible rape," said Kiania. "My mother is going to see to it that Marcus goes away for a very long time."

Tom thought Kiania was way too calm for a girl that had been held at gunpoint by someone who wanted to rape her.

"Burglary?" he found himself saying.

"Burglary is defined as breaking and entering into any building or structure with the intent to commit a felony," explained Kiania. "It isn't limited to theft."

After Tom popped the disk into the machine, there was a moment of awkward silence.

"I'm sorry I hit you, Tom," said Kiania. "But you could've been killed."

"And you couldn't have been?" asked Tom.

"I had everything under control," replied Kiania. "If I was scared of people with guns, I wouldn't be studying to join the FBI. Marcus was under the influence of methamphetamines. Like most bullies, he's a total coward. That's why he was accompanied by six other members of the football team when he confronted you after the honey incident. When he broke into the school yesterday, he was completely out of his mind."

Tom did think it was weird that Marcus held Kiania and the girls at gunpoint as long as he did without making a move. Now that he thought about it, Marcus had been twitching like he was having a seizure or something.

"You can't effectively molest someone with only one free hand," said Kiania. "My plan was to pretend to play along, disarm him, and then incapacitate him."

"Is that your way of saying, 'thanks for saving my life?'" asked Tom.

"No, this is."

Without warning, Kiania pulled Tom close and kissed him right on the mouth. Tom's brain shut down and exploded. His body instinctively kissed her back. It was only for a moment, but it seemed to last forever. When they broke off, it took Tom a full five minutes to process what had happened. The girl he loved had just given him his first kiss.

"Why didn't you do that yesterday?" was all he could manage.

"I wasn't going to do that in front of all the girls," said Kiania smiling. "Now shut up and watch the movie."

CHAPTER 9

(HALLOWEEN)

It was about six o'clock as Mrs. Tanya Diya made her way home. Her law firm had once again refused to take the case of Marcus Johnson, despite the desperate pleas of the boy's parents.

How a lunatic like that ever got into a private school, I'll never know. If it had been another day of the week, my daughter would've been in that locker room.

Jasmine's basketball practice would have ended about half an hour ago, but Jasmine would still be using the school's exercise equipment now; she always did that. Mrs. Diya wasn't worried that Jasmine might not get her homework done. Jasmine always got her homework done and got good grades in school. Sometimes Mrs. Diya was worried that her daughter might be pushing herself too hard, but the sad truth was that you could have a perfect GPA and still not get into the college you wanted. The issue wasn't necessarily about race anymore. In recent years, too many colleges, particularly the politically biased ones, tried to meet different kinds of quotas regarding their student bodies. That was one reason why Jasmine played girls' basketball.

We made it through slavery and Jim Crow; we'll get through this.

As she drove, Mrs. Diya was thinking about her daughter playing college basketball, becoming a lawyer herself, and having children of her own.

In your dreams, Tanya.

All Jasmine cared about was school and basketball. She really didn't have time for a man in her life right now. Someday after she went to college and got a good job, she might think about finding someone who was man enough for her.

I'd rather wait and have her meet Mr. Right than rush things and have her meet Mr. Wrong.

Due to Indiana's bizarre daylight savings time, it wasn't sunset yet, but it was beginning to get dark. Mrs. Diya had to slow down because the streets were packed with trick-or-treaters. The twins would be out trick-or-treating with friends right about now. Jasmine would still be working out. By the time they all got back, Mrs. Diya and her husband Charles would have some hot pizzas waiting for them. As she pulled up to the house, she saw that the lights were on. Charles usually got home first. His car was in the garage when she opened it, but when she went inside, she saw that the bowl of candy for the trick-or-treaters was untouched. Trick-or-treating usually started at five o'clock and ended at seven.

He can't still be taking a shower.

Tanya placed her things on the table and called out Charles's name. There was no answer.

Tanya started to make her way up the stairs to see what Charles was doing when her phone vibrated. Oddly enough, it was a text message from Charles.

Ever see the movie *Psycho*?

Before Tanya could respond, the bedroom door at the top of the stairs opened up, and someone dressed head to toe in black and wearing a green and black-spotted frog mask stepped out, clutching a bloody knife.

Tanya screamed and instinctively raised her arms to defend

---

herself. She screamed again as the knife was driven into her hand. The Dart Frog kicked her hard in the chest and sent her crashing down the stairs. The Dart Frog leapt down after Tanya and landed on her chest, breaking several ribs. Before Tanya blacked out, she used the last of her willpower to rip the mask from the person's face, and she couldn't believe her eyes.

CHAPTER 10

When Tom was younger, he would always rush home from school to go trick-or-treating on Halloween. A kid could never get enough free candy in two hours, so he would always race around the neighborhood like his life depended on it. Of course, Tom had long outgrown the most popular Halloween tradition. If Halloween didn't fall on the weekend, he'd spend his evening doing his homework, and then watch a scary movie if he had the time.

If I hadn't read that one book, I wouldn't even know what Halloween is really about.

Since it was a school night, Tom had just finished grinding out a paper about atrocities committed by Henry VIII and drawing parallels between him and all modern-day politicians who found the immutable laws of God inconvenient. He was in the middle of making popcorn when his little sister Britney walked into the room.

"Don't burn down the house, Smokey."

"I told you not to call me that," groaned Tom.

After the incident with Marcus, Tom got a new nickname. When word got around that his classmates called him the Teddy Bear, combined with how he had confronted Marcus, one news network rebranded him "Smokey." Tom wasn't pleased with his new nickname, not even after Samantha pointed out to him that Smokey the Bear had reduced forest fire damage by eighty percent in the first twenty years that his PSAs had been running.

Tom had become the school celebrity. Some of the boys thanked him for saving their girlfriends, and even Juno got a little too friend-ly with him when she thanked Tom for saving Kareen. Juno had walked right up to Tom, wrapped her arms around him, and kissed him on the cheek right there in front of everyone. Kiania was quick to reprimand her for it.

"Get your paws off my boyfriend!"

Juno's expression was one of a woman overcome with raw emotion.

"Sorry, Kiania, I got a little carried away. It's just that I've already lost my parents, and my boyfriend is in rehab. You'll have to forgive me if I properly thank Tom for saving my best friend."

"I did not encourage her!" said Tom.

To prove his sincerity, Tom had to take Kiania shopping. Of course, for Kiania, he would've happily shaved his head, painted a stripe around his neck, and volunteered his services as a hu-man bowling pin. It didn't change the fact that he would need to take dish duty at the bakery for a month to recoup his losses, and Thanksgiving was just around the corner, so there would be a huge traffic intake.

Tom sat down to watch his horror movie. He had made it twen-ty minutes in when he got the call.

Why would Samantha be calling me this late?

Tom had known Samantha long enough to know that she wasn't the kind of person to make social calls on Halloween. He knew for a fact that she had basketball practice today, and would've imme-diately gone home to do her homework. In all likelihood, she was more tired than he was. Samantha wasn't the kind of person to pull pranks either, that was something Rick would do.

"What's happened?" he asked, answering the phone

"Tom, there's been another double murder!" cried Samantha, utterly hysterical.

Tom felt the heat drain from his body. After the episode in the girl's locker room with Marcus, he had almost completely forgotten about the murders.

"Who?"

"It's Jasmine's parents..."

Ever since he started courting Kiania, Tom had been doing his best to keep himself from swearing; but he couldn't keep it in this time. He had been born and raised in the United States of America during a time of great civil unrest. He knew what was about to happen, and the reality of it overwhelmed him.

"Shit, things are about to get loud."

When Marcus held the girl's swim team at gunpoint, South Bend became the center of attention for every news outlet in America. Now two prominent African American citizens had been senselessly slaughtered in their own home, leaving behind three children. Within twenty-four hours, the entire country was in an uproar. The school was crawling with cops. Tom had to spend the rest of the week dodging journalists that wanted his thoughts on the tragedy. Meanwhile, Jasmine and her siblings' faces were all over every major news network, along with all the other surviving children of the Dart Frog's victims. South Bend officially had a serial killer on the loose, and the whole country knew it.

A mandatory curfew was now in effect throughout the city. No one under the age of twenty-one was allowed out after dark without an adult present. When it came time for Tom and Kiania's next date, she needed to be escorted to the Lime residence by her father. They were watching a movie Kiania had already seen, so she wouldn't be distracted while she talked to Tom.

"Same weapon, same mask, only this time it was green."

"Oh great," replied Tom. "Now they can make a traffic light."

"Once again, no signs of forced entry. According to the police, Mr. Diya got home at about 5:30. Jasmine's siblings had already left to go trick-or-treating with friends. Mr. Diya went up to take a shower. The murderer walked right in, killed him, and mutilated the corpse. But this time there was one difference."

"Dare I ask, what?" asked Tom.

"In addition to his extremities, the murderer removed Mr. Diya's right thumb. After the murderer was done, they waited for Mrs. Diya to come home. She walked in, made her way up the stairs, and the murderer sent her a text message with Mr. Diya's phone. The murderer used the momentary distraction to knock her down the stairs, and then finished her off."

"What was the text message?" asked Tom.

"Ever see the movie *Psycho*?"

Tom was about to ask Kiania if she was serious, but she had just said that Mr. Diya was killed while taking a shower, and Mrs. Diya was knocked down the stairs. It was some sort of twisted homage.

"That's all we needed," groaned Tom. "A serial killer with a sense of humor."

"Despite the fact that the victims were African Americans this time, the police are confident that it's the same person."

"Why would their race affect the issue?" asked Tom.

"My dear Thomas, you know as well as I do that serial killers have victim profiles. For example, one serial killer might only kill blonde women in their mid-twenties. Both the Simpsons and the Smiths were Caucasian. However, all the victims have one thing in common. In all three cases, the victims were the parents of a senior at our high school."

"And now our school is crawling with cops," said Tom.

"They've come to the same conclusion that I have," said Kiania. "Three pairs of dead parents can't be a coincidence. No, it is perfectly clear that the Dart Frog is a student at our school, in all probability, one of our fellow seniors."

"Are you sure?" asked Tom.

"As sure as I can be without any tangible evidence. Unfortunately, the Dart Frog has been very careful to not leave any. Nevertheless, it's highly improbable that the murderer could be an underclassman. The graphic and meticulous nature of these crimes suggests a very personal motivation. What motivation would a freshman have for killing Juno's parents to cap off the first week of school?"

"What about a member of the faculty?" asked Tom.

"The police started looking into the faculty after the second pair of murders. It is unlikely that any of the teachers or other members of the staff would harbor some sort of grudge against Juno, Fred, and Jasmine specifically. Even if that were the case, why would they take it out on their parents?"

It had occurred to Tom that it was possible that someone on the school's payroll might be a little too interested in the students, but then he remembered what Kiania said about victim profiles. Juno and Jasmine were both women, but Fred was a man. Kiania seemed to read his mind.

"Serial killers looking for some sort of sexual release from their crimes have sexual preferences. But the fact that there have been six different victims, half men and half women, four Caucasians, and two African Americans, creates too much inconsistency. No, I don't think the Dart Frog is some kind of pervert, they're only in this for the *thrill of the kill* as it were."

"And the removal of the eyes, reproductive organs, and the women's breasts?" asked Tom.

"Scare tactics and trophies," replied Kiania.

Tom didn't say anything for a long time. He had known a lot of the people in his class since middle school; he had even gone to kindergarten with some of them. But there were nearly two hundred people in his class, and he obviously wasn't acquainted with all of them. As a devout Catholic, he knew that evil was very real. In recent years, school shootings had become too frequent across the country; he prevented one a few weeks ago. If Marcus could do something as depraved as hold the swim team at gunpoint and attempt to rape Kiania, it was perfectly possible that one of his classmates could be the Dart Frog.

"Does anyone stand out?"

"Senior hall is occupied by nearly two hundred people," replied Kiania. "Let's see if we can narrow it down. We can eliminate ourselves, obviously. We were both at the movies when the Simpsons were killed."

"Okay," said Tom. "You're the aspiring criminal profiler. What are we looking for?"

"This person is in all likelihood a sadist who enjoys watching people suffer. We're looking for someone intelligent, someone who thinks things through. They knew how to commit three double murders without leaving any tangible evidence for the police to use. The fact that all the victims were mutilated post-mortem without much difficulty suggests a practical knowledge of human anatomy. All the victims were parents of someone on the high end of the school's social hierarchy. Whoever killed them knew exactly what kind of security system their houses had and how to disable them without sounding an alarm. I trust you know that hacking isn't anywhere near as easy as they make it look in movies and television?"

Tom nodded.

"With that in mind, I'm inclined to think that the Dart Frog is on the same social standing as his or her victims; but I can't say for sure without further data. It could just as easily be a socially awkward and intelligent stalker."

"That's nothing to go on," said Tom.

"Exactly," replied Kiania. "For the time being, let's examine each event one by one. Is there any reason to suspect any one individual for each double murder?"

"Juno is the queen bee on campus," said Tom. "Anyone she wronged could have a motive. The boys she dated, the ones she shot down, the girls that envied her, and the ones that straight-up hated her. That's no short list."

"Taking all the other facts into consideration, only one person comes to mind," said Kiania.

Kiania pulled up a list she had made on her tablet, complete with visual aids.

"Mark Xeg. The socially awkward president of the school's gaming club and possibly the most knowledgeable boy in school. Juno shot him down last year, and he was subsequently bullied by Fred, whom Juno has been dating for some time. No one was killed while he was on suicide watch."

Mark was one of the students in the running to be class valedictorian. With his knowledge of computers, Tom could easily see him hacking someone's home security system.

"But why would he kill Jasmine's parents?" asked Tom.

"I can't say for certain," replied Kiania. "I can only guess, and no good can come from wild speculation. But eliminating a suspect because you don't know their motive is a rookie mistake."

Tom saw that Kiania had the other members of the gaming club listed under Mark's name. Any one of them could've had a motive to hurt Juno after what she did to their friend. Courtney Peaches, Rachel Phillips, Elizabeth Holt, Darrel Edwards, and Haru Fukuda. Tom noticed that Kiania had crossed out Rick's picture and name.

"You're taking Rick off the board?" asked Tom.

"The mutilations inflicted on the Diya's were done by someone using their right hand," replied Kiania. "Your friend's right arm has been in a cast since the food fight."

"Yes, that is a good point."

Kiania pulled up the next person on her list.

"In a premeditated and calculated crime, the perpetrator usually has something to gain. So far, the person that has benefited the most from these atrocities is Isaiah James. He competed fiercely with Fred in football and in romance. He was turned down by Juno, just like Mark, and Fred was the one who became team captain. Now things have changed. Fred is in rehab, and Isaiah is team captain."

"But he was at the football game the night of the second double murder," said Tom.

"He could've had an accomplice, or he could've snuck out of his home later."

"But once again, why would Isaiah kill Jasmine's parents?"

"I do not know," replied Kiania. "I am only observing the fact that, at the moment, he has the most to gain from these crimes. I admit that there isn't sufficient data to confirm that he is the Dart Frog, but there isn't enough to prove that he isn't either."

Tom was going to bring up Isaiah's reputation, but then he remembered that Kiania had previously told him on one of their dates that serial killers were often people you'd never accuse of murder. Isaiah appeared to be a remarkable athlete and a model student, but Tom didn't really know him personally. He had no idea what could be lurking beneath the surface. Kiania placed a question mark next to Isaiah's name and picture but didn't take him off the board.

"Both of the suspects that we've looked at don't seem to have had any motive for killing the Diyas," said Kiania. "If anyone hated Jasmine, it was Kalin Doyle. When he was nine years old, his mother was killed by a man driving while under the influence of marijuana. He was actually in the car when it happened."

This took Tom by surprise. He knew that Kalin lived alone with his father, the sheriff, but he never knew the circumstances of his mother's death. He had been wondering why the Dart Frog was only killing the parents of Saint Thomas More High School students and not the students themselves. What if Kalin never got over his mother's death?

"Of course, Kalin isn't the only person in our class that is missing a parent."

Kiania had another image linked to Kalin's on her tablet.

"Lilian Andersen, Kalin's girlfriend. She's been in and out of foster homes since she was six. Her parents were killed by radical democrats while attending a protest against left-wing indoctrination in children's entertainment."

"How do you know all of this?" asked Tom.

"The death of her parents is a simple internet search. As for her foster care records, the police aren't always as stupid as they appear in horror movies. They've identified her as a person of interest."

"Are they going to take any action?" asked Tom.

"Right now, their suspicions are only suspicions. In a court of law, that is not enough. Unfortunately, the Dart Frog hasn't left much in the way of tangible evidence. For all we know, the Dart Frog could be someone we haven't even considered. Six people are dead, and now the entire country is watching the case unfold with bated breath. No one wants this person getting off on a technicality."

CHAPTER 11

Unlike Juno, Jasmine didn't need a week to recuperate from the loss of her parents. She was back in school on Monday morning, and the first thing she did was stomp over to Kalin's locker and slam her fist into it.

"YOU FILTHY MURDERING MONSTER!!!"

Kalin's face was utterly devoid of emotion. He didn't react in the slightest as Jasmine spat out a never-ending stream of obscenities.

"I haven't the foggiest idea what you're talking about," said Kalin calmly.

"DON'T GIVE ME ANY OF THAT!" exclaimed Jasmine, who thrust a newspaper into Kalin's face. "IS THIS HOW YOU GET YOUR SICK KICKS!?!"

The front page of the newspaper was about the murder of Jasmine's parents. Kalin's expression did not change.

"I never touched your parents."

"BULLSHIT!!!"

Before the situation escalated any further, the police officer that had been on duty pulled Jasmine away.

"That's enough!"

Jasmine swatted the man's arm away. If her actions could be considered assaulting an officer, she really didn't care.

"MY PARENTS ARE DEAD! MY LITTLE BROTHER, MY LITTLE SISTER, AND I ARE ALL ORPHANS! AND YOU'RE DEFENDING THIS PIG!?!"

Jasmine stuck both her middle fingers in the air and stomped off.

Despite Jasmine's outburst, there were no more violent incidents among the students. Between the police officers that now stood in the halls and Principal Miller's threat of expulsion, all the students were very quiet. Everyone just went from one class to the next hardly saying anything, and they all surreptitiously watched each other. Though the police obviously hadn't shared their theory with the public, everyone in the school had begun to suspect what was going on. The parents of three different seniors had been senselessly slaughtered in their homes. It couldn't be a coincidence. The Dart Frog was someone in senior hall.

How the hell are we supposed to think about polynomial functions and the half-life of plutonium? There's a killer on the loose!

Tom was finding it harder and harder to focus on schoolwork. Like everyone else, he was wondering who the Dart Frog could be and who was next.

Juno and Fred were dating, but there is nothing at all to link the Simpsons and the Smiths with the Diyas. Tom had been trying to establish why Mark or Isaiah might want to kill Jasmine's parents. As far as his memory served, Mark had never interacted with Jasmine at all. All of Mark's attention had been on Juno, who spurned his affection with extreme prejudice.

I can believe Mark killed Juno's parents because he couldn't stand being rejected, and I can see him killing Fred's parents because Juno dated him. He offered Juno a shoulder to cry on, and she beat the crap out of him and told him to kill himself. Did heartbreak and sorrow turn into rage while he was on suicide watch? Kiania said these crimes were all premeditated and calculated, not spur-of-the-moment crimes of passion. What would he gain by taking his frustration out on Jasmine?

Thanks to Jasmine and the African American community of

South Bend, the murders had become a national sensation. Maybe Mark killed Juno and Fred's parents in some sick attempt to get her to fall in love with him. When that failed, did he decide to keep killing because he enjoyed it? Did he enjoy the attention that the Dart Frog was getting, the attention he didn't get as a celebrity in the gaming community?

Then there's Isaiah.

Isaiah was a model student, a football star, and a hard worker that loved his family.

Allegedly.

Tom had been low on the school's social hierarchy since freshman year. He only knew Isaiah by reputation. Isaiah's whole golden boy routine might just be an act for all he knew. He had competed fiercely with Fred for the top spot on the school's football team, and they had both dated Juno at some point. Did Fred make Isaiah feel inadequate? Did Isaiah take extreme steps to knock Fred off his perch?

But why would he kill Jasmine's parents?

As far as Tom could tell, Kalin and Lilian were the only two people that might've had reason to attack the Diya family. Both had been social outcasts. Lilian had lost both of her parents, and Kalin had lost his mother. Tom had seen enough movies and TV shows to know that losing one or both parents at a young age could cause long-lasting psychological trauma.

Did Kalin and Lilian decide to celebrate senior year by killing their classmates' parents?

If this were a movie, Tom would've thought that the Kalin and Lilian theory fit a little too well. But this wasn't a movie, this was real life.

Occam's Razor, the simplest explanation is most often the correct one. But of course, there's no proof. I'll just have to keep my eyes on those two moving forward.

Fred may have descended into alcoholism and dropped out of school after the deaths of his parents, but it quickly became clear that Jasmine wasn't going to let her parents' deaths stop her from playing basketball. The first game after her parents' deaths was against their rival school, the Saint James Archers. Samantha told Tom that there were going to be talent scouts in the crowd, but the fact was that the whole country was going to be watching. Because of the curfew, Tom and Kiania were going to the game with their families. The school was swarming with onlookers and police when they arrived. Tom and his family had barely gotten out of their car when they were ambushed by reporters. Despite the media circus surrounding Mr. and Mrs. Diya's deaths, the world hadn't forgotten that Tom had saved the girl's swim team from a shooter. They were saved by the timely arrival of Kiania and her family. Kiania's mother used her position as county prosecutor to threaten to have their licenses pulled.

"Must be great being a county prosecutor," said Mrs. Lime.

"It has its perks," said Mrs. Martins. "But I'm glad I could finally get away from the office to meet the family of the boy who saved my daughter."

It quickly became clear that Tom and Kiania's parents would get on famously. They had a little trouble finding seats that would accommodate them all. The game was sold out. Not only was a significant portion of the student body present, but a large number of Jasmine's sympathizers from the city's African-American community were in attendance. As the party fought their way through the crowd in an attempt to find a place in the bleachers, Tom saw Isaiah being interviewed by some reporters in another corner of the gym. Tom couldn't make out what was being said, so he resolved to keep his eyes on the news later.

He has benefited the most from the murders so far. But looking at him, you wouldn't think he'd do it.

———————

The very next moment, Tom and Kiania were ambushed by Kareen, who hugged them both.

"And how is Saint Thomas More High School's favorite power couple this evening?"

"We're doing fine, Kareen," replied Kiania. "Finished your homework already?"

"No one does their homework on Friday night," said Kareen. "Juno is on cheerleading duty tonight. I'm here in case she needs some emotional support."

Tom and Kiania looked over where the cheerleaders were getting warmed up. Juno was working with an impassive countenance.

"It's amazing how she and Jasmine can keep going after everything that has happened," said Kareen. "If someone murdered both my parents, I'd probably end up like Fred. I just wouldn't know what to do."

Tom couldn't believe that Juno was still a cheerleader. He thought she would've been kicked out after what she did to Mark.

I guess having your parents murdered buys you a lot of clemency. The cheerleader coach is probably a Bergoglian.[1]

While Tom and Kiania's parents were busy shooting the breeze, both Tom and Kiania were scanning the crowd.

"Fifty-fifty chance the Dart Frog is here," whispered Tom.
"Serial killers do like to follow reactions to their crimes," replied Kiania. "But not every senior is here. The Dart Frog may be committing their next murder as we speak. In any event, we should be safe here. All the Dart Frog's victims were killed in their own homes. He or she wouldn't try to kill our parents in front of all these witnesses."

---

1   Bergoglian: A derogatory term used to refer to people who claim to be Catholics, but whose personal opinions, beliefs, and stance on certain issues are in direct conflict with true Catholic values and laws to the point of heresy and apostasy, both of which are crimes that warrant immediate excommunication from the Church. Alternatively, it can refer to criminally negligent or incompetent members of the clergy, particularly those that fail to excommunicate people who unabashedly commit heresy and apostasy.

It was for that reason that Tom volunteered to be the person to get snacks. As he made his way to the snack bar, he saw where Isaiah was sitting. Mark was not present; the only member of the gaming club that was present was Rick. He wasn't surprised when he didn't see Kalin or Lilian anywhere.

Jasmine would crucify Kalin in front of all these people if he were here.

When Tom left the gym, he finally caught sight of Adam Jones. He was dressed in his Paladin mascot costume and was being interviewed by more reporters.

They must be talking to every African American in the school. I'm sure he only cares about getting more views for his UBox channel.

Tom didn't get to the snack bar without being noticed by the reporters, but this time someone else came to the rescue. A tall woman dressed in the uniform of the sheriff's department walked up, flashed her badge, and told the reporters to get lost.

"Thank you, officer…"

"Captain, Captain Lopez."

"Thank you, Captain Lopez."

"I should be thanking you," said the captain, her tone suddenly becoming a lot more friendly. "You saved my daughter's life after all."

Kalin wasn't the only person in school with a parent in the sheriff's department. Tom had completely forgotten about Silvie Lopez, another member of the swimming team.

I think I just figured out where Kiania is getting her inside information on the Dart Frog investigation from.

"Well, to be perfectly honest, Captain, I was just trying to save my girlfriend," said Tom.

"And here I was thinking there weren't any real men in this school. This is for you."

Captain Lopez handed Tom a gift card.

"And if Kiania ever dumps you, I'm sure Silvie will be happy to have you."

Tom blushed. Silvie was a pretty girl, but she couldn't hold a candle to Kiania.

"I'll bear that in mind, Captain."

Don't get your hopes up.

Kiania was still scanning the crowd when Tom returned to the bleachers with everyone's snacks in hand.

"So how long has Rick been crushing on Samantha?" she asked.

Tom's face turned red again.

"What makes you say that?" he asked.

"He hasn't taken his eyes off her since he arrived," replied Kiania. "It's the exact same look that you have on your face whenever you look at me."

"I'm not at liberty to discuss that," replied Tom.

"Duly noted," said Kiania.

Before the national anthem, Principal Miller called for a moment of silence for the Simpson, Smith, and Diya families. The entire gymnasium immediately became as quiet as a church. Both Tom and Kiania's eyes darted around the room, trying to watch everyone's reactions. Adam had removed the helmet of his costume but displayed no emotion. Tom caught sight of Casey Rosewood. She had helped Jasmine out in her science classes over the years. She seemed to be crying a little. Rick was observing the moment with all due solemnity but still had his eyes on Samantha. Isaiah looked sympathetic, but like Adam, he displayed no obvious emotion. Tom spotted Randy tucked away in one corner of the room, and he seemed to be suppressing a grin. From her position among the cheerleaders, Juno was crying freely. Jasmine was putting on a strong front but was clearly struggling to keep her emotions in check.

Anyone who savagely murders six people and is still coming to this school must be able to put on a good poker face.

Saint Thomas More High School and Saint James High School had a long and colorful rivalry. Whenever the two schools competed in a sporting event, it was called a "Holy War." Everyone that had shown up in the gym that night had come to see a girls' basketball game, but what followed after the national anthem could hardly be considered a game. In the end, the Paladins had beaten the Archers fifty-five to seventeen. All the while, Jasmine was like an unstoppable juggernaut. She never let up, not even for a moment, and when it was all over, she had scored thirty-three points. When the final buzzer sounded, she couldn't hold her emotions back anymore and collapsed to the floor crying.

"Oh dear," said Mrs. Lime.

Jasmine's teammates all flocked around her. Juno fought her way through to give Jasmine a hug. The first person to make it to Jasmine from the bleachers, despite her infirmities, was Jasmine's grandmother.

As soon as the elderly Mrs. Diya had her crying grandchild in her arms, she started to sing. It was some variation of *Michael Row the Boat Ashore*. Little by little, the rest of the gymnasium started to join in.

Michael row the boat ashore, Hallelujah!
Preach the gospel and law forevermore, Hallelujah!
O poor sinner filled with woe, Hallelujah!
Sinner row to save your soul, Hallelujah!
They nailed Jesus to the cross, Hallelujah!
But his faith was never lost, Hallelujah!
Jordan's river is chilly and cold, Hallelujah!
Chills the body but not the soul, Hallelujah!
Jordan's river is deep and wide, Hallelujah!
Milk and honey on the other side, Hallelujah!
So Christian soldiers off to war, Hallelujah!
Hold the line forevermore, Hallelujah!

After everything that had happened over the past couple of months, this was a stunning moment of school unity. One could hardly believe that the *War Between the Butterflies and the Geeks* had ever taken place. But for some reason he couldn't explain, Tom's thoughts were disturbed by the song.

Where did I hear that before?

As Tom and Kiania's families made their way to their cars, they tried to read the faces of the police officers they passed. Nothing had happened during the game, and nothing appeared to be happening now, at least not yet.

Maybe the Dart Frog is waiting for an unsuspecting family to come home.

As soon as they made it to their cars, Mrs. Martins reminded Tom's parents to make sure the house was securely locked up when they got home. As they drove, Tom decided to text Rick. He hadn't expected Mark to show up at the game, but he was curious to see if Rick knew where he was. He proceeded tactfully.

How are things with the gaming club?

We're getting by. Of course, it's not easy for me to play Star Warrior with only one hand. Haru is doing the best that he can, but he's no Mark.

He's still AWOL?

He hasn't logged in since Juno nearly drove him over the edge. Most days he doesn't even talk to us. He's the reason we won the national tournament. I don't know how he spends his nights now.

The image of Mark dressed head to toe in black, wearing a frog mask, and wielding a huge hunting knife flashed across Tom's mind; but he didn't share his thoughts with Rick.

He was hopelessly in love, and Juno rejected him. It must've changed his priorities.

I guess… While we're on the subject of girls, can you keep a secret?

Certainly.

Do you think Samantha would go to the prom with me if I asked her?

Tom smiled.

Go ahead, flip that coin.

As soon as Tom and his family got home, they locked the house up tight. They then proceeded to carefully search all the rooms from the attic to the basement. There was no one in the house but their five selves. Tom texted Kiania that they were barricaded in until morning, and she promptly responded that it was the same at her house. Since he had a lot of homework to do tomorrow, Tom brushed his teeth, went to his room, locked the door, and tried to get some sleep. But sleep would not come easily. He knew that somewhere in South Bend, the Dart Frog was probably picking out his or her next victim, if they hadn't already made their next move.

CHAPTER 12

(MIDTERMS)

November passed without incident. The Dart Frog still hadn't been caught. For the students of Saint Thomas More High School, the chaos that usually accompanied the impending arrival of Christmas was mixed with a deep sense of dread, and not just because of the approaching midterms. For Tom, school was becoming unbearable. With swimming season in full swing and midterms around the corner, he and Kiania had to cut down drastically on their binge-watching sessions. With everything going on, all his teachers' lectures turned into nonsensical forty-five-minute streams of gibberish. Tom spent most of his time in school trying to observe his classmates, desperately trying to figure out which was the monster in human form.

Kalin and Jasmine spat hate at each other whenever they were in close proximity, but Mrs. Miller's threat of expulsion kept them from going any further. Football was over, and Isaiah had successfully earned his scholarship, but he still looked just as tense as everyone else. Casey seemed scared of her own shadow. Kareen was constantly on edge. She was almost always seen with dark chocolate in her mouth; something Kiania said only happened when she was nervous and didn't care about breaking out. Out of all the students in senior hall, both Adam and Randy seemed comparatively oblivious to the dark cloud of fear that hung over the campus.

Randy walked from class to class with an incredulous grin on his face. Adam was no doubt taking advantage of the media circus to attract attention to his UBox channel. He went around interviewing his fellow students, asking them who they thought the Dart Frog was and who they thought was next.

Mark looked like a zombie as he moved through the school. He had been avoiding Juno after her last rebuff. He couldn't even stand to look at her, but on the last Friday before midterms, Juno bee-lined straight for him, her face red with rage. She picked Mark up and slammed him against the nearest locker.

"DID YOU KILL MY PARENTS?!"

Mark had been hopelessly in love with Juno, but the only times she ever touched him was to hurt him. From the moment Juno approached, his face had gone from resigned depression to pure terror.

"No," he replied weakly, tears swelling up in his eyes.

"WHERE WERE YOU THE NIGHT THEY WERE KILLED?!"

"Nowhere."

"WHERE WERE YOU THE NIGHT FRED'S PARENTS WERE KILLED?! DID YOU KILL THEM BECAUSE YOU COULDN'T STAND THE THOUGHT OF FRED'S LIPS ON MINE AND HIS HANDS ALL OVER ME?! DOES DRESSING UP IN A FROG MASK AND CARVING PEOPLE LIKE PUMPKINS MAKE YOU FEEL LIKE A BIG MAN?!"

Before the gaming club could arrive and tear Juno apart, Isaiah stepped in.

"Unless you want to be expelled, I suggest you put him down and leave him alone."

Juno put Mark down and promptly slapped Isaiah across the face.

"Mind your own damn business!"

Juno's latest assault on Mark was all anyone was talking about at lunch. Rick sat with the rest of the gaming club to try to calm Mark down, leaving Tom and Samantha by themselves.

"Juno accused him of being the Dart Frog," said Samantha. "Do you think there's anything in it?"

"He certainly has reason to hate her," replied Tom. "But looking at him now, you wouldn't think him capable of these crimes."

"No arguments here," said Samantha. "He looks more like an injured puppy than a wolf stalking its prey."

And I still can't think of any reason he'd kill Jasmine's parents unless he wanted to cover his tracks. But after Juno's last rebuff, maybe his suicidal thoughts turned to frustration and rage, and he needed to take them out on something...

There were other suspects. Tom's eyes went around the cafeteria, observing his fellow students, wishing he could read their minds.

This is insane! How can anyone even think about Christmas or midterms with a killer on the loose?!

Protons, neutrons, electrons, compounds, elements, reactions, half-lives! If I ever have to take another chemistry class in my life, I might go on a killing spree myself!

My parents can't find out! If they do, it will ruin everything! My god! They can't find out!

I don't understand it. What does the Teddy Bear have that I don't? It's not fair...

It's him! I know it's him! Everyone else is going nuts, but he keeps walking around like it's just another day at school. I must be careful though...

My parents died too; I didn't get a scholarship.

She has the most to gain, and her alibi doesn't hold up. I don't doubt she'll do anything to get her way, those six people were just collateral damage.

Who's next?! What if it's my family?!

Tom spent the weekend revising for midterms like everyone else. There was little else to do with the Dart Frog still on the loose and the curfew still in full effect. He tried to tell himself that when the exams were over, he could spend plenty of time with Kiania over Christmas vacation. On Monday morning, he went in to take his first three exams like everyone else. At first, no one noticed that one member of the senior class was absent, but by the end of the day, word began to spread through the grapevine. Tom didn't get the news until after his third and final exam of the day. It came from Rick.

"Tom, did you hear? Randy's missing!"

"Missing?" asked Tom.

"He wasn't in school today and the police are looking for him."

"Why?"

"Apparently he went out to buy a video game on Sunday and never came home."

Tom couldn't think of any logical reason why Randy would run away from home and skip his midterms. In fact, he hadn't given Randy a single thought since he tried to interview Kiania and asked her some very insensitive questions, an interview that ended with Tom chasing Randy away like all the other times.

He still had four exams to take, so he tried not to think about it.

The next day, there was still no news of Randy. Tom had managed to confidently make it through two more of his midterms. He only had two left, and the thought of spending Christmas vacation with Kiania filled his mind. All in all, he was feeling pretty good about himself. When he went to school on the final day of his exams, he found a small mountain of gifts in front of his locker. They were all from members of the girl's swim team, their friends, their boyfriends, and his admirers throughout the school. He stashed them in his locker until the day was over. When Tom's final exam was over, he needed to ask Rick and Samantha to help carry the gifts to his car.

"Oh dear, this one's from Juno," said Samantha. "She's thanking you for saving her best friend, and tells you to open the gift in private."

"I tremble with anticipation," said Tom, sounding more apprehensive than excited.

"One day you're a nobody, then you stop a shooting, and suddenly you're Mr. Popular," said Rick.

"It's not Tom's fault you only know how to be brave in video games."

Tom guessed correctly from the conversation that Rick still hadn't asked Samantha out to the prom. They had just made it to Tom's car and he was pulling out his keys when he noticed something odd.

"What's that smell?"

Both Rick and Samantha sniffed the air. It was Samantha who smelled it first.

"God, it smells like bad meat! Where's that coming from?!"

It was coming from the present on top of the pile that Tom was carrying. It was about the size of a soda can.

I cannot wait to have fun with you.
-A friend

Tom opened the present and screamed. When Rick and Samantha saw what was inside, they screamed too. There in the box was the rotting remains of a human thumb.

Tom spent the better part of the next three hours answering questions for the police. The thumb had belonged to an African American man. They needed to do a DNA test for confirmation, but it was a pretty safe bet that it was the one missing from Charles Diya. There were fingerprints on the box, but they belonged to a very terrified and confused freshman named Tony Armstrong, who insisted that he had been paid one hundred dollars by someone in a black ski mask and sunglasses to place the box by Tom's locker. Before long, the police would start interviewing every person in the school. Tom wasn't going to get to have his date with Kiania that night. The Dart Frog was making his or her next move. In all probability, his parents were the targets.

When he was finally done answering the police's questions, Tom was taken home. Just like every night for the past few months, he and his family searched the house from top to bottom. The house was locked up tight, with no way in or out. But this time, police cars patrolled the neighborhood and blocked every entrance into it. Also, in the months since the first murder, the neighborhoods of Saint Thomas More families had formed watches. When Tom finally went to his room, he had his weighted wooden training sword at the ready. It was essentially a very heavy club, but it would serve him just fine. He was in constant contact with Kiania and his friends over the phone until they went to bed. Unable to sleep, Tom kept pacing his room for hours, jumping at the slightest sound and staring out the window. Eventually, it started to snow. Tom hadn't had a white Christmas in years. Old Man Winter had a reputation for coming to South Bend late and then never wanting to leave, but recent events had made Tom forget all about it.

We actually get some snow on the ground in December when there's a psycho on the loose. Merry fricking Christmas.

Eventually, Tom just couldn't keep his eyes open anymore and fell fast asleep. He didn't know how long he had been asleep when he was awoken by the sound of his ringtone. He flailed about in the dark to find his phone. It was just past seven o'clock. The sun wasn't up yet, but that was normal for South Bend in December. Tom's still sleepy brain suddenly processed that he had fallen asleep while waiting for the Dart Frog to make their move. Fighting off grogginess, he hastily answered Kiania's call.

"What is it?"

"The Dart Frog was screwing with us. He or she has killed Randy's parents."

It was all over the news. The Parkers had been found lying mutilated in the snow with a pink and black-spotted frog mask placed between them. The big difference from the previous murders was that the bodies had been dragged outside this time, and the house had been burned down. Randy himself was still nowhere to be found.

That evening, Tom was escorted to the Martins' residence for a date with Kiania. They waited until her parents left them alone before they began discussing the recent developments.

"I'd been wondering why the Dart Frog cut off Charles Diya's finger," said Kiania. "They were planning a misdirect. They send you a finger, everyone thinks your family is the next on the chopping block, and while the police are distracted, he or she caught the Parkers off their guard. Well, that trick's not going to work again."

"Why did the Dart Frog kill the Parkers anyway?" asked Tom. "All the other victims were parents of seniors high on the social ladder. Randy and his family don't fit the victim profile. And why did he or she burn the house down?"

"Serial killers typically don't change their MO unless they have to," replied Kiania. "It's possible that the Dart Frog is devolving and losing control. It's also possible that the Parkers weren't part of the Dart Frog's original plan. A great big fire usually does a good job at obliterating forensic evidence, so in all probability, the Dart Frog wanted to make sure the police didn't find something in the house."

As Tom had said, Randy was not high on the social ladder. The fact that he was still missing made everyone else think he must be the Dart Frog. After making sure her parents hadn't come back down, Kiania asked Tom what he thought.

"I don't believe in that story for a minute. Randy runs away; his parents tell the police that he's missing, and then Randy comes back, kills his parents, and then burns the house down? It doesn't make any sense. If Randy was the Dart Frog and wanted to kill his parents, he wouldn't have run away; he would've killed them outright."

Kiania smiled. Tom was no fool.

"If Randy were the Dart Frog, I imagine the police would've caught that little cretin by now. If you want my opinion, I'm sure the little rat stuck his neck out where it didn't belong, and this time he got his head cut off."

"Your argument is logical, but we can't confirm it until we've found his body. In the meantime, we must take into account every conceivable eventuality," said Kiania.

"I don't get you."

"My dear Thomas, there is such a thing as a double bluff. Let's assume for a moment that Randy is the Dart Frog. After the Diyas, these murders attracted the attention of the entire country. The whole town is under curfew. Whoever the Dart Frog is, he or she can no longer leave their home without adult supervision. Unless their parents were in on these crimes, the Dart Frog would need to take them out of the equation."

"So Randy runs away, tricks everyone into thinking he's dead, and then kills his parents to take all three of them off the board?" asked Tom.

"I admit its probability level is not high, but at the moment there's no evidence that says it didn't happen. I've told you before, serial killers are often people you'd never suspect of murder. Randy may have presented himself as a bumbling imbecile in the past, but for all we know it was all just an act. Sometimes it is wise to seem foolish."

Kiania paused a moment to see if Tom would catch the reference. He didn't.

"Aeschylus," she said smiling.

Tom was about to mention that Randy had no real motive for killing any of the others but stopped himself. Kiania had already told him after Halloween that you don't eliminate a suspect because you don't know their motive. Of course, there was a real possibility that there was no motive behind these killings at all, and the Dart Frog was just some sadistic psychopath getting their rocks off.

The fire. That's the real anomaly this time, the fire. The Dart Frog has always been careful not to leave any forensic evidence in the past. Either he or she is getting sloppy, or they wanted to make sure the authorities didn't find something. If Randy is the Dart Frog, he was probably destroying the evidence. If Randy isn't the Dart Frog, then he probably discovered their identity. Kiania's right; we can't be sure until the police have found Randy, dead or alive.

CHAPTER 13

(NEW YEAR'S EVE)

Tom was running on the treadmill in his family's basement. Christmas had passed without incident. It had been the first time he had spent Christmas with two different families, his own and Kiania's. Not wanting to miss his mom's cooking and unable to resist Mrs. Martins's, he had eaten until he was sick, which was why he was trying to burn off the excess calories right now. Whenever Tom exercised, he always had his favorite songs playing; but no matter how loud the music was, his thoughts always came back to the murders. The police still hadn't found Randy, nor had any other arrest been made. The Dart Frog was still on the loose.

When Tom got off the treadmill, he skimmed through his junior yearbook as he rested. He paused over the pictures of the suspects he and Kiania had identified. He also stopped over the pictures of the students whose parents had been killed. He also looked over the other students who were now seniors, wondering if there was someone that he and Kiania had overlooked, but no one jumped out at him.

Tonight is my last New Year's Eve as a student at Saint Thomas More High School. In a few months, most of us will be graduating, and one of us will be going to Terre Haute[2] to be put down like a sick dog.

---

2   As I write this book, the death penalty is still legal in the state of Indiana. Terre Haute is where the criminals on death row are executed.

No matter how hard he tried, Tom just couldn't wrap his head around it. There was so much about the murders that he still didn't understand.

The curfew is still in effect, and there are roadblocks; how is the Dart Frog getting around?

Tom looked at a map of South Bend. He had marked it with the locations of all the murders, the school, the homes of the suspects, his own house, and Kiania's.

Some of my classmates live on the other side of town. If the Dart Frog is alone, they can't get through a police checkpoint unless they have a convincing fake ID. Where would they even get a fake ID? For that matter, where would they get four large knives without raising suspicion?

The police had every sporting goods store in the county checking to see if anyone was buying thirteen-inch hunting knives, but Tom remembered what Kiania had said about all the murders being premeditated. In all probability, the Dart Frog already had all the knives they needed.

If Randy wasn't the Dart Frog, the real killer was still walking the halls of Saint Thomas More High School, hiding in plain sight. Tom had probably talked to the murderer without even realizing it. Tom and his family hadn't been victimized yet, but now Tom had been the first person to be singled out by the killer. Tom didn't know what he would do if his parents died. What little money he had to his name had come from helping them out in the bakery. He was months away from graduating high school, but he had no idea how to buy a house, even if he could afford one. He had no idea how phone plans worked. He had no idea how insurance worked, how to do taxes, or anything like that.

You'd think they'd teach those things in school instead of algebra.

Tom couldn't imagine what would become of his two sisters if anything happened to their parents. As he got up to exercise with his training sword, he imagined he was slashing at the Dart Frog.

When he was done exercising, Tom went upstairs to take a shower. He was going to be waiting for midnight with Kiania. Despite the fact that he and Kiania had already kissed before, he was very anxious to finally perform the time-honored New Year's tradition with her. He had just gotten out of the shower when he received a text message from Kiania.

Bring a swimsuit. (Be discreet)

Tom hadn't been expecting that. His brain immediately lit up at the possibilities.

When Tom finally left the house at nine o'clock, he had his best swimming trunks tucked inconspicuously into one of the interior pouches of his winter coat. It had been arranged for Captain Lopez to drive Tom to the Martins' residence so his parents wouldn't have to leave the house. As he left the house, he heard the door lock behind him. It was promptly followed by the shooting of a bolt and the sound of a chair being wedged into place.

No need to remind them to lock the door. I'd say they're safe until I get back, but I don't want to jinx it.

The drive to the Martins' residence passed mostly in silence. Captain Lopez asked Tom a few questions about his relationship with Kiania once or twice, but Tom wasn't feeling talkative. By this time next year, both he and Kiania would be in college. He wanted to cherish tonight, but his thoughts kept coming back to the murders.

Why does the Dart Frog wear a different colored mask to each murder? Do the colors mean anything?

As an aspiring comic book writer, Tom knew that different colors could mean different things depending on the artist's intent. But after four double murders, he didn't see a pattern forming.

Red, yellow, green, pink...

Red and yellow were both primary colors. Green was a secondary color. The pink mask was the real oddity.

Pink is just a lighter shade of red. There are no pink frogs, unless you believe those photoshopped images you see on the internet.

The Dart Frog was smart enough to avoid the police for five months; they should be smart enough to know that there weren't any pink frogs in the animal kingdom. The Dart Frog had made that pink mask deliberately, but why?

Captain Lopez drove through three different police checkpoints. Again, Tom found himself wondering how the Dart Frog was getting around.

Obviously, there's no way Kalin, Mark, or anyone else walked ten or more miles in the dead of night carrying a frog mask and a big knife. The Dart Frog isn't stupid enough to be using transportation services, they're too easy to trace. I'm sure the police know every car in senior lot, so disguises and fake IDs are useless. It's not like a high school student has an army of disposable and untraceable cars. UGH! If I were a homicidal maniac, I'd know how a homicidal maniac thinks!

Tom's train of thought was interrupted by their arrival at Kiania's house. Captain Lopez told him that she would pick him up after midnight.

"Make good choices!"

Like I'd really do anything under the county prosecutor's roof.

As Tom made his way up the driveway, fresh snow started to fall. He expected the door to be answered by one of Kiania's parents, but it was Kiania herself. For some reason, she was wearing a black sleeveless tank blouse and jeans. Tom would've wondered if she was cold, but the sight of her made him feel like he was melting. She was also wearing the necklace that Tom had gotten her for Christmas.

"Happy New Year," she said smiling.

"Happy New Year,"

Tom expected Kiania's mother to be all over him in a matter of moments, but she did not appear as Kiania locked the door behind them.

"Does your mother know you told me to bring a swimsuit?" he asked.

"My parents have gone to a New Year's party for all the bigwigs in the county. We have the house to ourselves."

The words struck Tom like a bolt of lightning.

"Is that safe?" he found himself asking.

"The Dart Frog isn't the Terminator. Thus far, he or she has only killed people in their own homes. Your neighborhood is still being watched, and my parents are in a place that's crawling with cops. But enough about that..."

Kiania took Tom into the living room, where there was a door to the enclosed pool. Kiania sat Tom down on the couch.

"Before we go any further, there's something I need to ask you."

"Ask away."

"Word through the grapevine is that Juno gave you a Christmas present on the last day before finals."

Tom's expression immediately changed, and all the color drained from his face. Either Samantha or Rick had broken their vow of silence, or Juno bragged to the entire school.

"What was it?" asked Kiania, beaming at him like a lioness ready to pounce. Tom had been nervous when Kiania told him they were alone. Now he was panicking.

What do I do? I can't lie to her; she'll know!

"That bad, huh?" said Kiania, still smiling.

"I didn't know what it was, if I did, I never would've opened it! I swear to God!"

"What was it?"

"It was a flash drive..."

"And what did this flash drive contain?"

Tom took a deep breath, swallowed, and said a silent prayer for mercy.

"It was a video of Juno doing a striptease, but I didn't watch the whole thing! As soon as I realized what it was, I ripped the drive out and smashed it! I wouldn't touch Juno if she was the last woman on Earth, I love you!"

Tom braced himself for either a punch in the face or a kick in the groin, but neither came. Instead, he felt a kiss on his cheek.

"Calm down, Teddy Bear. I believe you."

Kiania never called Tom by any of the nicknames that the class had given him. She knew how much he hated them, but right now, Tom was just too relieved to care.

"Kareen warned me that Juno might be doing more than playful flirting with you. She's been looking in your general direction ever since the incident with Marcus."

"I have no intention of being her latest sap," said Tom. "I prefer brunettes."

Kiania got off the couch and stood up.

"Good boy, here's your reward."

Before Tom's brain could process what was happening, Kiania pulled her blouse off over her head and pulled down her jeans, revealing that she was wearing a shiny purple string bikini underneath. Tom felt his heart leap into his throat. He had only ever seen pictures of Kiania in the school's regulation swimsuits. The bikini she was wearing was a lot more revealing. Kiania never stopped smiling; she was a confident woman. The fact that she was comfortable showing this much skin made her even more attractive.

"Since my parents are away, we can watch our sitcoms in the hot tub. You can change in the bathroom, I'll be waiting."

Kiania tossed her long black and blue streaked hair as she

walked gracefully out the door to the pool, leaving Tom absolutely dumbstruck.

Kiania was a confident woman, but Tom was VERY nervous. He seldom wore a bathing suit except during the summer when he went to the beach, the pool, or on vacation with his family. He had never worn a bathing suit around a woman as breathtakingly beautiful as Kiania. Tom had been keeping up on his exercises, but as he looked at himself in the mirror, he was suddenly conscious of every little imperfection on his skin.

What if she doesn't think I'm buff enough?

She has turned down men with more muscle mass than you, and you're the one she's been dating for five months.

I've never shown this much skin to a girl!

Shut up and grow a spine. The girl of your dreams is inviting you to watch British sitcoms in a hot tub. TIME TO BE A MAN!

Tom's swim trunks were decorated with palm trees silhouetted against a red sunset. He had picked this one out during his last vacation because all his research told him red was the color that attracted women. He tried to look confident as he walked through the door that led to the pool, but the sight of Kiania in the overflow hot tub was too much for him.

Dear God, she really is just like a mermaid...

For a long moment, Tom just stood there completely stupefied. Kiania gestured for him over with her finger. Tom wanted to pinch himself to make sure this wasn't all just a dream, but he didn't want to look like an idiot. He put the disk in the player and climbed into the hot tub with Kiania. His first instinct was to get in on the opposite side, but Kiania already moved closer to him before he was fully immersed.

"A few months ago, you tackled a man with a gun. Why are you suddenly shy?"

As the episode started, Kiania laid her head on Tom's shoulders.

He found it impossible to look at the TV and tried his hardest to keep his eyes above the neckline. All the while, Kiania continued to laugh her cute laugh as the British sitcom played out. After ten minutes, without thinking, Tom wrapped one arm around her. Thankfully, she didn't seem to notice. Tom didn't know how hot the water was, but he was sure that the skin-on-skin contact alone could've made the entire hot tub evaporate. After another five minutes, Kiania looked away from the TV and into Tom's eyes.

"I don't need to be an aspiring criminologist to know that you want me, Thomas Lime. The mystery is, why does it feel like you're holding back?"

Tom's mouth was working, but no words came out. Kiania never stopped smiling.

"You know, I'm not sure I can wait until midnight."

Kiania pressed her body against Tom's and the reaction was immediate.

OH MY GOD! I CAN FEEL THEM!!!

Kiania teased Tom with her lips before she kissed him. When she did kiss him, Tom kissed her back. Then she kissed him harder, too hard. An alarm bell went off in Tom's head. He broke the kiss. Kiania was genuinely surprised.

"Kiania, please don't misinterpret what I'm about to say, but we can't do this."

"Why not?"

Kiania was impossible to read. Tom had never seen her like this, but he got a distinct impression that she was still trying to be sexy.

"Freshman year, Augustus Welker and Bridgette Davidson," said Tom. "Remember that?"

One of the things they burn into your brain at Catholic schools is to abstain from having sex before marriage, but once in a while, there's one pair of seniors that just don't get the message. Such was the case with Augustus Welker and Bridgette Davidson.

Unfortunately, this little high school love story didn't have a happy ending. Neither Augustus nor Bridgette had been in any position to support a child. Augustus's affection didn't last. Even though it destroyed Bridgette to do it, the baby had to be given up for adoption.

"I don't want that to be us," said Tom. "I love you too much for that."

Tom tried to brace himself for whatever came next. He hadn't expected Kiania to throw herself at him this evening, and he had no way of knowing how she would react to his declination. Much to his surprise, she kissed him gently on the cheek.

"Congratulations, Teddy Bear, you passed your test with flying colors."

"Test?!" asked Tom.

"Before our relationship could proceed any further, I needed to be absolutely sure you were a real man."

"A real man?"

"Yes, because unlike certain men, you can actually control your penis."

Tom was not ready for tonight. He was under the impression that he would be waiting for midnight by watching sitcoms with Kiania. First, he had watched Kiania undress like it was the most natural thing in the world. Then he actually got in a hot tub with her, she tried to seduce him, and now she had mentioned his reproductive organ out loud. And this was all part of some crazy scheme to see if he could control his urges. It was all too much for him, and it showed on his face.

"I think somebody needs a cream soda," said Kiania.

"Yes, please."

After another episode, Kiania decided it was time to get out of the hot tub and take it into the living room. When she got out of the tub, she dried off and pulled on a full-length black plush robe. Tom got dressed, but Kiania was still in her suit and robe.

"It's your reward," she said, answering the question he didn't ask out loud.

She brought me here to test me, but I won't be able to control myself if she keeps behaving like this.

"What happens if your parents walk in on us?"

"Captain Lopez will be back to pick you up before they return. Besides, my parents know I can take care of myself. And Tom..."

Kiania pulled Tom's face close, as if to kiss him again. She was still smiling, and her voice was dangerously polite.

"If you ever tell anyone what happened here tonight, I will rip off your nose. Is that clear?"

"Yes, ma'am."

"Good boy."

Needless to say, it was a New Year's Eve that Tom would never forget. He and Kiania thought they were alone the whole time, but someone was watching.

Tom and Kiania sitting in a tree...

CHAPTER 14

It was a cold and dark night in early January. Sheriff Sam Doyle had just arrived home after a long day at the office. He shouldn't have been surprised that his son, Kalin, was not in his room.

Dammit, where is that boy? It's after curfew!

Sam pulled out his phone and pressed the app to see where Kalin's phone was. He was disappointed to see that the phone was nearby. He found it sitting on Kalin's nightstand.

Where does he go? He's probably off somewhere fooling around with that girlfriend of his. At least I hope so...

Jasmine Diya had been fingering Kalin as the Dart Frog ever since her parents were murdered on Halloween. This was causing a lot of tension between the department and the African American community of Saint Joseph County. Worse, the murders had attracted national media attention, so everyone in the country knew about them.

Sometimes free speech can be more dangerous than a nuclear weapon.

Sam took a shower and preheated the oven for a frozen pizza. He then sat in front of the TV with a bottle of his favorite whiskey. As he poured himself a glass, his eyes went toward the mantlepiece, where there was a picture of Sam's late wife. Alison had been so beautiful and so loved. Sam had met her when he was still just a deputy in the department, and Alison had been a student at Notre Dame, where she earned the nickname "Queen of the Billiards." Alison's skills on the table would eventually reach national recognition, but she always kept coming back to South Bend. Every day since the accident that caused her death, Sam had worked strenuously to discourage the use of marijuana.

Kalin had loved his mother. The death of a parent would come as a great shock to any kid, but Kalin had actually been in the car when it happened. Unfortunately, Sam's work schedule meant that he couldn't always be there for his son. Sam did the best he could, but he was beginning to think it wasn't enough.

Alison, would you even recognize our baby boy now?

The preheat alarm on the oven went off, so Sam went to put the pizza in.

The whiskey must be stronger than I thought, I already feel dizzy.

When Sam put the pizza in the oven, he thought he heard a creaking noise coming from upstairs, but he dismissed it. The house was locked up tight, and the old house was always creaking.

Sam took a photo of a young Kalin with Alison out of the end table in the living room, but he accidentally dropped it. He cursed himself as he picked it back up.

Why didn't we take more photos?

He tried to cut his son some slack. That poor boy had been through hell; they both had. Then there was Kalin's girlfriend, Lilian. That poor girl had been on her own since she was six. Her parents had been senselessly killed for no reason other than being God-fearing Catholics. Lilian then spent the better part of a decade bouncing between foster homes and schools. For the past four years, Lilian had been in the care of Leonard and Theresa Benedict, a very generous couple that couldn't have children of their own. They sent her to Saint Thomas More High School, and that was where she met Kalin.

Sam had to admit that Kalin and Lilian's mutual interest in horror stories was a little odd, but he couldn't see either of them as the person running around in a frog mask and turning their classmates' parents into shredded beef.

I still can't believe this is all the work of a seventeen or eighteen-year-old kid. It's been almost six months; the Dart Frog has managed to commit four double murders and avoid capture. Seems way beyond the talents of a senior in high school. I certainly couldn't have gotten away with it when I was in high school. Then again, who really knows with kids today?

Sam was suddenly aware of how drowsy he was. The image on the TV became a blur. He blamed the whiskey. He thought his tolerance level was higher than this.

What the hell?

Sam's breathing became a lot more labored, and then his heart started to jump in his chest. That's when Sam knew it was time to call an ambulance. He fumbled in the dark for his phone but couldn't find it. He fell off the couch and lay sprawled out on the floor.

There was somebody in the house. Sam could hear footsteps.

Kalin!

Sam tried to call out, but he couldn't. The pain in his chest was becoming unbearable; he felt tears welling up in his eyes. The footsteps were getting closer; they sounded muffled, like someone was wearing plastic bags on their feet. Even with his distorted vision, Sam could see the covered boots walking into the room. He forced himself to look up and saw someone in a blue and black-spotted frog mask staring down at him. There was a flash of movement, and then he felt the cold steel digging into his neck.

CHAPTER 15

Every student at Saint Thomas More High School had heard the news of Sheriff Doyle's murder before they went to school on the first day of the second semester. Naturally, Kalin wasn't in school. It was a dark and cloudy winter day. The wind howled in fitful gusts against the old windows. Everyone was very quiet, and every senior looked surreptitiously at someone else. The teachers did their best to proceed with their classes like normal, but no one was really listening. Lectures became nonsensical obscenities that seemed to drag on for hours on end. The school had become a prison. The forced inaction and dull monotony of sitting in one spot for the better part of an hour nearly drove the students insane. Everyone in the room always jumped whenever the bell sounded, signaling the end of the period.

The Dart Frog had now raised his or her body count to nine. Word quickly traveled through the grapevine that the city was calling for assistance from the FBI. In between classes, Tom did his best to eavesdrop on every whispered conversation he heard. The consensus of Tom's classmates was that he was above suspicion. It was well-established that he and Kiania had been at the movies on the night the Simpsons were killed, and if Tom was the Dart Frog, he wouldn't have drawn attention to himself by sending himself Mr. Diya's decomposing finger before Christmas. Many people were still dead-set on Randy since the authorities still hadn't found him.

I seriously doubt it. If he's still alive, I'm sure they would've found him by now.

Tom was making his way to lunch when he noticed Samantha talking to Jasmine. He kept pace so he could listen without looking suspicious.

"Do you still think Kalin did it?" asked Samantha.

"Of course I do!" said Jasmine, as angry as ever. "He's the only person who has lost only one parent!"

"His mother died years ago."

Yeah, and the trauma turned him into a psycho. Maybe his father found out about his new hobby, so he got rid of him! Or maybe his father was the real target all along, and he just killed my parents and all the others to make everyone think there was a serial killer on the loose and drive suspicion away from himself."

Tom had to admit that Jasmine's theory wasn't entirely without merit.

It's perfectly possible, but of course there's no proof.

Tom hadn't been the only person listening in on Samantha and Jasmine's conversation. At that moment, Lilian marched right up to Jasmine, looking angrier than Tom had ever seen her. Lilian knocked Jasmine's books out of her hands and sent them crashing to the ground.

"How do we know you're not the killer?!"

The accusation took Jasmine and everyone else completely off guard.

"What?!"

"Face facts, Ms. Social Justice Warrior, if anyone benefits from all this insanity, it's you!"

"How dare you?!" was all Jasmine could manage.

"Don't bother denying it!" said Lilian. "Thanks to all the publicity you've been milking from your parent's corpses, you've got a free ride scholarship to any college you want! Why should my boyfriend be the only one accused of parricide when he has nothing to gain?!"

Jasmine's expression was one of pure rage filled to bursting. It only got worse when Jasmine realized that Lilian's argument seemed to have won over some of the bystanders.

"You stupid bitch!"

"Where were you on the night of the first double murder?!" demanded Lilian.

"At home, doing my homework," growled Jasmine.

Lilian cracked a huge smile.

"We both know that's a lie. Kalin and I were going to pay you back for that little stunt you pulled with all that bacon. We went to your house during the window when the Simpsons were killed, but you weren't there."

Jasmine seemed to be struggling for a response, but one of the cops patrolling the school intervened before the argument escalated.

It didn't take long for word of Jasmine and Lilian's argument to spread throughout the entire school. Tom and Kiania met that night under the pretense of doing their homework together.

"Do you think there's anything in Lilian's accusation?" asked Tom.

"I wasn't going to say anything at school, because I didn't want to pour fuel on the fire," said Kiania. "Jasmine claims she stayed after basketball practice to exercise in the school's weight room when her parents were murdered on Halloween, but I know for a fact that she wasn't there. We had swimming practice after their basketball practice, and I saw her drive out of the parking lot."

Tom did the math in his head.

The girls' basketball practice started at four o'clock and ended at five-thirty. The Diyas were killed a little after six. If Jasmine left right away, she could've gotten home in time to kill her father and then wait for her mother to come home.

"There's no denying that Jasmine has benefited the most from the murders," said Kiania. "But it doesn't change the fact that the two people who stand out the most in the Sheriff's murder are Kalin and Lilian."

"But if Kalin is a suspect, so is everyone else whose parents have been killed by the Dart Frog."

Kiania noticed the distaste in Tom's voice.

"Patricide and matricide, crimes so foul that even the ancient Greeks in all their debauchery considered them to be taboo."

"And yet that's exactly what two generations of their deities did, among other things," said Tom. "But I can't see someone like Jasmine stooping that low."

"Statistically speaking, serial killers are usually white men," said Kiania. "But there are always exceptions. Jasmine is a good athlete, but in America, women trying to earn athletic scholarships are a dime a dozen. It's perfectly feasible that her parents had no intention of paying her tuition if she didn't get one. It's also possible that she had some other motive we don't know about."

"Such as?" asked Tom.

"No good can come from wild speculation," replied Kiania. "Suffice to say, we have reason to suspect Jasmine, and there is no tangible evidence to prove her innocence."

Most teenagers only dream of killing their parents, but people have killed for less. Did Jasmine do the unthinkable? Did she kill her own parents just to secure her future?

"We come now to the murder of Sheriff Doyle," said Kiania. "That took place last night. Unfortunately, I don't know very much about it, not yet."

"It doesn't make any sense," said Tom. "The first three double murders were all the parents of seniors high on the school's pecking order. Next, Randy goes missing, and his parents are murdered shortly afterward. Not only does this not match up with the victim profile, but this time the Dart Frog decides to burn the victims' house down. Kalin isn't high on the pecking order either, and he's the only person to lose just one parent to the Dart Frog. Then there's the issue of the masks."

"What about them?" asked Kiania.

"For some reason, the Dart Frog wears a different colored mask to each murder. After carefully wiping the mask of any potential forensic evidence, he or she just leaves it there for the police to find, along with the murder weapon."

"The killer is obviously taunting the authorities," said Kiania.

"But why is the color of the mask always different? Word around the school is that it was blue this time."

"That's what everyone has been saying, yes."

"So the mask colors thus far in order are red, yellow, green, pink, and blue," said Tom. "We have all three primary colors, one secondary color, and a shade of a certain color. I don't see a pattern forming."

"The Dart Frog may be playing games with everyone," said Kiania. "Giving us meaningless information to confuse us."

"Well, it certainly doesn't make sense to me," replied Tom.

"If criminology were easy, everyone would be doing it," said Kiania.

The FBI team arrived in South Bend within twenty-four hours of Sheriff Doyle's murder. Word quickly spread that the team was led by Special Agent Arthur Diamond. Tom got his first glimpse of Diamond on the news. Arthur Diamond had recently celebrated his fiftieth birthday. His features were as hard as his surname. He had well-groomed but balding silver hair, and a thin trimmed beard, giving him the appearance of an aging lion. He had the eyes of an owl, seasoned by a career of fighting the worst that the human race had to offer. He was probably tired, but he couldn't stop even if he knew how; if he did, the whole world would go to hell.

On Thursday, Tom got an early morning call from Kiania warning him that Agent Diamond was about to interview all the students in senior hall.

"Don't speak unless spoken to, tell him what you told the police, and remain calm. Remember, you've done nothing wrong."

Tom shouldn't have been surprised. Even though his parents hadn't been murdered, he was the person the Dart Frog had used as a distraction when the Parkers were killed. Still, when he was finally summoned to the principal's office for his interview, he found himself trembling in anticipation.

CHAPTER 16

AGENT DIAMOND INVESTIGATES
(TOM)

Tom was shown into Principal Miller's office, but Mrs. Miller was off for the day. Special Agent Diamond was sitting behind the desk. He was dressed head to toe in black. His expression was polite but stern.

"Thomas Lime," said Diamond in a deep and commanding tone, but also smiling. "People talk about you even in Washington. The boy who tackled a gunman while armed with nothing but a fire extinguisher and a fire axe. Not bad for an aspiring comic book writer."

Tom knew that Kiania had told him not to speak unless spoken to, but he was genuinely surprised by this comment.

"How did you know that I want to write comic books?"

"I'm a federal agent; I know everything," said Diamond, still smiling. "I apologize if I've inconvenienced you, Mr. Lime, but it would seem one of your classmates is a murderer. Nine people are dead, one of your classmates is still missing, and it seems the murderer has singled you out."

This guy doesn't waste any time. Well, if they're interrogating every senior, then he has to do this over and over again with nearly two hundred people.

"I understand; what can I do to help?"

Tom was asked to account for his whereabouts on the nights of the murders, which he answered readily and without hesitation. He was then asked if he could think of any reason the Dart Frog would single him out and if he had any suspicions about who the Dart Frog may be.

"You seem to have given this a lot of thought," said Diamond.

"I want this murderer caught as much as anyone else," replied Tom. "Being a senior in high school is stressful enough without having to worry that your parents might be murdered in the night."

Without warning, Diamond changed the subject.

"What is your relationship with Kiania?"

The question took Tom by surprise. He couldn't understand why it would be relevant.

"We've been dating for about six months. I love her."

The last bit had slipped out before Tom could consider the wisdom of divulging the information.

"I suppose you'd have to, especially after you attacked a lunatic with a gun," said Diamond chuckling a little. "Now, your first date with her just happened to be the night of the first double murder?"

"Yes, as I said, we went to the movies to see *Sherlock Holmes vs. Jack the Ripper.*"

"That doesn't sound very romantic for a first date."

"I know, but Kiania doesn't like romantic comedies. It was that or nothing."

"What time did you two go to the movie?"

Every moment of that night was burned into Tom's memory, both because of the murders and because it was his first date. He had his ticket stub and the receipts stored in a safe place at home.

"The movie was supposed to start at seven twenty, but we had to sit through fifteen minutes of previews."

"And you two sat through the whole movie?"

"We didn't stay for the credits, but yes. Afterwards, we went to get some frozen yogurt, and then I took Kiania home."

"Did you see any of your other classmates that night?"

Why would he ask me that? I thought the Simpsons were killed while we were at the movie. Can't let it slip that I know the time of death, I can't get Kiania into trouble.

"Juno Simpson was at the movie too. Casey Rosewood was at the theater, but she went to a different movie. Oh! I almost forgot, Randy Parker was tailing me and Kiania!"

"Why would Mr. Parker be tailing you?" asked Diamond.

"When Kiania agreed to go on a date with me, it was something of a shock to the entire school. Randy is, or was, a reporter for the school newspaper. He had delusions of becoming a great journalist, but I'm sure he would've ended up working for a gossip rag."

"You weren't on good terms with him?"

"Everyone knows he transferred to Saint Thomas More because he got caught peeping at his old school. He's also responsible for my first loathed nickname."

Thankfully, Agent Diamond didn't call Tom by his nickname.

"Do you have any idea where Mr. Parker might be now?"

"I haven't the least idea."

Tom reiterated the list of people he suspected of being the Dart Frog and gave his reasons. Diamond then thanked him for his cooperation and told Tom to call him if there were any developments. Tom had barely walked ten steps down the hall when he realized something.

Why did he call Kiania by her first name?

(ISAIAH)

"I hope I haven't inconvenienced you, Mr. James."

"I'm willing to do whatever I can to help, Agent Diamond," said Isaiah. "This monster needs to be stopped."

To Agent Diamond, Isaiah James appeared to be a well-built

young man and a model student. His family seemed to be upstanding members of the community. But Diamond's long career in criminology taught him that they were exactly the kind of people that might have one or two skeletons in their closet. It was no mystery that Isaiah had benefited from the murders. When Fred Smith dropped out of school, Isaiah became the football team's new quarterback and captain. He now had a football scholarship to the college of his choice. The question was, what part, if any, did Isaiah play in the terrible crimes that had been committed?

"I hope you understand, the questions I'm about to ask you are strictly routine. I intend to do this with every student in senior hall. I'm very thorough when it comes to my work. Now, I can appreciate that this hasn't been an easy year for you. Being the football team captain is a huge responsibility under the best of circumstances, but this hasn't been a conventional year for the Saint Thomas More Paladins."

"That would be putting it mildly," said Isaiah. "After his parents were murdered, Fred tried to drink himself to death. Then three of my teammates went and got themselves expelled, and one of them went nuts, held the entire girls' swim team hostage, and tried to rape one of them at gunpoint. Now we're up to our necks in dead bodies. Pardon my hyperbole, but if this goes any further south, we're going to fall off the bottom of the earth."

Isaiah gave a succinct account of his whereabouts on the nights of the murders. Whenever there wasn't football practice or a game, he was either exercising or doing his homework.

"You don't socialize much?" asked Diamond. "Not even now that football season is over?"

"Football is my life," replied Isaiah. "But there are plenty of other boys out there that will tell you the same. The only way to get ahead in this world is to be the best. I work hard year-round to make sure I am the best."

"But I understand that you have done a bit of socializing. You go out with girls?"

"Every once in a while, yes. But nothing serious."

"I understand that you used to date Juno Simpson."

Isaiah didn't dodge the issue.

"Yes, I went out with her a few times during junior year, but it only lasted about a month."

"What happened?"

"I know why you're asking, Agent Diamond. I've heard my classmates whispering behind my back. But the fact is that she came onto me. Football season was over, and she was one of the prettiest girls in school, so I figured I might as well take her for a spin and see where it went. As I said, we went on a few dates. Then one day, she told me that I was, and I quote, as interesting as a sack of toenail clippings. That was the end of it."

"What was your relationship with Fred Smith like?" asked Diamond.

"We've known each other since middle school. We had a mutual interest in football. We competed fiercely, but football is a team sport. It doesn't matter how many touchdowns you make or how many balls you pass. I learned long ago that I don't get anywhere unless the team wins."

"Were you aware that the Smiths owned a dog?"

"Of course."

"Were you jealous when you found out that Juno was dating Fred?"

"I've got my whole life ahead of me, and pretty blondes are a dime a dozen in America. And to be perfectly honest, I don't like the way Juno treats people."

"Do you like to hunt, Mr. James?"

"Football takes up all my free time. I'm not about to risk breaking my ankle or something like that in the woods."

"Do you have any idea where Randy Parker might be?"

"I don't know anything about that."

"Are you alright, Mr. James?" asked Diamond at random. "You seem... nervous."

Isaiah had played it cool throughout the entire interview, but there was a thin layer of perspiration on his brow. Though he tried to hide it, Diamond also noticed that Isaiah's right hand was twitching.

"Confidentially, Agent Diamond, I'm not nervous. I'm scared."

"Scared of what?"

"I've already told you; I've heard my classmates whispering behind my back. They think I had something to do with the murders, and now the whole country is watching South Bend. If the wrong person takes these rumors seriously, I might lose my scholarship. And it's not just that. What if the Dart Frog decides to come after my family next? I've heard what happened to the others. My parents are good people; they don't deserve that. Nobody deserves that..."

"You can rest assured, Mr. James, I'm going to do my best to make sure that doesn't happen. There's just one more thing I'd like to ask you. Do you know what acepromazine is?"

Agent Diamond watched Isaiah's reaction closely. His mother was a veterinarian.

"I haven't the least idea."

"Thank you for your cooperation, Mr. James."

(JUNO)

Special Agent Arthur Diamond could understand why Juno Simpson was the most popular girl in school. She was the kind of girl that most young men would kill for.

I've put away men who killed for less.

"I'm very sorry for your loss, Ms. Simpson."

"I've heard that more times than I care to count, Agent Diamond. Just catch the killer, if you can."

"You may rely on me, Ms. Simpson. Now, can you think of anyone who might have reason to kill your parents or do you harm?"

"Mark Xeg," said Juno without any hesitation.

"Yes, the inattentive president of the gaming club," replied Diamond. "Several of your classmates have told me the same. I understand there was some unpleasant drama between you and him."

"The little worm has delusions of getting in my pants. Obviously, his video game-riddled mind lost its reality button somewhere down the line."

"In my experience as a criminologist, Ms. Simpson, breaking a man's heart is more likely to drive him to murder than video games."

"Worms don't have hearts," said Juno, as if the very thought of Mark was poison.

"Actually, Ms. Simpson, worms have five hearts. But that's impertinent to my investigation."

Diamond offered Juno a chocolate truffle before he continued. Juno declined, but Diamond happily ate one.

"Now, you were at the movies on the night your parents were murdered."

"Yes," replied Juno. "I went to see *Sherlock Holmes vs. Jack the Ripper.*"

"Do you enjoy murder mysteries, Ms. Simpson?"

"Who doesn't? The whole school was going to be talking about it. I figured I should see it before someone else spoiled it for me."

"Did you sit through the whole movie?"

"No, I was thirsty. At one point, I got up to get a drink from the snack bar."

"What time was that?"

"I don't know. I wasn't wearing a watch and didn't look at my phone."

"Did you see any of your classmates at the theater?"

"Kiania and the Teddy Bear were there."

"You mean Mr. Lime?"

"Yes, of course."

"I'm going to respectfully ask that you refrain from using nick-names, Ms. Simpson. I don't need any unnecessary complications."

"As you wish."

"Did you go straight home when the movie was over?"

"No, I was hungry, so I stopped at a store to get some of my favorite licorice."

"I see."

Agent Diamond fiddled with his fingers, a curious habit of his when he was thinking.

"Ms. Simpson, many of the victimized families, including your own, had sophisticated security systems installed on their houses. But in each case, the Dart Frog was able to get in and out without raising the alarm or leaving a trace. This is generally outside the skill set of your average high school student. More often than not, it's an inside job. Is there anyone in your social circle who frequented your house?"

Juno thought for a moment.

"Well, there's my latest ex-boyfriend, half the cheerleaders in school, and my BFF, Kareen. But I can't see any of them wearing a frog mask and cutting people's guts out. Most of them struggle just to write a paper about the Civil War."

"Ms. Simpson, in my time, I've come face-to-face with the most depraved and perverse individuals that the human race has to offer. I speak from experience when I say that some people simply aren't who they pretend to be."

Juno didn't hesitate to answer any of Agent Diamond's questions. After her parents were killed, she started living with her aunt in Michigan. Because of the curfew, she couldn't leave the house if she wanted to. She had no idea where Randy Parker might be hiding. She told Diamond that after the incident with Marcus and the swimming team, she wouldn't be the least bit surprised if Mark, Randy, or anyone else tried to rape her. Diamond patiently took down the names of all the boys Juno had dated, the ones she rejected, and all the girls that may have had a reason to hate her. It was an extensive list.

"You really get around, don't you?"

"It's not my fault that most of the boys in this school turn out to be worthless and dull," said Juno.

"You seem to be holding up remarkably well for someone that has lost both her parents," said Diamond.

"My parents are dead. Moping and crying about it isn't going to bring them back or improve my situation in any way. In a matter of months, I'll be graduating. If I'm going to make it in the world, I need to be better than that."

"True," replied Diamond. "One last question, Ms. Simpson. Do you know what acepromazine is?"

"What's that, the latest designer drug?"

(KALIN)

Special Agent Diamond hadn't been around Saint Thomas More High School very long. If he had known these students since the year started, he would've said that Kalin Doyle looked even gloomier than usual. His countenance was impassive, but his eyes were red.

"First of all, let me say that I am very sorry for your loss, Mr. Doyle."

"I don't want pity," growled Kalin. "I want this sicko's head on a stick!"

"I can assure you; I'll do my best to bring this case to a satisfactory conclusion."

Agent Diamond approached the first line of inquiry with tact.

"Now, I hope you understand that in order for me to get at the truth, I need to establish the facts. I've spoken with several of your classmates, and it seems to me that you weren't on the best of terms with your father. Am I mistaken?"

Kalin growled again.

"There's friction between high school students and their parents under the best circumstances. There's also a difference between thinking your father is a pain in the ass and not caring when someone turns him inside out."

"True," replied Diamond.

"The last time I spoke to him, he told me he was going to work. My last word to him was, 'Whatever.' That's it..."

It looked like Kalin was doing his best not to cry.

Easy to fake if you know how.

"I need to know where you were on the nights of the murders."

Oddly enough, Kalin didn't give the same bland answers that most of his classmates had given. He said that the night the Simpsons were killed, he and Lilian had gone to Jasmine's to get even with her for vandalizing his car, but she wasn't there.

"What time was that?"

"A little after nine," replied Kalin. "If I wanted to get even with the feminazi, then I needed to work under cover of darkness. I don't know what it's like where you come from, but even in August, it doesn't get dark around here until well after eight o'clock. Daylight savings time is weird in Indiana."

"And, where were you on the other nights in question?"

"On every one of those nights, I was at the bowling alley with Lilian. Except for the night the Parkers were killed. That night, my father didn't let me leave the house."

"The bowling alley?"

"The Billiard Bowl. The owner was a friend of my mother's. He lets me play pool for free and sometimes lets me stay after hours. It helps me feel close to her."

Kalin insisted he was at the bowling alley on the nights when the Smiths, the Diyas, and his father were murdered; but he said that he couldn't remember the exact time he left each night.

Agent Diamond folded his hands. His voice was firm when next he spoke.

"Mr. Doyle, on the night your father died, he had a drink of whiskey."

"That's not surprising in the least."

"Investigation revealed that the bottle he drank from contained a lethal amount of morphine."

"What?!"

Kalin's reaction seemed genuine.

"This, combined with the fact that there were no signs of forced entry at your house, despite your father having his own security system, suggests that this was an inside job."

"I didn't kill my father," growled Kalin.

"I didn't say you did," replied Diamond. "The murderer did the exact same thing at all the other houses. Now, you are the only person to lose just one parent. But your father's death isn't the only anomaly. The Diyas are the only African American victims to date. When the Parkers were killed, their house was burned down. At first, it looked like the murderer was only targeting the parents of seniors high on the school's social ladder; now, it looks like they're just pulling names out of a hat. Someone is going to great lengths to confuse me and everyone else working on this case. This person is clearly insane, but not unintelligent. Do you have any idea who that person might be?"

Kalin's answer came promptly.

"Well, at a guess and with very little to go on, I'd plump for the feminazi."

"You mean Ms. Diya?"

"No, I mean Mrs. Claus," said Kalin, making no effort to hide his sarcasm.

"Is there any reason to suspect her, besides your little grudge?"

"I've already told you; I have no idea where she was on the night the Simpsons were murdered, but she wasn't at home. She benefits the most from all this insanity. In America, there are more female athletes looking for scholarships than rats. People like her will do anything to get their way and force their agendas on us, just like that guy who staged a hate crime."

By this point, Agent Diamond had already spoken with Lilian. Both she and Kalin had more or less told Diamond the exact same things.

They could both be telling the truth, or they could both be lying...

(KAREEN)

Three of the double murders had been the parents of students high on the school's social ladder. One theory was that the Dart Frog had killed the Parkers and Sheriff Doyle out of necessity, and he or she could return to their original victim profile soon. Given that three of the five victimized students had been male, there was a good chance the next victim may be female. Being Juno Simpson's best friend and captain of the girl's swimming team made Kareen Fabbrie an attractive target.

The girl in front of Agent Diamond looked exhausted, like she could easily go to sleep.

"Are you alright, Ms. Fabbrie?"

"I'm sorry," said Kareen, lifting her head up. "It's been a hell of a year. Now we've got the swimming championship coming up, and I'm often up late doing my homework."

"I understand," replied Diamond. "Would you like a cup of coffee or something?"

"I'd prefer a cola."

Diamond asked someone to bring a cola from one of the school's vending machines. While they waited, he typed something on his phone. When the drink arrived, Karren happily unscrewed the lid and took two thankful gulps.

"That's the stuff."

"I'll try to make this as painless as I possibly can, Ms. Fabbrie."

When asked to give an account of her whereabouts on the nights of the murders, Kareen gave the same general answers that most everyone else in the school was giving. Like most of the girls in school, she was trying to balance being a student and an athlete.

"One of your fellow seniors is a dangerous and insane criminal. Is there anyone that you have reason to suspect?"

Kareen answered Agent Diamond's question immediately.

"Mark Xeg!"

Diamond chuckled a little.

"That boy seems to be very unpopular."

"I've seen the way he looks at Juno. Who else would try to put the moves on her right after her parents were murdered and her boyfriend tried to drink himself to death?!"

"What is your relationship with Juno?"

This question seemed to take Kareen by surprise, but it didn't stop her from answering.

"I've known Juno my whole life. We were in kindergarten together. She's my best friend."

"I see," replied Diamond. "And you don't approve of Mr. Xeg's romantic advances?"

"Juno hasn't been waiting her whole life for a stick figure with glasses and hair that looks like something the cat spit up. If you looked up the word 'dork' in the dictionary, you'd see his picture. Who cares if he wins a national video game tournament? That just means he has more free time than countless other hopeless cases across the world. When someone like that forgets their place, you need to shoot them down without mercy."

"The last time Ms. Simpson turned the boy down, he almost killed himself."

"Juno wouldn't love him if he were the last man on Earth. She wants and deserves the very best. Mark Xeg couldn't pay a woman who was blind and deaf to have sex with him. It's not Juno's fault if the little maggot couldn't accept that."

Hearts of stone.

"What about Mr. James?" asked Diamond.

"Who?"

"Isaiah James, the man who replaced Mr. Smith as captain of the football team."

"Oh, him!" exclaimed Kareen. "Well, just about every boy on campus has been ogling Juno at one point or another. Obviously, he's leagues above the dork, but he doesn't meet Juno's standards. It's not because he's black, she just finds him boring."

"When she broke up with him, how badly did he take it?"

"Unlike the dork, he took it like a man. At least that's what Juno told me."

"Has Mr. Doyle ever made any romantic advances towards Ms. Simpson?"

"Who?"

"The late sheriff's son."

Kareen laughed hysterically at this.

"Absolutely not! He wouldn't have fared any better than the dork if he had. If Juno considers well-built football players to be boring, a goth who spends most of his time reading old horror stories has no chance. Besides, he already has that dark-haired slut of his. Mark my words: if she isn't already pregnant, she will be before graduation."

"Are there any other boys of note making romantic advances on Ms. Simpson at the moment?"

Kareen didn't answer immediately.

"No, everyone has been leaving her alone since the incident with the dork."

"But?" prompted Diamond.

"You didn't hear it from me, but she may be planning to steal Tom Lime."

"Why would she do that?"

"He's the school celebrity. After Juno's parents were murdered and she lost Fred to alcoholism, I was all she had left. After the episode with Marcus in October, she feels indebted to him for saving me."

"Thomas Lime already has a girlfriend,"

"And I feel sorry for Kiania, but Juno has a habit of getting what she wants."

(JASMINE)

Agent Diamond knew he had to be careful with Jasmine Diya. Following the deaths of her parents, the Dart Frog murders had become a national sensation. Her persecution of Kalin Doyle had caused intense friction between the African American community and the sheriff's department. Now the Dart Frog was a cop killer. The last thing Diamond wanted to do was make a bad situation worse, but he needed to know all the facts. He would need to proceed with care.

"Ms. Diya, let me just say how very sorry I am for your loss."

"Pity won't bring my parents back!" snapped Jasmine.

"No, it won't. Nine people are dead. It's my job to ensure that the murderer gets what's coming to them. Are you going to help me do that?"

"What do you want to know?" growled Jasmine.

Diamond decided to get the obvious question out of the way.

"You have openly accused Kalin Doyle of being the murderer."

"Correct," replied Jasmine.

"In light of recent events, has your opinion changed?"

"No."

"And why is that?"

"He's a racist pig."

"Ms. Diya, your parents are the only African American victims to date. My colleagues and I are confident that these crimes are not racially motivated."

"It's all smoke and mirrors," yelled Jasmine. "I was his target all along, he killed his father and all the others just to throw everyone off the scent!"

"Ms. Diya, I intend to do everything in my power to ensure the person who killed your parents is brought to justice. I've made a career out of criminology. But I did not get where I am today by jumping to conclusions. I establish the facts, I go through the possibilities without bias or prejudice, and the truth becomes clear. My job right now is to create a psychological profile of the murderer and point the local authorities in the right direction, but I can't do that if I don't have all the facts."

Diamond asked Jasmine his usual questions, but she didn't entertain for a moment that the murderer could be anyone other than Kalin Doyle.

Her mind's all made up. Some people love to hear themselves talk but hate to listen. She's going to feel like a real jackass if it's someone else.

"I hope you understand, Ms. Diya, that what I'm about to ask you is strictly routine. I am asking the same of every other student in senior hall. If this killer is to be caught, I can make no exceptions. Where were you on the nights of the murders?"

Jasmine suspected that Lilian or someone else had already told Agent Diamond that she wasn't at home on the night the Simpsons were murdered. After Lilian spilled the beans and cast doubt, Samantha confronted her about her movements on Halloween. Jasmine had said that she stayed after basketball practice to use the school's exercise room, but Samantha knew for a fact that Jasmine left school after practice that evening and never came back. The mutilated bodies of Jasmine's parents had been discovered by her siblings when they came home from trick-or-treating. Jasmine had been the last to arrive home, and no one knew where she had been before that.

Jasmine knew Samantha had already been interviewed; she had seen her being called out of class. For all she knew, the pig and his girlfriend had also been interviewed. Jasmine did the only thing she could. Jasmine told a well-rehearsed lie that she had made for her parents if they ever found out that she wasn't really staying after school. She had never had to use the lie on her parents, but she had told it to Samantha when she confronted her.

Lying to a federal agent was a felony, but Jasmine couldn't' risk losing her scholarship. When she was done, Agent Diamond's expression was unreadable.

"Thank you, Ms. Diya," said Diamond smiling. "I think that's all I need to know. If you find out anything else about the murders, be sure to contact me."

"Happy to help."

Jasmine didn't go back to class right way. She went to the nearest girl's bathroom. After making sure no one was there, she locked herself in one of the stalls, where she promptly buried her face in her hands.

"DAMMIT! DAMMIT! DAMMIT!!!"

(MARK)

Mark Xeg was a little toothpick of a man. Most of the students that Diamond had already talked to had approached the interview with passive indifference. This boy, however, was like a turtle retreating into its shell in a desperate attempt to avoid a predator.

"Good afternoon, Mr. Xeg. I am Special Agent Diamond of the FBI. I'm here because someone in this school is a dangerous and insane criminal. I'm hoping you can shed a little light on that."

"I'll do what I can," whimpered Mark. "But I'm afraid I won't be able to tell you much."

"You're the president of the school's gaming club, are you not?" asked Diamond.

"No, I gave it up."

"You were a national gaming champion. That takes a lot of skill. You also earned a substantial amount of money. Why would you give that up?"

Mark bowed his head.

"It does take a lot of skill, but some people don't look at it that way. Having your heart broken has a way of changing a man's priorities."

"You're referring to Juno Simpson's violent rebuff of your affection."

Underneath his glasses, tears began to form in Mark's eyes.

"She's the most beautiful girl I've ever seen in my life. I should've known I didn't stand a chance with her, but I let winning the national *Star Warrior* tournament go to my head."

"What made you approach her again after the murders of Mr. and Mrs. Smith?"

Mark was too upset to question why an FBI agent was even asking him this.

"I had to try. After everything that had happened, I thought she would appreciate having a shoulder to cry on. But she didn't just reject me again; she made me feel like I didn't deserve to live. She treated me like I wasn't even human. It nearly pushed me over the edge."

"What stopped you?" asked Diamond.

"I couldn't... My parents... When they found me with the gun in my hands... I just..."

Mark was weeping openly now. Diamond passed him a box of tissue paper.

"I hope you understand, Mr. Xeg, that I need to ask certain questions of every senior in this school. I need to know where you were on the nights of the murders."

Like most of his classmates, Mark claimed to have been at home on the nights of the murders. Diamond knew right away that the boy was lying. He decided to press the issue in this particular case.

"Are you aware that lying to an FBI agent is a federal offense?"

"What are you talking about?" asked Mark.

"You're avoiding my eyes when you talk. The tone of your voice has changed, and you're twitching when you speak. All tell-tale signs of falsity. As you can plainly see, I miss nothing."

When Diamond spoke again, his tone was polite but stern.

"Mr. Xeg, many of your fellow seniors are pointing their fingers at you. If anyone had reason to hurt Juno Simpson and her boyfriend, it was you. Your best friends no longer know what you do with your spare time. And now you've lied to me."

All the color had drained from Mark's face. He sunk into his seat.

"Unless you want to spend the next five years in federal prison, I suggest you tell me the truth. Where were you on the nights of the murders?"

Mark was crying again.

"You wouldn't understand."

"Try me."

(AGENT DIAMOND'S NOTES)

Serial killers without a sexual preference are rare. This is going to make it hard to determine the unsub's[3] gender.

---

3   Unsub: abbreviation for "unknown subject." Criminologists often use this term to refer to the unknown perpetrator of a crime, preferring not to immortalize them with nicknames.

Despite the nature of the mutilations, I'm confident that these crimes aren't sexually motivated.

Serial killers that kill outside their own ethnic group are also rare. Only two of the victims thus far have been African Americans, the rest were Caucasian.

These aren't spur-of-the-moment crimes of passion, these are cold and premeditated acts of violence and terrorism.

Can't rule out the possibility of material gain as a motive.

Parricide is a very rare crime. Statistics show that perpetrators are typically white middle-class males with no prior history of convictions. But there are always exceptions.

Motives for parricide include mental illness, antisocial disorders, or dysfunctional and/or abusive family systems.

The only seniors with any known history of serious mental health issues prior to the murders are Kalin Doyle, Lilian Andersen, and Marcus Johnson (incarcerated). Mark Xeg became suicidal after the incident following the second double murder.

Several students suffer from Asperger's syndrome, but being socially awkward isn't proof-positive of homicidal mania.

Most students in the school suffer from depression, stress, and anxiety; but that's normal.

Adolescents typically don't think things through, but the

unsub has managed to avoid capture after killing nine people.

The unsub uses a knife because they're almost impossible to trace, and because they like to get up close. They like to watch their victims die.

The thrill of the kill isn't enough. This person gets a sadistic pleasure out of watching their classmates suffer in the aftermath of the crime. Most serial killers end up hurting complete strangers. This person is doing this to people they see five days a week, and has known some of them for over four years.

The mutilations are constant, almost ritualistic.

Frogs are symbols of death in many cultures, but can also be symbols of transformation.

For the seniors, this year is a transition period. They're not kids anymore; soon they'll have to make their way in the world.

It's possible the unsub is acting out some bizarre coming-of-age ritual.

This person knows exactly what they're doing. You can't make cold and calculated decisions when you're detached from reality. This person knows the difference between right and wrong, but they don't care.

The unsub has a disdain for authority and religious law.

"Thou shall honor thy father and mother."

"Thou shall not kill."

The unsub is a violent, hedonistic, and organized sociopath. They have knowledge, skill, and foresight beyond their years. This person is confident, but their arrogance is in check. Whoever he or she is, they aren't who they pretend to be.

In the case of material gain or revenge, if the unsub has already accomplished his/her objective, the smart thing to do now would be for them to stop.

Going from my own experience, this person will not stop killing until they are caught or killed.

CHAPTER 17

Tom was glad that he didn't have much homework that evening. Even though he had nothing to do with the murders, his interview with Agent Diamond had really taken its toll on him. He couldn't have spent more than an hour thinking about classical literature or the French Revolution if his life depended on it. He had barely finished storing things in his backpack when he got the call from Mrs. Martins.

"Thomas, dear, I know it's a school night, but could you come over for a bit? I think Kiania needs a pick-me-up."

Tom was once again given a police escort to the Martins' residence. When he arrived, he found Kiania looking paler than he had ever seen her. Though she had done her best to hide it, there were signs that she had been crying. Once they were alone in the living room, Kiania wrapped her arms around Tom and buried her face in his chest. Tom wondered if she could hear his pounding heart. He turned on a British comedy, but Kiania wasn't really paying attention.

"Why are you so handsome?" she said dreamily.

Tom had never seen his girlfriend like this. She wasn't the strong independent ice queen he had first seen in freshman year. She looked like a little girl whose pet had just died.

"Forgive me if this sounds impertinent, but how do you know Agent Diamond?"

Kiania knew that Tom wasn't an idiot. She knew he would've put two and two together eventually.

"I've met him before, years ago."

"What happened?" asked Tom.

"On our first date, I told you I didn't know you well enough to tell you why I wanted to join the FBI. I suppose I can tell you now."

Kiania left the room and came back with a framed photograph. The picture displayed a young Kiania on a beach in Florida with another girl her age. The other girl was Caucasian with long brown hair. Kiania didn't have the blue streaks in her hair yet, but the girl beside her was wearing a blue dress.

"The other girl is Faye Paczkowski," said Kiania. "She was my best friend; we were almost like sisters. We did everything together."

Tom felt a sudden chill. He had read enough comic books to know where this was going.

"We were eight years old. It was the last day of school. We were supposed to celebrate the start of summer vacation with a sleepover, but Faye never showed up. She never even made it home."

Kiania struggled to keep speaking.

"The police looked and looked. Eventually, the case went cold. For two long terrible years, there was nothing... Then the FBI arrested a man named Ben Jodie."

Ben Jodie, the Leopard-Man. Tom remembered hearing about him on the news. The story shocked the entire country. Over the course of ten years, he kidnapped, tortured, and killed sixty-six children.

"They knew it was him because he kept trophies and videos... One of those trophies was Faye's dress."

Kiania started to cry. It was a full ten minutes before she found her voice again.

"During his trial and execution, he never showed any remorse or guilt. God, justice, the law, right and wrong, it all meant nothing to him. All he cared about was his own sadistic self-indulgence. He didn't care that his victims were all eight years old; he didn't care that they had families and friends who loved them. They weren't human beings to him; they were just toys for his amusement... He knew the parents of all the children he had killed would watch him die. He smiled at them, and his last words were, 'Thanks for the fun.'"

There was a long silence.

"I never got over it. My mom got a job with a firm here in South Bend, and we left Florida to start a new life. But now I knew that monsters were real. An FBI agent named Arthur Diamond helped rid the world of a monster, but it didn't give me my best friend back. It was years ago, but seeing him again makes it seem like it only happened yesterday."

Kiania went through her seventh piece of tissue paper.

"I know I have a reputation for being an ice queen. But that's just because it's not easy for me to let people in, not after what I've been through."

"So why did you let me in?"

Kiania looked like she had been dreading the question. Tom braced himself.

"On our first date, I told you that you were the least objectionable of all the boys that had ever asked me out. That's the truth. But I must confess I had two ulterior motives. One: after three years of turning down every boy that asked me on a date, people began to question my sexuality. I couldn't stand it. Two: my parents still want me to have a normal life, especially my mother. If I didn't find someone to take me to the prom, I'd never hear the end of it. I didn't expect to fall in love."

There was another long silence.

"Tom, don't you have anything to say?" asked Kiania.

"You just said that you didn't expect to fall in love, but you did?" replied Tom.

"Does it matter? I used you. Aren't you hurt?"

"Maybe a little."

Tom checked to make sure Kiania's parents weren't listening in. Then he leaned in close to Kiania and whispered.

"But after what happened on New Year's Eve, I believe it's a moot point."

Kiania giggled a little.

"I guess so."

Once again, Kiania buried her head in Tom's chest. She wished he could stay longer, but they had school tomorrow. He'd need to leave when the episode they were watching was over.

Monsters are real, but thank God there are still some good people in the world too.

CHAPTER 18

Tom's senior year was officially a nightmare. Despite the assistance of the FBI, the Dart Frog still hadn't been caught. Most nights, Tom couldn't sleep, thinking his parents might be murdered in their beds. Things weren't any better at school. By this point, most of the students weren't even trying to hide their state of nervous tension. They were afraid to remain at Saint Thomas More, but they were also afraid to transfer out, worrying the Dart Frog might single them out. In one week, three different seniors suffered breakdowns and ran out of their classes screaming. Two juniors were expelled for starting a betting pool on who they thought the Dart Frog was and who they thought the next victims would be. Finally, a few freshmen accidentally caused an explosion in the chemistry lab. Naturally, this happened when it was below freezing outside. Now Tom knew why they didn't have fire drills in winter. If it weren't for Kiania, Tom's life would've been unbearable.

Eventually, February came, and with it, the swimming state championship. Having saved the girls' team from a shooter, Tom was excused from his classes on the appointed Friday and was invited to Indianapolis to watch the competition. The preliminaries would be on Friday afternoon, and the finals would be on the following Saturday. His mother came along as a chaperone, while his father stayed in South Bend with his sisters. With the change in scenery came a change in the mood of the students that had made the trip. Normality seemed to return to their lives. Yes, there was still a killer on the loose, but South Bend was now over two hours away.

In total, twenty-two students made the trip to Indianapolis on Friday. In addition to Tom, there were ten students on both the boys' and girls' respective teams, and Adam had accompanied them to carry out his duties as the school mascot. The preliminaries on Friday went well. Tom spent Saturday morning getting his homework done. His calculus homework, in particular, turned his brain to mush.

I know calculus is used in economics, business, and various other fields, but I'll wager that less than half the students in my class will use it in their day-to-day lives.

When Tom arrived at the finals, he was ambushed by a small mob of journalists who questioned him about the incident with Marcus in October. He told them the same thing he always told people when they asked about that day.

"When a man is in love, he doesn't worry about his own neck."

He avoided any questions about the murders and made his way to the bleachers. Tom had brought a bouquet of flowers with him. He had another gift for Kiania back at the hotel, but he wanted to see how the finals went, and then he wanted to give it to Kiania in private.

Tom knew how to swim if the occasion called for it, but he wouldn't dream of competing with athletes like these. It was a very close competition. Kareen and several other girls had scored enough points in their events to put Saint Thomas More in a position to take the title. Eventually, it was time for the final event, the five-hundred-yard freestyle. It was time for Kiania to show everyone why she was called the Icy Mermaid. As the girls took their positions, time seemed to stand still.

The buzzer sounded. The girls leapt into the water and took off like torpedoes. The pool was twenty-five yards long, and the girls were on the other side in twelve seconds.

Twenty laps in total. This is nuts!

Kiania seemed to be trailing behind the other girls. She wasn't last, but she wouldn't score any points for the team if she didn't pick up the pace. Tom's mind started to run amok with the possible consequences if Kiania lost. For four minutes, Tom felt like his heart would jump out. When there were only three laps left, Kiania made her move. In a race, the uninitiated think the best course of action is to move like the hordes of hell are on your heels from start to finish, but experienced athletes knew how to pace themselves, which is what Kiania had been doing. She shot into the lead as some other girls began succumbing to exhaustion. And then it was over.

"THE PALADINS WIN!!!"

When Kiania got out of the water, the first thing she did was take off her cap and flaunt her hair. Tom broke through the crowd and handed Kiania the bouquet. Much to his surprise, she kissed him on the cheek in front of everyone. Once all the awards had been handed out, the next thirty minutes were spent taking various pictures.

Tom was invited to join the girls for dinner that night. Thankfully, they had voted to hit up the best pizza parlor in town. Most of the men at Saint Thomas More High School would've killed to have been in Tom's position. He was surrounded by ten of the best girls on campus: Kiania, Kareen, Saeko Haga, Silvie Lopez, Dasha Ivanko, Nikki Bell, Felecia Marie, Moka Rosé, Vivian Nabarro, and Renetta Ricci. Of course, being the only rooster in a house full of hens rarely played out the way it did in a man's mind. Some of the girls fawned over Tom, much to Kiania's annoyance, but Tom didn't encourage any of them. The real issue arose when the girls all started talking about this, that, and the other thing, and Tom couldn't follow a word of it.

"So, Tommy!" said Moka, "What are your plans after graduation?"

"I'm going to learn how to make comic books," replied Tom.

Moka gave him a lewd look.

"You know, there are easier ways for men with artistic talents to make money. I'd be happy to pose for you."

"Get your own boyfriend," said Kiania angrily.

"It's not my fault he's the only real man on campus."

Tom excused himself by saying that he had to go to the bathroom.

I swear to God, sixty percent of the time, it's like they're speaking a foreign language backwards. So this is what it's like to be on the other side of it.

At that moment, the stall opened. Tom immediately recognized the person who came out of it.

"Mark? What are you doing here?"

"Tom Lime?" replied Mark. "I didn't expect to see you here."

"I came to watch the swimming championship; you still haven't told me what you're doing here."

"I came for the anime convention," said Mark. "I figured there was a one-in-a-million chance there might be some attractive women who shared some of my interests. Might as well have been one to ten billion."

Anime convention? That would explain all the people in outlandish costumes that I saw on my way to the championship.

"How did you do it?" asked Mark.

"How did I do what?"

"Nearly every boy at school has asked Kiania Martins out on a date at one point or another, and she turned them all down. How did you break the streak?"

Mark was comparing Tom's love life to his own. What Mark didn't seem to realize was that Kiania Martins was nothing like Juno Simpson.

"I just told her that she had beautiful hair, and I asked her if she'd go to a movie with me," said Tom.

"And that worked?" asked Mark.

"I didn't think it would either. I guess I just got lucky."

Compliments would never be enough to sway Juno Simpson. Tom wasn't a male model, but at the end of the day, he was a lot more attractive than Mark, and Mark knew it.

"I guess you did," he said as he left the bathroom.

When Tom had left the girls at the table, they had been happy and were thoroughly enjoying themselves. When Tom returned from the bathroom, it looked like the cloud of fear that awaited them back in South Bend had fallen anew.

"Did you just see Mark Xeg in the bathroom?!" asked Vivian.

"He says he's here for the anime convention," replied Tom.

"And I'm the Queen of England!" exclaimed Kareen. "That little freak is the Dart Frog! You mark my words!"

The other girls quieted Kareen down before she made a scene.

"Who else had reason to hurt Juno?" said Kareen, reducing her voice to a whisper.

"Do you want the short list, or the long?" asked Nikki.

"Besides, he's a ragdoll," said Silvie. "To effortlessly cut people up the way the Dart Frog does, you'd need powerful limbs."

"You don't need muscle mass to wield a knife," insisted Kareen. "And you have to remember that anyone who's insane has a great deal of unnatural strength."

"Okay, let's assume Mark is the Dart Frog, and he wanted to get back at Juno," said Felicia. "Why would he kill her parents and the parents of four other people?"

"Maybe there's no reason at all," said Kareen. "Maybe he's just doing all this for laughs!"

Tom wished they could just eat dinner in peace, but it was painfully clear that wasn't going to happen.

"I don't think so," whispered Silvie. "You didn't hear it from me, but a lot of my mother's colleagues think the Dart Frog has something to gain from all this. I think it's Jasmine."

Most of the other girls were genuinely surprised.

"Why?" asked Dasha.

"She's the one who drew the entire country's attention to the murders," replied Silvie. "Her parents are the only African American victims. She now has a free ride to any college she wants. Why should goth boy be the only one accused of parricide?"

"You think she'd kill her own parents to guarantee a scholarship?" asked Moka.

"Who knows? Maybe her parents molested her and her siblings."

"Please, I'm trying to eat here," said Renetta.

"You'd think there would've been at least one witness on Halloween," said Felecia. "There must've been children running around the neighborhood trick-or-treating that night. Someone must've seen something."

Tom and Kiania had taken no part in the conversation, having privately discussed the murders in great detail. But Kiania finally broke her silence.

"Eye-witness testimony is notoriously unreliable anyway."

"What do you mean?" asked Dasha.

"Any experienced criminologist will tell you the same," replied Kiania. "Memories are time-sensitive, witnesses can be misled, and anyone can lie."

After dinner, everyone went back to the hotel. The girls were tired and had a two-hour drive back to South Bend tomorrow, but Kiania still wanted to cap off the day with Tom. He had a movie picked out when she came knocking.

"I'm legitimately surprised that you kissed me in front of everyone after the event."

"I was exhausted and didn't care," said Kiania smiling.

"Well, I know you'd destroy my manhood if I did this in public."

"Did what?"

Tom left the room and returned carrying a foot-long bear made entirely of chocolate. On the bear's torso was the message "Prom?" written in jelly beans.

"Did you make that yourself?"

"The bear was my mother's idea," said Tom.

"I certainly never pictured this scenario playing out like this."

"Is that a yes?" asked Tom.

Kiania kissed him on the lips.

"Thomas Lime, I'd be positively thrilled to go to prom with you."

CHAPTER 19

Tom woke up in a cold sweat. He had dreamt that he and Kiania were swimming up at Lake Michigan when the Dart Frog attacked them. In the dark, he fumbled for his phone. It was only two-thirty in the morning. The room was bitterly cold, as hotel rooms usually were. Outside, the wind howled. The nightmare had made Tom uneasy. He crept over to his mother's bed; she was sleeping peacefully. Her chest heaved gently up and down. There was another strong gust of wind outside. Tom crept to the window and saw the snow coming down.

I hope we don't get snowed in.

Tom went back to his bed but didn't fall asleep. He always had trouble sleeping in a strange bed. He reached for his headphones and tried putting on an audiobook, but he still could not sleep. The nightmare had made him wary, and he suddenly felt the same cold dread that he felt on the night he took Kiania to see *Sherlock Holmes vs. Jack the Ripper.*

KIANIA! THE DART FROG KILLED FRED'S PARENTS AFTER THE FIRST GAME!

Tom didn't care that it was only a quarter to three. He needed to check on Kiania. He grabbed his phone and called her.

"You better have a damn good reason for waking me up this early."

"ARE YOU ALRIGHT?!"

"No, my boyfriend is screaming at me over the phone, and it's not even three in the morning."

"ARE YOU SAFE?!"

Kiania could sense the urgency in Tom's voice.

"The door is locked, and we have a chair wedged under it."

"And your parents?"

"My parents are fine. I can hear my dad snoring."

Tom breathed a sigh of relief.

"I'm sorry. I just woke up from a nightmare. I can't get back to sleep, and I have that feeling…"

"Your concern is deeply appreciated," said Kiania, lowering the tone in her voice. "But I don't think the Dart Frog would be stupid enough to kill someone here. There are only so many students from Saint Thomas More in Indianapolis. If he or she were to make a move right now, it would really narrow it down."

"I hadn't thought of that," replied Tom.

"Try to get some sleep."

"I'll try," said Tom. "I love you."

"I love you too."

Sleep would not come easy for Tom. He tried to reassure himself by thinking about what Kiania had said.

What was I thinking? The Dart Frog never stays at the scene of the crime, and they couldn't leave the hotel in this weather. Even if they could, anyone leaving the hotel would immediately be under suspicion. They couldn't get in anyone's room without a key anyway.

Tom looked at the door. Seeing the wisdom in Kiania's course of action, he had wedged the chair in his room under the handle. It could not be broken open by force, at least not without vociferously drawing attention to what was going on. He tried to think of ways the Dart Frog might try to gain access to his or her victims in this scenario.

If the Dart Frog can't get in, they'll make their victims come out. They might do what I did and call someone on the phone, saying that they're in trouble... No, that doesn't make sense. If someone is trying to kill you, you call 9-1-1, not random people. No one would fall for that.

Tom remembered the explosion in the chemistry lab.

That might work. Set the hotel on fire, and then pick someone off in the chaos. But then they wouldn't have time to carry out their mutilations.

Tom suddenly realized that the Dart Frog could've easily stolen a master key from one of the hotel staff and snuck into someone's room while they were all at dinner.

It's three in the morning. The Dart Frog has never waited that long to make their move. If their aim was to kill Kiania's parents, or anyone else's, they would've done it by now.

Again, a fierce gust of winter wind beat against the window.

They wouldn't get far in this weather anyway.

Tom didn't know when he fell asleep again, but eventually he did. This time he was awoken by a nightmare of the Dart Frog breaking through the walls of his room with a fire axe.

HERE'S FROGGY!

Tom sat bolt upright in his bed and screamed. His mother was there beside him.

"Bad dream?"

"The worst," replied Tom. "What time is it?"

"Almost time for breakfast."

A shower wasn't enough to wake Tom up. Even if he had a cup of coffee or two with breakfast, he was sure he would fall asleep on the drive back to South Bend. He got dressed and went to meet up with Kiania.

Everyone was meeting in the lobby. Kiania seemed to have gotten plenty of sleep, despite the fact that Tom had woken her up at a quarter to three.

"I don't need to be a criminologist in training to know you didn't get enough sleep last night."

"I had another nightmare," replied Tom.

Tom got in line at the breakfast buffet and took a seat with Kiania. He had just eaten a slice of bacon and was about halfway through his first cup of coffee when Saeko made a diversion.

"Where's Kareen?"

Every other girl on the swim team suddenly realized that their captain was absent.

"I thought we all agreed to meet for breakfast," said Dasha.

"She's probably just slaving away in front of the mirror."

"I'll call her."

Kiania rang Kareen up on her phone, but there was no answer. She tried calling her again, and that's when the sound of someone screaming echoed through the hotel. Before their parents could stop them, every Saint Thomas More High School student was either cramming into an elevator or running up the stairs. They found Kareen in the hallway, still in her pajamas and screaming hysterically, her face contorted in horror. Tom shouldn't have looked in the door, but something made him do it anyway. A moment later, he stumbled out and puked all over the floor. Mr. and Mrs. Fabbrie were lying on their bed, their eyes missing, their entrails tossed here and there, with a bloody knife and an orange and black-spotted frog mask placed between them.

The police searched the hotel from top to bottom, but the organs that had been taken from Mr. and Mrs. Fabbrie were nowhere to be found. Somehow the Dart Frog had managed to get into their room, incapacitate Kareen, kill her parents, mutilate their bodies, and get their organs out of the building without drawing attention to what was happening. The students didn't make it home until late afternoon. Tom and Kiania didn't get a chance to discuss the matter in private until a week later.

"Twenty-three of us were in Indianapolis last week. One of us has to be the Dart Frog," said Tom.

"Twenty-three that we know of," said Kiania. "Randy is still missing."

Naturally, Kareen and several other students had immediately pointed their fingers at Mark. Mark had been staying in another hotel, which had also been thoroughly searched. The organs were still nowhere to be found, nor was there any other incriminating evidence to be found on Mark or anyone else. What bothered Tom and Kiania was that as far they could tell, almost none of the people at the hotel were on their list of suspects.

"There's no way Kalin, Jasmine, Isaiah, or anyone else could've driven all the way from South Bend to Indianapolis and back in a blizzard, and certainly not without other people noticing their absence," said Tom.

"I admit, its probability is not high. But there's no evidence that says it didn't happen," said Kiania. "The fact that no one saw their registered vehicles leave town doesn't mean they didn't hitch a ride. The deputy that has taken custody of Kalin since his father's murder has voiced that it's hard to keep track of his movements, and he frequently breaks curfew. If Jasmine decided to leave town for a day, it's highly unlikely that her grandmother would tell the police."

"Even though there's been another double murder?"

"Never underestimate the love of a grandmother or a parent," replied Kiania. "I don't imagine any of the surviving parents want to believe their little boy or girl is a psychotic serial killer. Some may even go to great lengths to protect them."

"One of the main motives suspected by the police is parricide," said Tom. "You don't think Kareen would kill her own parents, do you?"

"At this point, I'm prepared to think anything of anyone," replied

Kiania. "But Kareen's parents kept a close eye on her bank account and her credit cards. She didn't buy six hunting knives. Besides, if she was the Dart Frog and wanted to get rid of her parents, she picked a very sloppy time to do it. Mark is the only main suspect that we know for a fact was in Indianapolis. If Mark is the Dart Frog, why didn't he wait until Kareen and her family got home, at which point there would've been plenty of other suspects in the area? If Mark isn't the Dart Frog, why didn't the killer take advantage of the situation and plant evidence on him?"

Tom didn't have an answer to either of those questions.

"This is what I overheard the police and the hotel staff saying," said Kiania. "At about midnight, someone opened the Fabbries' room with a master key stolen from one of the staff; the same key was later found in a random trash can on the second floor. When we found them, I saw that Kareen had a syringe mark on her arm, and her parents had marks on their necks. Hence the three syringes that were found carelessly discarded on the floor."

"What drug was used?" asked Tom.

"I can't say for certain without seeing the coroner's report, but at a guess, I'd say morphine, the same as Sheriff Doyle and the Smiths."

"So, he or she gave Kareen enough to keep her incapacitated and gave her parents each a shot they wouldn't wake up from, and then went to town with their knife?" asked Tom.

"Looks that way. The Dart Frog has to be someone who is knowledgeable about drugs. He or she doesn't want Kareen to die; they want her to suffer. Kareen isn't a morphine addict or even a user. I know because we were all tested for drugs before the championship."

Tom wasn't a drug addict or user either, but he was smart enough to know that too much morphine could easily be fatal. Even drug dealers knew better than to give their junkies more than their bodies could handle. The Dart Frog wouldn't care how much they used on Mr. and Mrs. Fabbrie because they were trying to kill them, but they needed to be careful with Kareen.

"So, the Dart Frog is someone who is knowledgeable about drugs and has access to them. Unfortunately, most people that handle drugs at Saint Thomas More don't make it to senior year. It's one of the leading reasons why students get expelled."

"That doesn't mean they all get caught," said Kiania.

"I acknowledge that I may not want to know the full answer to this one, but how did the Dart Frog get the organs out of the hotel? I still can't believe anyone could've left the hotel that night," said Tom.

"I overheard the manager saying that there was a guest named Elias Voorhees who checked out after midnight and paid in cash. The snowfall didn't get serious until about an hour later."

Tom knew right away that "Elias Voorhees" was just an alias. But at that moment, something clicked in his mind.

"Jordan's river is deep and wide, Hallelujah! Milk and honey on the other side, Hallelujah!"

Tom had previously wondered where he heard that spiritual at Jasmine's basketball game, and now he remembered.

"Oh my god!"

"What?" asked Kiania.

Tom pulled out his phone and pulled up UBox. He searched for a specific channel and started scrolling through the videos until he found the one he was looking for.

"Durendal Pictures?" asked Kiania, reading the channel's name.

"It's Adam's channel, he was in Indianapolis for the championship too. And check this out."

The video Tom was hovering over was dated June 13th, the summer before their junior year. Months ago, when he looked over the channel to see Adam's review of *Sherlock Holmes vs. Jack the*

Ripper, the video he was looking at only had one hundred and fifty views. Now there were over five million.

Friday the 13th Parts IV-VIII: Children & Teenagers That Survived Their Parents

Predictably, Adam was wearing a Jason Voorhees mask in the video.

"Hi guys! It's Jason's birthday, and I know everyone wants to see a good Friday the 13th movie, one that gives the franchise the justice it deserves. But today, we'll be looking at an often-overlooked aspect of the movies. Tommy and Trish Jarvis, Reggie Winter, Megan Garris, Tina Shephard, Rennie Wickham, and Sean Robertson. They all survived an encounter with Jason Voorhees, but their parents or guardians did not.

At the end of Friday the 13th Part VIII, having survived Jason's rampage, Rennie and Sean are reunited with Rennie's dog in Times Square, but I'm not buying the happily ever after vibe this movie is trying to give. I know these kids are just about to graduate high school, but are they really going to be able to make it on their own in the world with this sort of psychological trauma hanging over their heads? There should be movies about what these kids go through after Jason's attack. We saw something like this with Tommy Jarvis in Friday the 13th Part V, but as is typical of Hollywood, sequels often have different writers, directors, etcetera. It's next to impossible to maintain a consistent and cohesive narrative."

The video trailed on, but Tom and Kiania were interrupted by her phone. Kiania saw that it was Silvie and answered it. Tom read the expression on her face and immediately knew something was up.

"They found a body."

CHAPTER 20

Agent Diamond sat in his hotel room, lost in thought. A hunter had found the remains of Randy Parker in a patch of woods along the Saint Joseph River. The boy needed to be identified by his dental records. After being wrapped in a couple of garbage bags filled with kitty litter, buried in a shallow grave, and left to rot, there wasn't much left of him. Several of the boy's bones had been smashed. Agent Diamond had seen enough bodies throughout his career to know that this wasn't done by animal predation or the elements. The boy had been tortured.

Randy Parker's parents weren't just killed; the unsub burned the house down. The frog mask left at the scene is exactly the same as all the rest, but all the other masks were primary or secondary colors, and this one was pink. The mutilations are the same as all the other murders, but according to the coroner, the mutilations on the Parkers looked rushed. Obviously, the aspiring journalist saw something he wasn't supposed to see and tried to blackmail the person or persons involved, not realizing the person he was trying to blackmail either was the unsub or knew them. If he had evidence of the Dart Frog's identity, he would've just gone to the authorities. I need to look for students with dirty secrets.

The Parkers weren't the only anomaly in the Dart Frog's victims. Sheriff Doyle was the only single parent to be killed. Investigation proved that he wasn't any closer to uncovering the Dart Frog's identity than anyone else, so it was improbable that was the reason he was killed. Then there was the Fabbries. Richard and Sarah Fabbrie were the only victims killed outside South Bend or Saint Joseph County. The knife and mask found at the scene were the same as those found at all the other crime scenes. All the mutilations were the same as well. It was highly unlikely they were dealing with a copycat. The question haunting Diamond's mind was whether his unsub was still in control of their actions or if they were devolving.

Five double murders and one single, it's perfectly possible this unsub is getting cocky. But there still isn't a single piece of tangible evidence I can work with. That suggests they're still in control.

One would've thought the list of suspects would've been substantially reduced with the latest murder. Randy Parker had been dead for about two months, and the only people that stood out were Kareen Fabbrie and Mark Xeg, but Agent Diamond wasn't convinced. The Dart Frog was someone who thought things through. Killing anyone when there was a limited number of potential suspects in the vicinity only made sense if you were trying to frame someone. Kareen had been quick to point her finger at Mark Xeg, but there was no concrete evidence against him. In fact, there wasn't anything concrete against any of the other students.

Mark Xeg had been suicidal, and he had reason to hurt Juno Simpson. He was highly intelligent but socially awkward. Agent Diamond could easily see the boy lashing out against other students high on the social ladder, but Diamond still didn't commit himself. In the case of the Gainsville Ripper, the police identified a certain eighteen-year-old boy as a potential suspect. The real killer was eventually arrested, but not before the other guy's face was plastered all over the news. By the time the killer was caught, the damage had been done. With no solid evidence to fix him as the killer, Agent Diamond wasn't about to put Mark Xeg and his family through any unnecessary grief.

Earlier, the hotline received an anonymous tip about Adam Jones, the school mascot. He had been in Indianapolis as well. Apparently, there was a suggestive video on the boy's UBox channel. Diamond had interviewed Jones and the rest of the seniors in the school. Out of all the students he had spoken to, Jones seemed the most enthusiastic about the interview. It was the boy's ambition to become a famous filmmaker. When asked how he would pay his tuition at the University of Southern California, he said that he had received offers for advertisements on his channel. The channel had experienced a huge traffic intake since the murders started. Of course, this was all circumstantial, and it didn't fit Diamond's profile of the killer. Anyone smart enough to kill a dozen people and avoid capture wouldn't leave an old but potentially incriminating video on their UBox channel. Jones had benefited from the murders, but Diamond had been a criminologist long enough to know that there was such a thing as coincidence.

According to the hotel security records, no one left and reentered their respective rooms during the window when the murders were committed. This suggested that someone else was in Indianapolis when the Fabbries were killed; but as far as anyone knew, none of the other seniors at Saint Thomas More left Saint Joseph County that weekend.

Which brings us to the non-existent Elias Voorhees.

There were ways to sneak past roadblocks. No vehicles registered to a senior at the school and not involved in the championship had left South Bend during the event, but that didn't mean someone didn't hitch a ride. If someone were to go all the way to Indianapolis and back unnoticed, they'd go from being a potential suspect to an impossibility. It sounded like something out of a book or a movie, a murderer giving themselves an alibi that was above reproach. The only issue was how a student's absence would go unnoticed. Diamond could easily see some of the parents lying to protect their children. With twelve gruesome murders under their belt, the Dart Frog was looking at the death penalty, and Diamond was still convinced that this person wouldn't stop until they were caught or killed.

CHAPTER 21

(SPRING BREAK)

No one that was at Saint Thomas More High School during the murders would ever dispute that the winter months were the worst. Being confined to your house when it was cold and dark outside was bad enough when there wasn't a psychotic killer on the loose. As is typical of South Bend, Old Man Winter kept his habit of arriving late and then never wanting to leave. When spring finally came, it was a huge relief. The change in the mood it brought over the students wasn't just because of the weather, but because they knew the school year was almost over.

On Monday night during Spring Break, Dasha Ivanko sat in her living room with a bowl of triple chocolate ice cream and watching her favorite movie in French; she needed the practice. Dasha couldn't wait for the year to be over. Once she graduated, she'd be off to the University of Florida. She would finally be out from under her mother's thumb when that happened. Dasha's mother was the chemistry teacher at Saint Thomas More High School. She had raised Dasha on her own since her father died serving in the Marines. Dasha had been too young to remember her father, but his death profoundly impacted her mother.

Mrs. Olva Ivanko was a rigid disciplinarian and was overprotective of her daughter. She made Dasha promise that she wouldn't have any boyfriends until she graduated from college. She wasn't aware of it, but Dasha hadn't kept this promise. It wasn't love at first sight, but eventually, the boy in question had managed to charm Dasha into giving him a chance. No one knew about her boyfriend, not even her teammates on the swim team. She had to come up with a different convincing lie each time she met with him. When she finally got down to Florida, she would be able to go where she wanted when she wanted.

It was twelve minutes past ten o'clock when the movie ended. Dasha was just getting up to go to bed when her phone started ringing. She picked it up and saw that it was Silvie.

Why would she be calling me this late?

Dasha answered the phone, but what came through wasn't clear.

"Das... the... dral... on... ire..."

"What?"

"Ca... ou... ar... e... aid... dral... on... ire..."

The line cut out. Dasha tried texting Silvie to see what was going on, but it didn't go through. She had lost the signal. That's when she heard the sound of the garage door opening. The garage door could be opened with a remote or from the keypad outside. But Dasha's mother was upstairs, and no one else would be coming in through the garage, especially not this late. Before Dasha could process what was happening, the door burst open. Dasha turned to face the kitchen and saw someone dressed head to toe in black and wearing a violet and black-spotted frog mask.

Dasha screamed and screamed, it was all she could do. Her body had frozen, just like it had when Marcus held her and the other girls at gunpoint in the locker room. As she screamed again, she heard muffled footsteps rushing towards her, and then she felt a sharp prick in her neck. As she sunk to the floor, she heard her mother screaming.

The Dart Frog turned to face Olva Ivanko, who immediately

raced back up the stairs. Olva's mind was racing. She couldn't think of any reason why someone would want to kill her, but right now that didn't matter. She didn't know if anyone had heard her or her daughter screaming. She had to call the police, but first she needed to get away. The only sounds she could hear were the Dart Frog stomping after her and her own pounding heart.

WHAT DID HE DO TO MY DAUGHTER!?!

She needed to call the police, but as she made it to the top of the stairs, a white-hot pain exploded in her throat. The Dart Frog had thrown their knife all the way up the stairs. She opened her mouth to scream again, but no air escaped her ruined throat. She collapsed to the ground choking on her own blood. She maintained consciousness just long enough for the Dart Frog to climb the stairs, bend over, and rip the knife out of her throat.

CHAPTER 22

Tom had been fitted for the suit he would wear to the prom. He spent the rest of the day working on his dance steps so he wouldn't embarrass Kiania. As he practiced, he couldn't get the murders out of his mind. March passed without incident. It almost made everyone forget that there was a killer on the loose. But Tom had the image of Richard and Sarah Fabbrie's mutilated bodies, eyes gouged out and entrails pulled out of their chests, burned into his memory.

Over a month and nothing. Either the Dart Frog has already accomplished his or her goal, or they're waiting for the heat to die down.

Kiania had told Tom that the fact that Agent Diamond hadn't had anyone arrested yet meant that they didn't have any solid evidence. Tom couldn't believe that they were up to their necks in dead bodies, yet the authorities didn't have anything they could use to get a warrant for someone's arrest. Kiania had calmly explained to him that hunting serial killers wasn't like a cartoon.

"Organized serial killers don't leave blatantly suspicious and incriminating items just lying about."

Adam's video was suspicious, but Kiania explained that it was circumstantial evidence at best. True, Adam had benefited from the murders. Tom certainly wished he had a UBox channel that could get advertising offers; very few channels did. But if Adam wanted to make some fast cash and didn't care about the legality of it all, there were easier and a lot more secure ways to get it that didn't involve killing a dozen people. The fact also remained that Adam had no known connection to any of the victims. The police would likely keep an eye on Adam but could do little else.

Tom tried to imagine ways for Kalin, Lilian, Jasmine, or anyone else to sneak out of South Bend and go to Indianapolis and back without raising suspicion.

Who in their right mind would let their child leave town while there's a murderer on the loose?

Isaiah was the only suspect whose birth parents were still alive. Kalin was supposed to be under the roof of one of his father's friends from work. Everyone in the sheriff's department wanted this killer caught as much as anyone else, so it was highly unlikely this man would cover for Kalin if he decided to take a trip to Indianapolis without telling anyone.

I wonder how suggestive Jasmine's grandmother can be.

It was no mystery that Jasmine had benefited the most from the murders, and now she and her siblings were staying with their grandmother. Tom supposed that Jasmine could've told her grand-mother that she was staying at a friend's house for the night. But she still couldn't have left town in her car or any car that belonged to someone in senior hall.

I'd make a very lousy criminal.

Tom and his family made sure the house was all locked up before it got dark. Tom sat in his room watching old TV shows on his laptop. There weren't any good shows on TV today, not since all the major en-tertainment companies had gone woke. It was one of the reasons why Tom wanted to be a comic book writer. All the comics he had enjoyed growing up had been ruined. It wasn't long before he got bored.

Now that swimming season was over, Tom and Kiania had much more time to spend together. Senior year was almost over, and Tom intended to make the most of it. Unfortunately, Kiania and her family had gone to The Bahamas for spring break, so Tom was on his own.

My last spring break as a student of Saint Thomas More, and I have to spend it here alone.

Almost on cue, Tom got a text from Kiania.

Wish you were here.

The text was accompanied by a picture of Kiania by a pool in her string bikini. Tom didn't need his girlfriend to tell him that he'd never have children if he shared the picture with anyone. Tom's mood improved for a few minutes, but then the grim reality struck him.

Senior year is almost over.

It seemed like only yesterday that Tom got up the courage to ask Kiania out on a date. He really wished he had done it in freshman year. Soon they would be graduating. Tom was going to one college to learn how to make and sell comic books. Kiania was going to another college to earn her bachelor's degree, which she needed if she wanted to join the FBI. Tom knew in his heart that no force in heaven or hell could stop Kiania from pursuing her goal.

We've had one year together, and it was spent with a psychotic killer on the loose.

Tom knew that he should've been grateful just to get one date with Kiania, let alone a whole year, but it wasn't enough. He wanted more, so much more.

Tom's train of thought was interrupted by his phone ringing. He picked it up and saw that it was Samantha.

Tom had lost track of time while watching TV; it was past ten o'clock. Only one thing could make Samantha call this late.

"What is it?" asked Tom, dreading the answer.

"The cathedral is on fire!"

Saint Matthew's Cathedral was where the seat of the Bishop for the Diocese of Fort Wayne-South Bend was located. It wasn't exactly the grandest Catholic Church in the county, but the prospect of it catching fire would still be a local media circus. The fact that this was happening when the students of Saint Thomas More were on spring break could only mean one thing.

"The Dart Frog is making their next move," said Tom.

"Whatever you do, don't open your door or leave the house!" exclaimed Samantha.

"I know; I'm not an idiot,"

After the deaths of the Fabbries, the seniors of Saint Thomas More had adopted a plan of campaign. They had a phone tree ready to put everyone on alert if anything suspicious happened. In all likelihood, the Dart Frog didn't have their phone on their person. Anyone who didn't answer their phone would immediately fall under suspicion. Tom contacted all the people he was supposed to call and pulled out the retractable self-defense baton that Kiania had gotten him for Christmas. His sword was too impractical indoors. Tom's parents were still awake; they had been watching a late game show when the neighborhood watch contacted them. When Tom was sure they were securely locked in their room, he returned to his own.

Alright, who drew the short straw?

As Tom stood waiting in his room, he tried to make a mental list of all the people he knew were out on vacation.

Kiania and her parents are in The Bahamas, the Bells are in Hawaii, the Rays are in Florida, and the Williams are in South Carolina. Did I forget anyone?

If Tom's information was correct, no one on his list of suspects was supposed to be out of town at the moment. Unable to stand the suspenseful silence, Tom called to check on Rick. His friend answered almost immediately.

"Anything on your end?" asked Tom.

"Nothing yet," replied Rick.

"Did you make contact with Mark?"

"I think I roused him from sleep," said Rick. "He says that he and his family are all locked up."

"That's good to hear."

"You don't think he's the killer, do you?"

"I won't commit myself," replied Tom. "But the facts have got to be faced. He could've done every one of these murders. He's certainly smart enough and had reason to hate Juno and Fred."

"If he's a suspect, so is everyone else in the gaming club," replied Rick. "We all had reason to hate Juno after what she did. Except maybe Lizzie, she couldn't work up the courage to ask a boy out, much less kill somebody."

"Who do you think the Dart Frog is?"

With all due respect to his childhood friend, Tom didn't expect Rick to come up with an intelligent answer. He was just trying to make conversation while he waited for something to happen.

"Well, if we're going by the rules of horror movie logic, Kalin and Lilian are too obvious. If the motive is parricide, I'm definitely going with Jasmine. You can't get over the fact that her parents are the only African American victims, and she got a free ride to Harvard out of the deal."

"And how could she have gotten to Indianapolis and back without anyone realizing?" asked Tom.

"She could've figured out a way. Her grandmother probably doesn't even know what year it is."

BOOM!!!

The Lime residence could only fit two cars in the garage. Tom's used sedan was often parked in the driveway. When Tom mustered the courage to look out the window, he was shocked to see that his car had gone up in flames.

"What the hell was that?!" screamed Rick over the phone.

"THAT FILTHY PSYCHO JUST TOTALED MY CAR!!!"

Tom's first instinct was to race downstairs and beat the brains out of whoever just wrecked his beloved car, but he was smart enough to realize that was likely what the Dart Frog was counting on. This was probably a ploy to lure him out of the house or get him to open the door. Tom was sure someone on the neighborhood watch had seen what had happened, but he called the fire department anyway.

Within an hour, the entire neighborhood was crawling with police and fire officials. Someone had placed a homemade firebomb on Tom's car, but it had only served as a distraction. When the bomb on Tom's car was remotely detonated, the Dart Frog had already claimed Olva Ivanko as their latest victim. Tom got hardly any sleep that night. In the early morning, he debated whether or not he should bother Kiania with this latest development while she was on vacation, but one of her friends from the swim team had spared him the trouble. Tom spent most of the day filing an insurance claim with his father. Needless to say, he remained in a very bad mood.

Due to the Dart Frog's inactivity during March, Agent Diamond and his team returned to Washington to await results. When news of the latest murder had spread, they were back in South Bend in a matter of hours, and everyone learned how scary Diamond could be when he was mad.

"Please explain to me how a serial killer gets away with arson and murder when every local police officer and state trooper in the county is supposed to be on alert!" yelled Diamond.

"Shit happens?" said one of the frightened cops.

"Well, shit *does* happen," said Diamond. "I can't exactly argue with that, but it doesn't have to be in your pants! Now I suggest you bring me something I can work with before any more shit happens!"

A thorough investigation revealed that the firebombs at Saint Matthew's Cathedral and the one in Tom's car were all the same. Unfortunately, they weren't made using anything traceable. The bombs were all detonated remotely. While the fire at the church left everyone distracted, the Dart Frog attacked the Ivanko residence. When the Dart Frog was done, they detonated the bomb on Tom's car to cover their escape. When Kiania finally returned home from The Bahamas, Tom was ready to discuss everything in detail with her.

"So now we have five double murders and two single murders, three if you count Randy. That makes thirteen altogether," said Kiania.

"And now we're looking for a sadistic sociopath with access to drugs and sufficient knowledge and aptitude necessary to assemble firebombs with remote detonators," said Tom. "This just gets better and better. The fire department told us the bombs were made using homemade napalm. How would anyone at our school know how to make napalm?"

"It's actually pretty easy if you know how," replied Kiania. "The ingredients are cheap. All you need is something to stir and store it in. You won't get anything out of that. Is there anyone we can eliminate from suspicion based on the facts?"

"The phone tree was broken up when Dasha didn't answer her phone. Unfortunately, none of the people that branch off after her are on our list of suspects."

"I don't think any judge will be able to issue warrants for nearly two hundred phones," said Kiania. "Even if they could, I doubt it would reveal anything. Some serial killers are caught through sheer stupidity, but I don't think this one is dumb enough to take their phone with them."

"What else could they have done?" asked Tom.

"Every phone has a different GPS tracking chip. If the Dart Frog cloned their own phone, they could take the cloned phone with them and leave their real phone at home. Any calls they made would still show up on their account. All they would need to do is dispose of the cloned phone afterward, and no one would be any the wiser."

As expected, Mark, Isaiah, Jasmine, Kalin, and Lilian all denied having anything to do with Mrs. Ivanko's murder. It was proven that Kareen couldn't have done it because she was staying with Silvie and hadn't left the house that night.

"Who else is there?" asked Tom.

"There's Adam," said Kiania.

"But you said his video is circumstantial evidence at best."

"It is, but now Mrs. Ivanko is dead, and he has a motive."

"And that would be?"

Kiania smiled.

"I'm ninety percent sure that he and Dasha have been dating in secret."

Tom was genuinely surprised.

"Since when?"

"He's been trying to win her affection since junior year. The body language they've both been displaying in school since the year started suggests she decided to give him a chance."

"Why have they kept it secret?" asked Tom.

"Mrs. Ivanko was VERY protective of Dasha. She would often complain about her in the locker room. She made Dasha promise that she wouldn't have any boyfriends until she got a college degree. Even if she were to allow her daughter to have a boyfriend, there's no way she'd accept an African American."

Tom suddenly remembered that one of the most watched videos on Adam's UBox channel was his review of *Guess Who's Coming to Dinner*, where he listed the reasons for the stigma against interracial relationships and angrily complained that society still frowned on them and yet forced people to accept relationships that were objectively immoral.

"So, Adam bumps her off so they can be together and kills twelve other people to cover his tracks?" asked Tom. "I don't pretend to understand what goes through the mind of a serial killer, but that just doesn't sound rational to me."

"Most serial killers aren't rational in the accepted sense of the term," replied Kiania. "But he could've done every single one of these murders."

Tom's only argument was that Adam killing twelve other people to cover his tracks seemed like serious overkill, but there was no concrete evidence that it didn't happen. That seemed to be the common problem with every theory Tom and Kiania came up with.

Innocent until proven guilty, but the Dart Frog is too smart to leave any evidence, or else the police and the FBI would've caught them by now. So how are we supposed to catch him or her?

CHAPTER 23

One of the things perplexing everyone was how the Dart Frog was getting to the sites of their murders. It wouldn't have been an issue when the murders started, but now the entire county was under lockdown. No one under the age of twenty-one was allowed out after dark without supervision. There were police checkpoints stationed throughout South Bend and the surrounding areas, and they knew the make and model of every car owned by the students of Saint Thomas More High School.

Services purchased with transportation apps were too easy to trace. But if one looked around the dark web, they could find transportation services that were much more discreet. These services were mostly used by cheating spouses, smugglers, and other such individuals. The drivers and the clients never knew each other's identities, and the drivers never asked any questions as long as the money was good. For the Dart Frog, money was never an issue. It was easy to make money when you weren't weighed down by a conscience.

The Dart Frog was traveling in a white SUV with the driver under the pretense of being a night shift delivery boy. There was a secret compartment in the back seat. The Dart Frog just had to cram inside and wait until they arrived at their destination. They had already arranged for a different ride when the job was done. The Dart Frog wasn't killing anyone tonight. Things were getting too hot, and they needed supplies, things you couldn't get in any store.

The SUV stopped at several traffic lights and no less than three police checkpoints. But eventually, the vehicle came to a complete stop. Within moments, the red light in the secret compartment turned green, signaling that the coast was clear. The Dart Frog got out and paid the driver, who promptly drove off without a word.

The Dart Frog had selected an abandoned repair garage on the outskirts of town for the drop-off point. Once inside, the Dart Frog stood against the wall by the door and waited for the man with the goods to arrive. Ten minutes later, the sound of footsteps became audible. The muffled sound of clanking metal accompanied it. As soon as the man entered the garage, the Dart Frog pulled a gun on him.

"Don't move."

The voice that came out from behind the black ski mask was heavily modulated. It was impossible to tell if it was disguising a man's voice or a woman's voice.

"Put the box on the ground gently, then put your hands above your head and get against the wall. You'll get your money if the box contains what I ordered."

The man did as he was told. The Dart Frog had ordered the items in question on the dark web. The arrangement was to pay half the money in advance and the rest upon delivery. The man who brought the box was just a delivery boy and had no idea what he was carrying; that way, he'd get to deny everything if he was caught.

The Dart Frog opened the box and examined the contents. At first glance, the box appeared to contain a half dozen metal canisters full of rubber cement, which was exactly what it was supposed to look like. The Dart Frog sniffed each container for verification.

Hello, gel-based explosives.

The Dart Frog tossed the delivery boy a thick wad of money and told him to get lost. The Dart Frog picked up the box and started making their way to the pick-up point for their ride back. It was time to make the final preparations.

This will be one prom South Bend will never forget.

CHAPTER 24

(PROM NIGHT)

Agent Diamond claimed that he knew the Dart Frog's identity, but he didn't have any tangible evidence to prove it and couldn't legally obtain any. No one wanted the Dart Frog to get off on a technicality, so there was only one course of action available to the authorities: they needed to catch them in the act. And so, the prom was allowed to take place.

It was a beautiful spring day. The sun was shining, the birds were singing, and there were brightly colored arrangements of flowers throughout the city. One could hardly believe there was a psychotic killer on the loose. Years later, everyone would say they could feel it in their bones that it was almost over. Everyone involved could feel the cold dread and anticipation despite the warm spring sun.

Tom had already said his daily Rosary and had just gotten into his suit. As always, he needed his father's help with the tie. He stood in front of the mirror in his room to examine the final product. He almost didn't recognize the handsome and well-groomed young man that stared back at him.

Only the best for Kiania.

It seemed like only yesterday that Tom was graduating from grade school. To celebrate the occasion, Tom's class had gone to Chicago to see a musical. On the bus ride, Tom and some other boys talked about how some of them would be finding girlfriends in high school. Tom never dreamed that on the first day of freshman year, he would find a girl as beautiful as Kiania. Once again, he wished he had worked up the courage to ask her out then and there. They could've had four years together instead of one, and three of those years wouldn't have been spent with a serial killer on the loose.

Now, they would be going to separate colleges in a matter of weeks.

No use crying over spilled milk.

Tom didn't care that the Dart Frog was still out there; he wouldn't let it ruin his special night with Kiania. They didn't have much time left, and he wanted to make every moment last.

The day was passing fast. After allowing his mom to take pictures, Tom got into the limo that would take him to the Martins' residence, where Kiania's mother would undoubtedly take more pictures before they went to the prom. The limo hadn't even made it out of the neighborhood when Tom got the call from Rick.

Let me guess, Samantha bailed on him at the last minute.

Rick had managed to successfully ask Samantha to the prom, but only after convincing her that he wasn't just asking her as a last resort.

"What is it?" asked Tom.

"I thought you should know, Mark is missing," said Rick. "He isn't at home or anywhere else. No one can get a hold of him, and his parents have already called the cops."

That was not good to hear. Juno and Kareen had both openly accused Mark of being the Dart Frog, and Tom and Kiania had never crossed him from their list of suspects. He was one of the few people who could've committed every one of the murders. Every police officer in the county would be out tonight, as would every concerned citizen, all with guns and itchy trigger fingers. This could get ugly very quickly.

"Okay, thanks for the heads up."

When Tom arrived at the Martins' residence, Mrs. Martins greeted him even more enthusiastically than usual. When Kiania came down the stairs, Tom felt like he had just stepped into one of his dreams. She was dressed in a stunning sleeveless purple mermaid dress. Predictably, her long hair was in an elegant mermaid braid and seemed even shinier than usual. Her perfume was utterly intoxicating, but Tom became hopelessly lost the moment she smiled.

"Are those flowers for me?" she asked half-jokingly, indicating the bouquet of roses he carried.

"Yes," was all Tom could manage.

"Do you need a drink or something?" asked Kiania's father. "You look a little flushed."

Tom was suddenly aware of how red his face had become. Fortunately, he was saved by Kiania's mother, who was all too eager to take pictures before it got dark. As they made their way to the living room, Kiania pulled him aside.

"You look very handsome, Tom," she said smiling.

"You look amazing," replied Tom.

The next twenty minutes were spent taking pictures. They took pictures indoors and outside, with more poses than Tom cared to count. Being so close to Kiania with that divine perfume almost proved too much for him. Her skin was so warm, Tom thought her given nickname was a grave injustice. When they were finally done taking pictures, it was time to head to the prom.

When the limo exited the neighborhood, Kiania broke the silence.

"You've hardly said anything since you arrived."

"I'm just having a hard time believing all this is real," replied Tom. "Why would a girl as beautiful as you ever agree to go to the prom with someone like me?"

Kiania kissed Tom on the cheek and then laid her head on his shoulder. Once again, Tom was nearly driven insane by the scent of her hair. He had to keep reminding himself to keep his eyes above the neckline.

"Thomas Lime, there isn't anyone else in the world I'd rather be with right now."

Tom was fairly sure Kiania was putting on a strong front for him. In all probability, the Dart Frog was going to try something tonight, and Kiania was probably just as tense as everyone else. But Tom had been waiting for this day for a long time and was determined to enjoy himself; sadistic psychopaths be damned.

Tom and Kiania passed four police checkpoints before they arrived at the Century Center, South Bend's flagship convention venue, where the prom was being held. There were even more cops strategically placed around the building. At the front door, students were searched for weapons.

"Do they really expect the Dart Frog to come here?" asked Tom.

"Not to kill anyone," replied Kiania. "That would be suicide. But they've been relishing in everyone's terror all year long, and tonight is the big night. We'll have to be on our guard."

The theme for the prom was Camelot. There were shields along the wall representing the different Knights of the Round Table, a sword in the stone, the Holy Grail, and even a dragon. Tom hadn't been expecting anything too flashy in terms of decor, not after all the damages incurred at school due to the numerous pranks pulled earlier that year. As Tom and Kiania entered, they turned a lot of heads. The boys in senior hall had nearly a year to make peace with Tom being the boy who successfully asked Kiania on a date, and now they were jealous of him all over again.

Tom and Kiania scanned the crowds to see who was and wasn't present. As expected, Mark was nowhere to be seen. Dasha wasn't present, and neither was Adam. Casey Rosewood was almost unrecognizable without her glasses. She was dressed in a stunning blue dress; her usual pigtails had been replaced with a single elaborate braid. Both

Isaiah and Jasmine were dressed in red. At length, Tom spotted Rick and Samantha. Samantha was dressed in green; Rick's suit was white. Rick's hair had been cut, and he was wearing a substantial amount of gel. A quick look around the room told Tom that Rick was the only member of the gaming club in attendance that night.

"She insisted that our colors go together," said Rick. "And I wasn't wearing pink."

"Any sign of Mark?" asked Tom.

"Nothing," replied Rick. "Look, I know this looks bad. I can see Mark as the person who filled Juno's locker with cow manure, but I can't see him as the maniac that's been going around carving everyone's parents like jack-o-lanterns."

"Many serial killers aren't who they pretend to be," said Kiania. "Without any tangible evidence to the contrary, we can't make exceptions based on character, perceived opinions, or probability."

The entire room fell silent when Kalin and Lilian entered the room hand in hand. Both were dressed head to toe in black, but Lilian's dress was trimmed with scarlet. Lilian's figure was unmistakable, but Tom almost didn't recognize Kalin. Kalin had cut his greasy black hair and looked very well-groomed. They drew several reactions as they walked in, but they ignored them all. Tom and Kiania were close enough to Jasmine to hear her comment.

"A pig dressed in a suit is still a pig."

Kalin and Lilian were immediately forgotten when Juno entered the room. For months after her parents were murdered, she seemed inconsolable and lost. But tonight, she seemed like her old self again; she was once again the queen bee she had always been. She was dressed in an elaborate white dress embroidered with gold. Her long golden hair was decorated with matching ornaments, which looked like they cost even more than the dress. She walked right up to Tom and Kiania, wearing that same cat-like smile that the school knew so well.

"You look very handsome, Tom. And Kiania, for an icy mermaid, you make one very spicy jalapeña."

"Thank you, where's your date?" asked Kiania.

"I decided to come alone," replied Juno. "The only real man on campus already has a date."

Juno was looking at Tom again.

"I know Kiania plans to join the FBI, but what will you do after graduation, my dear Teddy Bear?"

Tom remembered what happened when he mentioned his plans to the swim team; he didn't want to give Juno the chance to extend him the same offer.

"I plan to learn how to make and sell comic books. What are your plans?"

"I'm heading off to Syracuse; I'll see where it goes."

"You're holding up awfully well under the circumstances," observed Kiania.

Juno's expression immediately changed.

"My parents are dead; wallowing in self-pity won't bring them back. After witnessing Jasmine's self-determination at that basketball game, I decided that I would not stop living my life."

Juno turned her attention back to Tom, this time undressing him with her eyes.

"I hope you'll save at least one dance for me; this might be the last chance we get."

"Get your own dance partner," said Kiania.

"Well, we'll see who gets crowned King and Queen," said Juno.

Very few people seemed to be in the mood to dance. Agent Diamond and the lingering police officers in the background were a constant reminder of the reality of the situation. After Principal Miller officially allowed the festivities to begin, two songs passed awkwardly with no one taking to the floor. At this point, Tom and Kiania decided to break the ice. All eyes were on them, but Tom didn't pay any attention to them; it was just him and Kiania. As they began their slow waltz, the DJ played Gus Black's cover of *Don't Fear the Reaper*, which seemed strangely appropriate.

Tom kept his eyes locked on Kiania's, completely blocking out everything else. Kiania was the better dancer, so she took the lead. After weeks of careful preparation, Tom was competent enough to follow. His mother's words echoed in his mind.

You'll be fine as long as you don't step on her feet.

It didn't take long for Tom to get lost in the dance. He had dreamed of this night since he first saw Kiania during freshman year. Now that his dream had actually come true, he couldn't believe it. When the DJ started playing *How Long Will I Love You*, Tom's emotions started to show on his face.

"Are you alright?" whispered Kiania.

"I've waited a long time for a moment as happy as this."

"Then let's make it last."

Tom never wanted it to end, but he knew it would. Kiania would be hundreds of miles away in a matter of weeks, and he didn't want to let her go. Tom had successfully taken Kiania to the prom, but having achieved this, he knew it would never be enough.

This is the girl I want to marry.

Up to this point, most of the other students were just watching in awe as Tom and Kiania danced. The first couple to follow their example was Kalin and Lilian. Kiania's eyes locked with Lilian's, and the unspoken message was clear.

Are you challenging me?

I'm not calling you out for dinner.

Both Tom and Kalin gave their partners their full attention as they were led through the dance steps. Tom was nearly overwhelmed by Kiania's fast movements more than once. At one point, when she took a dip, his proximity to her bust left him flustered; but he would not embarrass her in front of all these people. When this little dance duel finally ended, both couples got a loud round of applause.

"Watch out, Morticia," said Samantha looking at Kalin and Lilian.

Thanks to Tom and Kiania, the prom became a lot livelier. There were dances, pictures were taken, and friends talked about their plans for the future. But Tom didn't care for some of the songs.

"Is this supposed to be music or attacking the walls of Jericho?"

Tom went to the DJ to make a request.

"Well, that's not usually on the playlist, but I'll make an exception for you."

Tom took Kiania back out onto the dance floor. For years, Tom had been trying to identify the song playing in the background of Martini's Bar in *It's a Wonderful Life* during the scene where George Bailey was praying. It had been driving him nuts for years. Back in December, Tom finally learned the name of the song. It was called, *Vieni Vieni*. Once he knew the full song, it always made him think of Kiania.

Palm trees are gently swaying
My heart is saying, how much I love you
Ah, moonlight is softly gleaming
My heart is dreaming of you.

Finally, the moment of truth came.

"Ladies and gentlemen," said Principal Miller taking the stage. "It's time to crown this year's Prom King and Queen!"

The whole room immediately fell silent. Of course, being the prom king or queen just meant you were more popular than everyone else, and as long as your grades weren't bad and you behaved in school, the staff wouldn't offer any objections. Tom expected the king to be either Isaiah, the boys' basketball captain Joey Red, or soccer captain Zane Wyvern. He expected the queen to be either Juno or Jasmine. A drum-roll played as the envelope was handed to Principal Miller.

"The winners are… by a landslide… Thomas Lime and Kiania Martins!"

It took a minute for Tom's brain to process what he heard. He had been trying so hard to savor his time with Kiania that evening that everything else had seemed irrelevant. When he finally found his voice, he could only manage two exclamations.

"OH MY GOD! WE WON!!!"

As soon as Tom and Kiania got on the stage and were crowned, the lights went out. Several people screamed; the police officers moved instinctively to the doors. Suddenly, images were projected onto the wall. Tom felt his stomach lurch. One by one, the mutilated bodies of all the Dart Frog's victims were displayed.

"SOMEONE SHUT THAT OFF!" screamed Agent Diamond.

The projector was mounted on the wall and was too high to reach. Juno fainted at the sight of her parent's bodies, and the images of the Smiths followed shortly after. Jasmine screamed at the sight of her parents. There was a substantial amount of vomit on the floor when the projector displayed the Parkers. Kalin started shouting obscenities when his father's body was displayed, and Lilian tried to restrain him. After the projector cycled through the Fabbries and Mrs. Ivanko, it displayed a video of the Dart Frog wearing a black mask. Whoever it was waved at the terrified students and started singing in a heavily modulated voice.

"Tom and Kiania sitting in a tree. K-I-S-S-I-N-G. First comes love, then comes the bed, then comes the Dart Frog for their heads!"

CHAPTER 25

Tom and Kiania were the first people to leave the Century Center. Agent Diamond personally escorted them out. They both made frantic calls to their parents, warning them not to open the doors for anyone but the police, who were already on their way.

"Where are you taking us?" asked Tom as they sped off in Diamond's SUV.

"We have an FBI safe house all set up," replied Diamond. "If this son of a bitch wants you or your parents, we're not going to make it easy for them."

The SUV had its lights and siren on and didn't stop for anyone or anything. Tom and Kiania held hands but weren't talking. There were no words for this situation. Ten minutes passed in intense silence, then Diamond got a call while the driver sped on.

"Good news, your families are safe and are en route to join us. One way or another, this ends tonight."

After another ten minutes, they arrived at the safe house. It was a two-story building on the outskirts of South Bend. There were already four police officers on the scene. They were all that could be spared that night.

"Agent Diamond, we've swept the building from top to bottom. There's no one here."

"Good, get these two inside."

Ten minutes later, Tom and Kiania were joined by their families, who brought them a change of clothes. Diamond dismissed his driver and the other officers that weren't part of the protective detail. Once Tom and Kiania had changed, Diamond gathered everyone in the living room. Both Tom and Kiania's parents were given armored vests to wear.

"This isn't going to do us any good if they stab us in the head," said Mr. Martins.

"Thank you very much for that mental image," said Mrs. Lime.

"They won't get that far," said Diamond. "All the windows have bars, and all the doors are made of iron and are locked. There will be five of us down here, and we're all armed. You'll be safe, locked in your rooms."

"If amphibian face shows up, he's one dead frog," said one of the officers.

Tom's sisters were immediately sent to bed, but Tom doubted if Britney or Jennifer would actually sleep. They waited for an hour, but there were no updates, good or bad. It was Mrs. Martins who broke the silence.

"Kiania, was it a good prom?"

"Before it went to shit, yes," said Kiania, trying to smile.

Just as Tom, Kiania, and their parents were going up the stairs, something came in over the police radios. Everyone froze where they were and listened.

"Some officers just picked up Fred Smith," said Diamond. "He was out unsupervised with his dog and a gun."

"Let me guess, no frog mask and no knife," said Kiania.

"Exactly," replied Diamond.

Tom sat on the bed in his designated room, but he wouldn't go to sleep. He'd be incapable of sleeping until this was all over. At his request, his parents had brought his baton over. He kept it close in case anything happened. Agent Diamond had confiscated everyone's phones in case the Dart Frog tried something.

Every cop in the county is on alert. Roadblocks and police checkpoints may not have stopped the Dart Frog in the past, but there are four armed police officers and an FBI agent downstairs, and this place is a fortress. Are any of my classmates really crazy enough to attempt something like this?

In the silence, Tom could hear the clock strike downstairs. It was eleven o'clock. He laid down on his bed but didn't close his eyes. As he stared up at the ceiling, he tried to go over everything that he and Kiania had talked about since all this insanity started.

Juno's parents were killed on the night I took Kiania to the movies. Juno was in the theater with us when it happened.

He remembered how Juno fainted at the Century Center when the images of her murdered parents were projected on the wall.

She said she was going to Syracuse to see where it goes. She probably has no idea what she's going to do with her life now.

Juno had no shortage of enemies. But if anyone had reason to hate her, it was Mark Xeg. Juno had broken his heart and had almost driven him to suicide. Mark was in Indianapolis when the Fabbries were killed, and no one knew where he was now.

Fred's parents had been the next ones to die. At first glance, Fred was one of the strongest people that Tom had ever known. But after his parents were murdered, he dropped out of school and descended into alcoholism. According to the other boys around school, Fred had been in rehab for months afterward. He couldn't have killed the Diyas on Halloween. Sure, the police had just found Fred running around with a gun, but he was probably just doing what half the city was doing right now.

The person that had benefited the most from the murders was Jasmine Diya. The deaths of her parents had sensationalized the murders throughout the country. Jasmine's whereabouts on the nights of the murders had been called into question. Now Jasmine had a free ride to Harvard.

I know who else went to Harvard.

Tom couldn't get the image of Jasmine breaking down after that basketball game out of his mind. But was that all just a bunch of amateur dramatics? Did she fool her grandmother so she could go to Indianapolis under the alias of Elias Voorhees?

"Jordan's river is deep and wide, Hallelujah! Milk and honey on the other side, Hallelujah!"

Tom started thinking about Adam and Dasha. Neither of them showed up for the prom. Tom had no idea where Adam was on the night the Simpsons were killed. The alias Elias Voorhees and the way the Diyas were killed suggested the Dart Frog had a thing for horror movies; then there was the video Adam had posted on his UBox channel. Did Adam take a page from the D.C. sniper and make everyone think there was a serial killer on the loose just so he could put his girlfriend's mother out of the way? If he did, why did he wait so long?

Downstairs, the clock struck thirty minutes past the hour. Prom night was almost over. As Tom lay on his bed, lost in thought, his ears were unconsciously listening for something. If he strained his ears, he could hear his father pacing in the room he and Tom's mother shared down the hall. Down the other end, he could hear Britney crying. He could hear nothing from Kiania's room or the one shared by her parents. He wished Agent Diamond hadn't confiscated their phones. He could hear Diamond and the police officers moving about and talking downstairs, but he couldn't make out what was being said. He could hear leaves rustling in the wind outside. Every little noise seemed magnified.

Either Kalin or Lilian could've killed Sheriff Doyle easily. All the other victims were parents of someone higher on the school social ladder. But then again, Randy didn't fit the profile either.

It was clear that Randy and his family hadn't been intended targets. That slippery little worm had seen something he wasn't supposed to see, so the Dart Frog silenced him.

If Randy knew the Dart Frog's identity, he would've just gone to the police so he could be the big hero. He may have been dumb, but he wasn't dumb enough to blackmail a serial killer. No, someone on campus has a dirty little secret that they don't want anyone else to know about. But what kind of secret would anyone at a Catholic school have that they'd kill to protect?

Since the Catholic Church got a new pope, one that was doing everything in his power to bring the Church back from the brink of complete annihilation, Catholic schools had become a lot stricter regarding the conduct of their students. Since his freshman year, Tom had lost track of how many students had been expelled from Saint Thomas More for drug possession or use.

Morphine is a controlled substance. Maybe Randy was spying on someone and saw a drop. It's perfectly possible.

One thing that Tom couldn't get over was the Dart Frog's choice to wear a different colored mask to each murder. Why weren't they all red? Was the Dart Frog just trying to screw with everybody?

Red, yellow, green, pink, blue, orange, violet, and now black. It doesn't make sense.

The black mask that the Dart Frog wore in the video could've been entirely for intimidation and stealth purposes, or it could've had a symbolic meaning. Black could've meant the complete absence of light and, by extension, color, or it could've meant every color combined. Tom had been a student of the arts long enough to know that if you mixed a bunch of different colors, the result just kept getting darker and darker. It all depended on the killer's intention.

Why did the Dart Frog wear a pink mask when they killed the Parkers?

The Dart Frog was an organized serial killer. Everything they did had a purpose. It didn't really matter what color mask the Dart Frog wore when they went to kill the Parkers. The fact that they set the house on fire let everyone know that something was off. But the Dart Frog had chosen to wear a pink mask for some reason.

If they had gone with cyan, they would've had all the spectral colors. Pink is just a shade of red. I think it's a pretty safe bet that the Dart Frog didn't wear it for breast cancer awareness. What does it mean? Femineity, good health, charm, playfulness, childishness, romance?

Somewhere in the back of Tom's head, something clicked. A huge piece of the puzzle seemed to fall into place.

"Oh no, don't tell me…"

Tom sat up, suddenly alert. He heard the sound of footsteps in the grass outside, damnably unmistakable to someone listening with all his senses as he was. Agent Diamond had given strict orders that no one was to leave the house. It couldn't have been one of the officers. Tom felt his hair stand up, and sweat formed on his forehead. He resisted the temptation to look outside his barred windows. The Dart Frog had referred to him and Kiania by name. Every cop in the county was on their toes tonight, not to mention an army of concerned citizens with guns. Agent Diamond claimed that he knew the Dart Frog's identity; he just couldn't prove it. The noose was tightening, and the Dart Frog might abandon their modus operandi altogether for the sake of speed.

Tom stood up, careful to keep his form out of the window's line of sight. His baton was in his hand. He listened, but he didn't hear any more footsteps. Downstairs, the clock struck a quarter to midnight.

BOOM!!!

The whole house shook, and the lights flickered out. A moment later, thirteen similar bombs were remotely detonated harmlessly across South Bend as distractions. Tom could hear everyone screaming.

"WHAT THE HELL WAS THAT!?!"

There was a loud reverberating crash of metal and a sharp hissing. Then the house was filled with the sound of gunshots. Tom could hear both his sisters screaming. He lost count of how many shots were fired before they stopped, then he heard the sound of someone running up the stairs.

Agent Diamond had told Tom not to open his door under any circumstances, but his urge to protect his family, his girlfriend, and her family overrode that order. To say that Tom wasn't scared out of his wits by the explosion and the gunshots would be untrue, but his father's words echoed in his ear.

God hates a coward.

He quickly unlocked the door and slid back the bolt. He heard someone running down the hall.

I need to time this just right.

He raised the baton over his head, threw the door open, and brought the baton down on the Dart Frog's head as they ran past his door.

"MONSTER!!!"

Tom didn't give his opponent any time to react. Using all his body weight as a battering ram, he rammed the Dart Frog against the wall. He heard something drop to the floor but didn't stop to look at it. His martial arts and self-defense training had taken over. He got his arms under the Dart Frog's to prevent them from reaching for another weapon. The Dart Frog tried to use their own weight to push Tom off, but he was much too heavy. They wrestled down to the other end of the hallway. Without warning, the Dart Frog slammed their head into Tom's face. Tom reeled back in pain and dropped his baton. The Dart Frog pulled out a knife and charged, but Tom kicked the knife out of the Dart Frog's hand and followed up with another kick to their chest, causing them to stumble backward. Tom seized his opening.

"YOU WANT A PIECE OF ME!?!"

Once again, they wrestled, but they had both forgotten where they were and went tumbling down the stairs.

As Tom fought to remain conscious, he felt warm blood gushing out of his nose. His whole body ached. He wasn't even aware of the thin cloud of smoke at the bottom of the stairs. Suddenly his eyes started to burn, as did his throat. His nose discharged a large quantity of blood and mucus.

WHAT THE HELL?!

After the Dart Frog had blown the front door down with gel explosives, they had thrown a homemade tear gas bomb inside to incapacitate Agent Diamond and the four police officers, making it much easier to beat them in a firefight. Unfortunately for Tom, the gas hadn't fully dispersed.

Tom felt a pair of hands close on his throat. Tom forced himself to open his eyes, and though his vision was obscured, he saw that part of the Dart Frog's mask had broken, exposing one of their eyes. At that moment, Kiania came rushing down the stairs with Tom's baton in hand and smacked the Dart Frog in the head, causing them to collapse. Tom pushed his attacker off him, and the Dart Frog didn't get up.

Tom rubbed his eyes, and his vision cleared enough for him to see that the police officers were lying in pools of their own blood.

"Tom, are you alright?!" exclaimed Kiania.

"Everything aches, I've got a bloody nose, and my eyes and throat feel like they're on fire, but I'm good. Thanks for the help."

"I'd kiss you, but you've got blood all over your face," said Kiania.

"Fair enough."

Tom got up and stood on both of the Dart Frog's arms while Kiania went to grab a pair of handcuffs from one of the dead cops.

"Not so tough when someone actually fights back, are you?" asked Tom, wiping off a thick wad of blood from his face.

Tom and Kiania heard their families running down the hall upstairs.

"Careful! There's some kind of gas!"

As Tom's parents simultaneously scolded him for doing something so stupid and thanked God that he was still alive, Kiania rushed over to where Agent Diamond was lying on the floor. He was still breathing. The Dart Frog had gotten off one good shot at him, but he had been wearing a vest. Mrs. Martins picked up one of the dead police officer's radios while the men cuffed the Dart Frog.

"Suspect is at the safe house, officers down, send an ambulance now!"

Mr. Lime and Mr. Martin held up the Dart Frog while Tom checked to see if there were any more concealed weapons on their person. There weren't, but he discovered something else.

"A woman?"

Tom pulled the mask off. Everyone stood there, staring at Juno Simpson.

"JUNO!?!"

"Who were you expecting? Jason Voorhees's father?" groaned Juno, still smiling her cat-like smile.

Tom couldn't believe it, but Kiania seemed to be putting the pieces together.

"That night at the movie," she said. "You weren't the person who came back into the theater with that drink. That was your partner in crime, wasn't it?"

Juno didn't stop smiling. At that moment, everyone was startled by the sound of a gun cocking behind them.

"Let her go!"

They all turned to see Kareen standing in the doorway with a gun.

"LET-HER-GO!!!"

At that moment, Tom knew. He knew without being told, and any fear he had felt went up in a white-hot blaze of anger.

"YOU FILTHY ROTTEN SODOMITE!!!"

BANG!!!

Tom felt an explosion of pain somewhere on his body, but his brain didn't process where. As he fell backward, he heard the clock striking midnight; he heard Kiania and his parents screaming, then more gunshots, and then he heard nothing at all.

CHAPTER 26

Awareness came very slowly. At first, Tom couldn't move any part of his body, not even an inch.

Am I dead?

It took all Tom's courage and effort just to open his eyes. When he did, Jesus was there, staring down at him. He could hear voices, but they sounded far away, and he couldn't make out what was being said. A sharp pain in his shoulder jogged his memory.

Kareen shot me. I died. I'm being judged.

Tom was raised a devout Catholic but was taught never to presume God's mercy. Mercy could not exist without justice. At the moment, Tom couldn't remember the last time he had gone to confession. It must've been before Easter. He tried to think of what sins he could've committed since then. Was he too attracted to Kiania? Was it the time he dreamed about skinny dipping with her on an island? Was it the intense hatred he felt in those final moments before Kareen shot him? Was it sins of omission? Did God never really forgive any of Tom's past transgressions? Whatever it was, Jesus just kept staring down at him with the same expressionless face. Tom kept repeating the same thing over and over again.

"I'm sorry."

Tom kept apologizing until he drifted back into unconsciousness. Jesus was still looking down on him when he awoke, but the rest of his vision was a hazy whirlpool of obscure images.

Knights charging across the horizon on fire-breathing bears?

The knights were fighting an army of giant technicolor frogs led by Juno. The scent around Tom didn't match up with anything he was seeing. It was too clean, with a faint aroma of disinfectant. He wondered where he had smelled it before. Wherever he was, it was cold. He called out for his parents and Kiania, but nobody came.

When Tom woke again, he found he could move his left arm when he put his mind to it. Suddenly, his senses were stimulated by an unmistakable scent.

"Ki... a... nia"

She came into his line of vision. Her eyes were red from tears.

"I told you never to do that again."

The sensation of her kiss was enough to convince Tom that she was real, but something still didn't add up.

"Why are you dressed like a belly dancer... and why is Mothman juggling pies on a unicycle?" he said, pointing behind Kiania. There was no one there.

"That's the drugs," replied Kiania.

It took a minute for Tom's foggy brain to process what she said. He looked up; what he thought had been Jesus was just a Sacred Heart portrait hanging over the bed he was laying on.

"Where am I?"

"You're in the hospital. Lucky for you, Kareen wasn't a good shot. You blacked out from shock and hit your head."

Tom looked around. His vision cleared enough for him to make out the table on his left-hand side, which was covered with gifts and get-well-soon cards. A sharp jolt of pain in his right shoulder brought another flash of memory.

"Mom and Dad!"

"It's alright," said Kiania. "Our families are fine; it's all over."

Kiania showed Tom the newspaper that had been sitting on the other table.

SOUTH BEND DART FROG CAUGHT!

Tom saw from the pictures on the paper that the police officers that had tried to protect them were all dead.

"What happened to Diamond?"

"He's down the hall," replied Kiania. "He was wearing a vest, the tear gas spoiled Juno's aim, and she only wounded him. His wife is demanding that he retire early."

"That dude is married?" asked Tom.

"It's not public knowledge, but yes. Apparently, she was quite a dish back in the day."

"What happened?" asked Tom. "I don't remember anything after Kareen shot me."

"Kareen is dead," said Kiania. "I picked up Diamond's gun and shot her."

Tom couldn't hide his shock.

"You killed her?!"

"She shot my boyfriend, and she was going to kill the rest of us because we were witnesses," said Kiania. "I did what I had to do, and the hospital's resident priest told me not to lose any sleep over it."

Kiania certainly didn't look like killing her team captain had any impact on her conscience.

"Juno?"

"She's in another hospital, chained to a bed and surrounded by police officers. After Kareen shot you, she tried to get away in the chaos. I shot her three times. I don't know how she's still alive. I could've sworn I hit a lung."

"Why did you shoot her three times?" asked Tom.

"After I shot Kareen, there were only three shots left."

Tom knew that Kiania was training to join the FBI, but the fact that she could easily kill someone she had known for years and unload three shots into someone else was a little unsettling. But the truth was that Tom was too relieved and zonked out from his painkillers to care.

"Remind me never to get on your bad side..."

As Tom drifted back to sleep, he felt Kiania's kiss again.

"Eu te amo, Thomas Lime."

Kiania wasn't around long enough to see Tom cry.

I love you so much... I never want to let you go...

A few hours later, Tom was visited by his family. For months he was afraid that his parents might be murdered in their beds, and now it was over. He felt waves upon waves of relief to see them alive.

"Hi Mom... Dad..." he managed.

Tom knew they wanted to tear him a new one for almost getting killed, but they didn't. He couldn't remember the last time he heard his sister, Jennifer, cry.

"Tommy, baby," said his mother, kneeling down beside him. "You know how much I love you."

"I love you too..."

"Do not EVER let anyone call you a geek because you want to write comic books," said his father. "No one compares with you."

"Thanks... dad."

It was hard for Tom to keep track of time. At one point, between waking and sleeping, he was visited by Rick and Samantha.

"Tom! Are you okay?" exclaimed Rick.

Tom hated being confined to a hospital bed. He was right-handed, and Kareen had shot him in his right shoulder. By this point, the doctors had told his parents that it could take months before he would be back to one hundred percent. He would be graduating with a brace and sling on. He also dreaded saying goodbye to Kiania when they both went off to college. All this, combined with the drugs the doctor had him on, made him very irritable.

"I have a freaking hole in my shoulder," said Tom. "I'm also tripping on painkillers, and I'm not looking forward to coming down."

"Well, this will make you feel better," said Samantha. "Three different teachers have already decided to give you an exemption from your finals."

"You're screwing with me," groaned Tom.

"Nope."

Tom's brain cleared enough for him to remember what had happened before the prom.

"Did the police ever find Mark?"

"They found him after Juno was arrested," said Rick. "He was bound and gagged in the late Mayor Simpson's sex dungeon. Apparently, Juno and Kareen were going to make him their scapegoat. They bragged about how they would shoot him and make it look like a suicide."

"How did he take it?"

"He looked even worse than you."

Asshole.

"He looked much better after Kiania spoke to him," said Rick.

"What?" asked Tom

"I don't know what your girlfriend said to him, but he really perked up afterward," said Rick.

I'll be sure to ask her about that.

Samantha must've read Tom's mind because she smacked the back of Rick's head.

"I suppose now is as good a time to tell you as any," said Samantha. "You have a new nickname."

"O lord, what now?" asked Tom.

"You are now, the Mighty Arctodus!" said Rick.

"The what?"

"Arctodus simus is the largest species of bear known to man," said Samantha.

"Whatever," said Tom, trailing off to sleep again.

When Kiania came again, Tom asked her about what she had discussed with Mark.

"Just tying up loose ends. I wanted to know where he was on the nights of the murders, and he really needed a pep talk."

I suppose having your heart broken, nearly being driven to suicide, and then having that same woman use you as a scapegoat for her crimes will do that to a person.

"Where was he on the nights of the murders?"

"Can you keep a secret?"

"Yes," replied Tom.

"So can I," said Kiania, smiling.

After Juno's devastating rejection of his advances in junior year, Mark took his mother's advice and tried to broaden his horizons. He had stopped playing *Star Warrior* because he was taking salsa lessons. He had kept this little extracurricular activity a secret because he was horrified to think how the rest of the school would react.

"If anyone found out, they'd make my existence hell with 'Mark the Dancing Dork' jokes for the rest of my life."

Kiania had promised she would never tell a soul. She then told Mark that the girl he fell in love with was only a mask, one that fooled the entire school. After assuring the poor boy that pretty blondes were a dime a dozen in America, she invited him to her graduation party to give him more experience talking to girls.

Tom decided he was strong enough to listen to Kiania put all the pieces of the puzzle together. Even if he wasn't, he wanted to listen to her talk.

"What's happening out there?" asked Tom.

"My mother is getting ready to ensure Juno gets what's coming to her. Juno may have been too smart to leave much in the way of evidence, but Kareen kept a diary."

Even if she pulls through, she has nothing to look forward to but three needles.

"So, they were really..."

"Yes," said Kiania. "Kareen had a history of depression, but her parents didn't know why."

"Did you know?" asked Tom.

"I had my suspicions but didn't want to assume. Turns out she'd been obsessed with Juno for years, and last year she got up the nerve to tell her, and Juno seemed to reciprocate those feelings. Unfortunately, for both of them, their parents were post-crisis[4] Catholics, and they wouldn't have condoned their behavior. That's when Juno told Kareen her big idea."

From disobedience to murder, just like in Genesis.

"That night at the movies, Kareen told her parents that she would be training in the school pool like she usually did. As team captain, she had privileged access to the pool after hours. In reality, she just left her phone in her locker, placing her miles away from the movie theater if anyone asked. She went to the movie theater with a ticket for the romantic comedy, which she had paid for in cash. After Juno left the theater to buy that soft drink, she went to the bathroom and changed clothes with Kareen. In a dark movie theater, one blonde girl looks like another. Kareen nonchalantly joined us in the theater, and Juno went home and murdered her parents."

No signs of forced entry.

"When the movie was over, the two of us saw someone matching Juno's description leaving the theater in haste. To make it airtight, Kareen has Juno's phone just in case the police get a warrant to check her GPS. Just like that, Juno goes from being a suspect to an impossibility. All that's left for her to do is to meet up with

---

4   This term is used under the assumption that the Catholic Church survives the dark age of apostasy, heresy, moral relativism, and moral insanity in which I am currently living; which I have come to call *The Twilight of the Church*.

Kareen, change clothes, drive back home, call 9-1-1, and scream the house down."

"Why didn't they kill Kareen's parents right away?" asked Tom. "Why kill all the others?"

"They took a page from the D.C. snipers," said Kiania. "John Allen Muhammad wanted to kill his ex-wife, but he'd immediately be a suspect if she was the only person killed. Instead, he made it look like she was one random target of a serial killer. Juno and Kareen needed more victims, and Fred Smith was unfortunate enough to be their first pick."

"But how was Juno getting around? I thought she was staying with her aunt in Michigan."

"As to how she got from point A to point B and back each night, the police are looking into it. As to how she got around her aunt's supervision, it's not hard to pull one over on someone who spends their nights with Mary Jane."

Oh, I forgot about that.

"One week after the Simpsons were killed, Kareen went to the football game while Juno went to the Smith residence. She had been dating Fred, so she knew how to get in. Dasha was babysitting down the street. She didn't hear the Smith's dog bark because it recognized Juno. Once inside, all she had to do was kill time. When the game was almost over, Kareen used a burner phone to let her know. At this point, Juno gives the Smith's dog a shot of acepromazine to ensure that he isn't going to complicate things. Then she hid in the basement, waited for the Smiths to come home and go to bed, crept upstairs, and killed them. In all probability, the acepromazine was meant to cast suspicion on Isaiah. His mother is a veterinarian, and he stood the most to gain by Fred dropping out of school."

"How did she get ahold of the drug?" asked Tom.

"Animal tranquilizers aren't controlled substances, and you can get just about anything online these days."

"Where did she get the money to pay for all this stuff?"

"Diamond's team has been going through Juno's laptop. Apparently, she was selling pornographic photos and videos of herself on the dark web under the alias Horny Heather."

Mental note, never name your daughter Heather.

"How did Fred take the news?"

"About as well as you'd expect," replied Kiania. "It doesn't help that he was caught breaking curfew and carrying a loaded weapon."

Ouch...

Tom still remembered how Fred looked when he walked into the gym on the first day of school. He was a big strong man with a promising future ahead of him, but then he was the victim of a terrible tragedy, and he couldn't handle it. Now he was a high school dropout.

"After that, they took a break until Halloween. Things got crazy at school, Mark was placed on suicide watch, and Juno was probably using that time to gather info on her next target. She knew someone like Jasmine would ignite a media powder keg and blame Kalin. I'm confident that Juno and Jasmine's relationship never developed beyond acquaintance, so breaking into her house would've been her first real challenge. This is where her hidden talent for hacking came in handy."

No one in Saint Thomas More High School had ever taken Juno Simpson for the Kevin Mitnick type.

If you knew how to steal a million dollars without getting caught, you wouldn't tell anyone either.

"Once she knew how to bypass their security system without getting caught, she had to pick a date where she knew there would be reasonable doubt as to Jasmine's whereabouts."

"Jasmine lied about staying after basketball practice to use the school's exercise equipment. What was she really doing?"

"I'm not at liberty to say," said Kiania, smiling.

Kiania had interviewed Jasmine earlier. Naturally, Jasmine was feeling like a complete jackass for jumping the gun and pinning her parents' deaths on Kalin, and she had already issued a public apology in front of the entire country. Since Kiania's boyfriend had been shot while apprehending the real killer, she was willing to talk, but only after Kiania promised her silence. Jasmine's dirty little secret was more embarrassing than Mark's but not as bad as Juno and Kareen's. High school was stressful under the best of circumstances, even more so when you're trying to earn a basketball scholarship. It turned out that Jasmine dealt with her stress by patronizing a local nudist club. No one knew about this, not even her parents.

"I've done my homework; at no point in the Bible does God or anyone else condemn nudity![5] It's not like I strut my stuff in a public street, and I never touched anybody! It's not about sex!"

But others might not have looked at it that way, and Jasmine couldn't risk losing her scholarship, which was why she kept it a secret. As she had done with Mark, Kiania promised she wouldn't tell anyone.

"We come now to the murder of the Parkers," said Kiania. "By this point, the murders were a national sensation, and the whole school was on edge. As you may recall, Kareen, in particular, was very anxious about something."

"Let me guess," said Tom. "Randy had obtained a picture or video of her and Juno in a compromising position."

"Bingo," replied Kiania. "Evidence enough to get them both expelled. Randy planned to make a little money from his discovery, but the little worm didn't know who he was screwing with. On the weekend before the midterms, he went to pick up his first payment and was ambushed by Juno. She then took him to her late parents' house and took her sweet time torturing the location of the video

---

5   While Jasmine isn't incorrect here, I feel obligated to point out that the *Catechism of the Catholic Church* states: "Purity requires modesty, as an integral part of temperance."

out of him. Since killing the Parkers wasn't part of the plan, they used Mr. Diya's finger, which Juno had kept just in case she needed a distraction, to ensure everyone's attention was on you. For good measure, Juno burned the house down when she killed Randy's parents. After that, she just got rid of him."

Tom never liked Randy. But the thought of him bound and gagged in Juno's basement, helpless and alone, tortured, killed, and then dumped in the middle of nowhere and left to rot was very unpleasant. No one deserved that.

"Next was Sheriff Doyle. Once again, Juno needed to put her hidden hacking talents to use. Suspicion would immediately fall on Kalin and Lilian if there were no signs of forced entry."

"But Sheriff Doyle was single, and Kalin wasn't high on the social ladder," said Tom. "Why did they break their victim profile?"

"Investigation into his files confirmed that Sheriff Doyle wasn't any closer to discovering the Dart Frog's identity than anyone else. It's possible they were already planning to kill Dasha's mother later, and they wanted to keep an even number of victims. But the immediate effect was to create chaos and confusion. When the Diyas were killed, Jasmine and the African American community brought the murders to national attention, and she openly accused Kalin of being the Dart Frog. Now the Dart Frog had become a cop killer. At this point, the FBI became involved in the investigation, and everyone began to suspect parricide as a possible motive for the murders. It was only natural that Kalin and Lilian accused Jasmine of being the Dart Frog."

Get everyone else to point fingers at each other to draw attention away from the real murderer.

"Next was the death of the Fabbries," said Kiania. "Until now, Juno had been doing all the heavy lifting, but it was time for Kareen to prove her devotion. Juno somehow arranged transportation to Indianapolis so she could check into the hotel under the pseudonym of Elias Voorhees. From there, Juno stole a master key from one of the hotel employees, so she could make it look like someone broke into the Fabbries' room, and then watched as Kareen killed her parents with the morphine she had so generously provided. All Juno did was mutilate the corpses when she was done. From there, she gave Kareen a dose of morphine that would make it seem like she had slept through the ordeal and walked out with the stolen organs. After that, she somehow arranged for someone to drive her all the way home in a blizzard."

Juno's aunt must not have been questioned after the Fabrries' deaths, or she was so stoned that weekend that she either didn't remember a thing or notice Juno's absence.

"The murders couldn't stop yet, that would mean the Dart Frog had accomplished their objective, and the authorities would make educated guesses as to what that objective was. But Juno and Kareen did wait until spring break to make their next move. I doubt they picked Dasha randomly. Maybe Kareen knew about Dasha's romantic troubles and, in some misguided act of mercy, decided to relieve her of them, or maybe they just wanted an even number of deaths. They had already killed a single father and needed a single mother to finish the set."

Tom wondered what Dasha and Adam would do now that it was all over. Adam had talked about horror movies on his channel, but now Dasha was living in one. Their relationship would never be the same, even if they didn't go off to college. Try as he might, Tom couldn't see this little love story having a happy ending.

Kiania kept talking, but Tom stopped listening. The thought of Dasha and Adam's uncertain future made him think about his own.

"And for the grand finale, they were going to kill the parents of the prom king and queen. Once this was accomplished, they would kill their scapegoat and make it look like a suicide. They had a note typed out and everything. Juno even accounted for the possibility of metal security doors. The police are trying to figure out how she got her hands on gel-based explosives."

Kiania suddenly noticed that Tom was crying.

"Are you in pain, Tom? Should I call the nurse?"

"Why didn't I ask you out in freshman year?"

Kiania knew immediately that this wasn't a side-effect of Tom's painkillers; he was being serious.

"I love you. You know I love you," said Tom.

Yes, she knew.

"I know I should be grateful for the time we've had together, but we've spent this year with a murderer on the loose... It's not enough... I want more..."

Kiania came over and kissed him on the lips. It was a long kiss.

"You want to stay with me forever, don't you?"

Tom didn't answer with words; it was written all over his face. Kiania smiled.

"Thomas Lime, you tackled a gunman while armed with nothing but a fire extinguisher and an axe. Then you fought a psychopath that had killed fifteen people. Do you really think I'm ever going to find another man like that?"

"Well, when you put it like that..."

"And, most importantly, you showed me that despite all the evil in this world, there are still some good people worth fighting for."

She kissed him again.

"I want my own house with an enclosed pool someday, and my parents know from experience just how expensive that is. So, you go learn how to make your Arthurian legends comic book while I learn to be a better criminologist."

Kiania bent down and whispered in Tom's ear.

"And before we leave, I'll show you how much I love you."

"I'm suddenly VERY motivated," said Tom.

CHAPTER 27

(FIVE YEARS LATER)

Tom and Kiania stood outside the Annis Copley Memorial State Mental Hospital. They had spent the previous day at Kalin and Lilian's wedding. It had been a very solemn occasion. After the ceremony, but before the reception, Kalin and Lilian had gone to visit the graves of their respective parents. When they reached the place where Kalin's father and mother were buried, they found a bouquet of flowers with a note signed in the name of Juno Simpson.

Tom could still remember the trial like it was yesterday. For over a year, the trial of Juno Simpson was all anyone talked about. The lawyers got fat, the judge got famous, and Juno was sentenced to death in the end. But during the trial, the nature of Juno's relationship with Kareen became public knowledge, and that was when all the innumerable enemies of Christ came rushing to her defense. They twisted the story of Juno's crimes into a sentimental tale that painted both her and Kareen as the victims of outdated ideologies and toxic social conditioning. As usual, they just kept complaining and complaining until they got everything they wanted. At her appeal, Juno was found legally insane and was sent to the Annis Copley Memorial State Mental Hospital for "rehabilitation."

No one could believe it. Together with Kareen Fabbrie, Juno Simpson had been responsible for the deaths of seventeen people, and she was going to walk away. Juno hadn't said a single word since her trial started, but after the appeal, she laughed. It was a loud, long, shrill, and inhuman laugh that would've made the devil proud.

In the years that followed, Tom's family was constantly harassed by people who came into the bakery to order items decorated with rainbow-colored frogs or obscene messages like "Pro-Murder and proud of it." When Tom's family refused to serve these people, they took the matter to court. Thanks to some very dedicated Catholic lawyers, Tom's family retained their right to refuse service, but it didn't stop there. One person had gone as far as to set the bakery on fire. When Tom finally got a replacement for the car that Juno destroyed, it was vandalized on a regular basis. It wasn't just happening to Tom's family. Anyone related to Juno's victims felt compelled to carry guns for fear of their lives.

"You don't have to do this," said Kiania.

"You said that Juno didn't even react when you killed Kareen, she just bolted for the exit," said Tom. "Kareen may have lusted after Juno and killed her own parents to start a new life with her, but I think we both know Juno was just using her. If I'm going to tell our story, I need to know what she was really after."

Tom had met with all the families of Juno's victims. No one was happy that Juno escaped justice or that all the enemies of Christ were painting her and Kareen as the tragic victims of Catholicism. The real story needed to be told, and Tom was the only one who could be counted on to tell the truth. Tom had started writing a comic book about the murders with everyone's blessing. If he was going to finish the book, he needed to know the real reason why Juno did what she did. He would've preferred to do this alone, but he knew Kiania would've given him hell if he did.

As soon as Tom and Kiania walked through the doors, the temperature dropped at least five degrees, and it only seemed to get colder the deeper they went into the building. They passed through one steel gate when they saw an inmate being subdued by orderlies.

"VROOM! VROOM! VROOM!!!"

The orderly escorting Tom and Kiania saw the confused expressions on their faces and answered the question they didn't ask out loud.

"He identifies as a car. Don't worry; he's harmless, just crazy."

Mental hospital nothing, this place is a nut house.

Tom and Kiania were escorted past two more steel gates and an electronic door. This was where the most dangerous inmates were kept. The air was cold and sterile down here, and there wasn't a trace of natural light. The pale overhead lights were caged and cast eerie shadows on the walls. As they made their way down the row of cells, Tom walked so he stood between Kiania and the cells. The first inmate they passed futilely clawed at the reinforced polymer walls as they walked by. The second inmate appeared to be in a catatonic state and was huddled in the corner of his cell. The third inmate had drawn some weird circles on the floor of his cell, but with what, Tom couldn't guess. He had his hands raised in the air and was chanting something, but the walls were soundproof, so Tom and Kiania couldn't understand what was being said.

When they finally came to Juno's cell, they found her asleep on her cot. A moment later, she smiled, opened her eyes, and looked right at them. Tom hadn't seen Juno since she escaped justice, and being this close to her made his skin crawl, even if there was a reinforced polymer barrier between them. Juno stood up, tossed her hair, and walked over to the intercom. Even after being riddled with bullets and spending years in the nuthouse, she still looked like a pop star, only now the mask had been lifted. Tom could see the sadistic hunger behind her soulless eyes. Those eyes darted back and forth between him and Kiania.

When Juno spoke, her voice was raspy, presumably from disuse.

"What's this, a conjugal visit? I don't think it's my birthday."

Tom didn't let the image enter his mind. Juno kept smiling.

"I see you two are still drawn to each other like magnets. But you haven't done the deed with the seed yet?"

Juno turned her head so all her attention was focused on Tom.

"Are you waiting until she finally joins the FBI? If she's got her bachelor's degree, that's still at least two years away."

Tom didn't respond.

"You really have got a lid on it, don't you, my dear Teddy Bear? When most people want something, they just take it. I'm sure both of you must've met plenty of other people in college. Why spend the better part of a decade waiting for something that may never come?"

"I don't expect someone like you would be capable of understanding the difference between love and self-indulgence," said Tom.

Juno turned away and chuckled. It wasn't as bad as the laugh she made when she escaped the needle, but it still sent a chill down Tom's spine.

"I heard that Kalin and Lilian tied the knot yesterday. How was the reception? Did anyone catch on fire?"

"Why would you ask that?" said Tom, unable to control himself.

"My dear Teddy Bear, if you browse wedding videos on the internet, you'll see that anything that can go wrong at a wedding will go wrong. Cameramen aren't paying attention to where they're walking and fall in baptismal fonts, people pass out and catch on fire, and in one case, a couple dozen helium balloons fly into powerlines and explode!"

She tried to kill our parents, I wrestled her down a flight of stairs, Kiania shot her three times, and she's talking to us like we're old friends.

"Did you catch the garter?"

Tom put on his best poker face, but Juno saw right through him.

"Well, that's wonderful news. It's a pity you need to wait about two more years."

Juno pressed her bust against the glass.

"I'd offer to help you vent some frustration, but I'm afraid inmates aren't allowed conjugal visits. And if they were, they certainly wouldn't let me have any. Two years ago, one of the new orderlies tried to molest me. I gouged his eyes out and bit his fingers off one by one.".

Kiania had had enough.

"The whole world knows what Kareen wanted. But you didn't even react when I killed her."

Juno was still smiling, but now she showed her teeth.

"I was wondering when you'd get to the reason you came here. Dear Kareen. I must admit, I wasn't sure she was capable of killing her parents that night in Indianapolis, but it's amazing what women will do for you when you make them cum."

Tom didn't need that mental image. He still remembered what he had seen in Kareen's diary.

I don't know how much longer I can keep up this charade. I'm supposed to act like my world is unraveling, but I'm free! I'm in ecstasy! I thought killing my parents would've been harder, but I just thought of our first night together, when my parents were out of town, and how I want nights like that for the rest of my life. All I had to do was stick a needle in both of them, and it was the easiest thing in the world. I now know I can live without my parents, but I can't live without Juno. She says we're not done yet, more people need to die, or else it will look like the Dart Frog accomplished their goal. I'll do whatever I have to do so I can be with her. It doesn't matter what happens to the other people in school. Nothing else in the universe matters, only us.

Kiania continued, undisturbed.

"Why did you kill all those people? Why did you try to kill our parents?"

"You've already got your degree. All you need now is two years of full-time work experience before they accept you at Quantico. You're not writing a paper about me, which means Teddy Tommy here is writing a book. I hope you don't leave out that romantic evening you two shared on New Year's Eve."

All the color drained from Tom's face.

"Don't rip his nose off, Kiania. Nobody told me about it; I was there."

This caught Kiania off guard.

"You were spying on us?"

"It was either that or stay at home watching my aunt get stoned. I remember once when my parents went to check on her. She attacked them, believing them to be chihuahuas that were armed and dangerous."

Tom didn't want to stay here any longer than Kiania.

"Why did you kill all those people?"

Juno never stopped smiling.

"I'll tell you if you both kiss the glass."

Not happening.

Juno waited a whole five minutes.

"You're no fun. Very well, I can't keep any secrets from you, Teddy Bear. Some people have accused me of being possessed by the devil. Some have asked if my parents abused me. Some people even asked if a priest or anyone else molested me. The correct answer is none of the above."

"Why did you kill all those people?" asked Tom, losing his patience.

"There's that word again," replied Juno, showing her teeth as she smiled. "The question isn't why. It's why not? Because God wrote it on the Ten Commandments? I don't know if you've noticed, but people don't want to believe in God or obey his laws anymore. If you tell them their feelings or their opinions are wrong, they refuse to accept it. Hell, in California, it's now legal to kill a baby even if it escapes the womb. As soon as God's laws become inconvenient, they're chucked like a live grenade; and many politicians, priests, and bishops are just too happy to oblige the teeming masses."

"The floor of hell is paved with the skulls of erring priests, with bishops serving as their signposts," quoted Tom.

"You actually paid attention in Sister Joan's class?" laughed Juno. "I guess that makes one of us."

"Two of us," corrected Kiania.

"I killed those people because I felt like it," continued Juno. "And I wanted to see how their children would react to their sudden loss of security. Fred thought he was going to go out and conquer the world. But as soon as Mommy and Daddy snuffed it, the big strong quarterback collapsed like a house of cards. It was priceless."

"You're a monster," said Tom.

"Not according to the powers that be," replied Juno, still smiling. "In a world where feelings justify absolutely everything, the Catholic Church is nothing but a fading light in the dark. I'm just ahead of my time. So you go ahead and write your book, my dear Teddy Bear; it doesn't really matter. The world has chosen my point of view over yours. You can't possibly hope to take on the whole world."

Tom and Kiania turned to leave.

"In the world you will have tribulation, but take courage, I have conquered the world," quoted Kiania.

"We'll see," said Juno.

After they left the asylum, Tom asked Kiania if she wanted coffee, to which she heartily assented; but they didn't talk at all on the drive over. For ten whole minutes, Tom didn't even touch his coffee. He had read Kareen's diary. Kareen had been afraid that she and Juno would get caught, but there had never been any guilt or remorse in her words. He shouldn't have expected anything less from Juno. Even after spending years locked in a box, she seemed to relish in her crimes.

"She tried to kill both our parents, she killed four police officers, orchestrated the deaths of thirteen innocent people, and ate their organs for shits and giggles. And what do our courts do? They let her escape with her life because 'we need to respect other people's choices.' It's enough to make anyone lose faith in the human race."

Kiania held his hand.

"The world is full of horrible people; I learned that when I was only eight. But someone reminded me that there are still good people in this world that are worth protecting."

Juno's words echoed in Tom's ear.

The Catholic Church is nothing but a fading light in the dark.

Political organizations, celebrities, entertainment, food, toy, and tech companies were doing everything in their power to turn people away from Christian values. Tom used to love reading comic books when he was a kid, but he gave them up when the companies that published them started bowing to the enemies of Christ. It was why Tom wanted to make his own comic books, but he didn't know if anyone would care what he had to say. Kiania seemed to read his mind.

"Remember the oath we took at graduation?"

Tom would never forget that day. Thanks to Kareen, he needed to graduate with his arm in a sling. Due to Mark's diminished performance in school, Kiania was class valedictorian. Their school patron, Saint Thomas More, was martyred for defying Henry VIII and the English Reformation. Henry VIII wanted to change the laws of God because he found them inconvenient. Thousands of Catholics were martyred for refusing to renounce their faith. Ultimately, Henry's first wife died, and Anne Boleyn didn't give Henry the son he wanted. Despite this, England never turned back to Catholicism; in the present day, less than ten percent of people in the United Kingdom identified as practicing Christians. For this reason, all Saint Thomas More High School students took a solemn oath at graduation.

We were forged in persecution
Kingdoms, empires, and tyrants come and go.
But the glory of our Lord Jesus Christ will endure forever.
Wherever we go, whatever befalls us,
We swear to uphold true Christian values
and the immutable laws of God.
In days of peace, in nights of war
In safety, in persecution,
Even unto our dying breath!
Christus nobiscum; state![6]

The graduating students promised to ensure that what happened to them that year never happened to anyone else. Jasmine would become a lawyer like her mother, and Kalin would become a police officer like his father. Kiania was going to join the FBI. And now Tom had to do his part.

"I know the world is insane right now, but I still want to have children someday," said Kiania. "We need to make sure that it's a world where Catholic women shouldn't be afraid to bring a child to life."

Five years of being persecuted by the enemies of Christ had taken its toll on Tom, but he also wanted to marry Kiania and start a family with her someday. He couldn't do that if things remained as they were. The Catholic Church was founded on the blood of

---

6   Christ is with us; stand firm!

martyrs, but there were no martyrs today. Too many Catholics were too weak and cowardly to stand up for the immutable laws of God in the face of persecution. Tom didn't know what the future would bring, but his father's words echoed in his ears.

God hates a coward.

If Tom hadn't mustered up the courage to ask Kiania out on the first day of senior year, he wouldn't be in a relationship with her today. If he hadn't mustered up the courage to face Juno on prom night, she would've killed both Kiania's parents and his own. When he got home, he said his daily Rosary, and then he went straight to work on his new comic. Thinking back on his conversation with Juno, he decided to paraphrase Agatha Christie on the first page.

People say their feelings justify everything, but that is not true.

ENDING EXPLAINED

Justice is left howling at the moon. This is the sad and horrifying reality of the world we live in. People don't want to believe in God and they want his laws abolished. People don't want to believe in good and evil, right and wrong; they want to be free to do whatever they want without consequence. For the better part of a decade, I have had to watch helplessly as everything I ever loved was desecrated and destroyed with impunity by the enemies of Christ. But my sorrows are nothing compared to the evil that afflicts the entire Church.

In October 2019, the pagan idol Pachamama was venerated in the Vatican. This was a direct violation of the first and greatest of the Ten Commandments.

"I am the Lord your God. Thou shalt have no other gods before me."

In the Catholic Church, apostasy and heresy are crimes that warrant immediate excommunication, by force of the law itself, at the moment it is contravened. For this offense and others, by all rights, the men responsible should've been forced to resign from their positions in shame. I will go further and say their names should be blotted out from under heaven, which is the only reason I'm not referring to any of them by name. And yet, they walked away, just as the enemies of Christ have walked away from their crimes.

A few months after the Pachamama incident, the Coronavirus pandemic descended on the world. At the height of the pandemic, faithful Catholics couldn't even attend Mass. For years afterward, we couldn't receive the Blood of Christ[7] at Communion for fear of spreading the disease.

In the Bible, whenever the people of Israel turned away from God, he delivered them into the hands of their enemies and afflicted them with all manner of curses. And now history is repeating itself. God's vengeful hand is plainly seen if one simply bothers to open their eyes, and yet the enemies of Christ are no less relentless in their conquest. And the Church is still being led to annihilation by apostates and heretics.

I used to dream of a future where I would share all the wonderful things in life with a family of my own. Now whenever I look to the future, I see only blood and fire. I see a world where faithful Catholics are forced to fade away into the darkness. Our enemies are legion. We Catholics can't take on the whole world when we're too busy fighting in our own house. If the Church is going to survive this dark age of moral relativism and moral insanity, it must be cleansed. The Church needs leaders as well as laymen with the courage and will to stand up to the enemies of Christ, whatever form they take. We cannot be weak, we cannot be negligent, we cannot be incompetent, we cannot be submissive, we cannot be indifferent, we cannot be tolerant, and we cannot be cowardly.

God hates a coward.

Think of my actions what you will, but don't doubt the reality. Passive indifference and willful ignorance will not protect the Catholic Church from extinction.

---

7   "Unless you eat the flesh of the Son of Man and drink his blood, you do not have life within you."

ROBERT CANTER'S PRAYER TO REMOVE CORRUPTION IN THE CATHOLIC CHURCH

Hoshi'a na, El Shaddai

Holy Mary, Mother of God, Mother of Sorrows, Our Lady of Fatima, Our Lady of Lourdes, and Our Lady of Victory, pray for us!

Saint Michael the Archangel, pray for us!

Saint Joseph, Terror of Demons, pray for us!

Saint Peter, pray for us!

Saint John, pray for us!

Saint Andrew, pray for us!

Saint James the Lesser, pray for us!

Saint Jude, pray for us!

Saint Philip, pray for us!

Saint Bartholomew, pray for us!

Saint Matthew, pray for us!

Saint James the Greater, pray for us!

Saint Thaddeus, pray for us!

Saint Simon, pray for us!

Saint Matthias, pray for us!

Saint Paul, pray for us!

Saint John the Baptist, pray for us!

Saint Mary Magdalene, pray for us!

Saint Anthony, Hammer of Heretics, pray for us!

Saint Athanasius, pray for us!

Saint Augustine, pray for us!

Saint Pius X, pray for us!
Saint Thomas More, pray for us!
Saint Charles Lwanga, pray for us!
Saint Thomas Aquinas, pray for us!
Saint Bernadette, pray for us!
Saint Teresa of Calcutta, pray for us!
Sister Lucia of Fatima, pray for us!

Lord Jesus Christ, only begotten Son of the Almighty Father, Lord of Heaven and Earth, and all things under the Earth. Accept this our humble prayer of reparation. Deliver us from this dark age of moral relativism, moral insanity, and self-indulgence. Make your glory known in the destruction of the wicked. Cleanse your Holy Church on Earth from the heresy, blasphemy, and apostasy that now corrupts it, as you cleansed the temple in Jerusalem.

(Recite the Rosary)

How to pray the Rosary
(To be prayed using the standard Rosary)

Recite the **Joyful** Mysteries on Monday and Saturday, the Luminous Mysteries on Thursday, the Sorrowful Mysteries on Tuesday and Friday, and the **Glorious Mysteries** on Wednesday and Sunday (with this exception; Sundays of Advent and Christmas – the **Joyful Mysteries**; Sundays of Lent – the **Sorrowful Mysteries**)

1. Make the Sign of the Cross.
2. On the crucifix and say the "Apostles' Creed"
3. On the first bead, say the "Our Father"
4. On the next three beads, say three "Hail Marys"
5. One next bead Say the "Glory Be"

6. Announce the First Mystery and then say the "Our Father"
7. Moving counter clockwise along the beads, say ten "Hail Marys" while meditating on the Mystery
8. Say the "Glory Be"
9. Say the "O My Jesus" prayer
10. Announce the Next Mystery; then say the "Our Father" and repeat these steps (6 through 8) as you continue through the remaining Mysteries.
11. Say the closing prayers: the "Hail Holy Queen" and "Final Prayer"
12. Make the Sign of the Cross

Joyful Mysteries: The Annunciation, The Visitation, The Nativity, The Presentation, The Finding of Jesus in the Temple

The Luminous Mysteries: The Baptism of the Lord, The Wedding at Cana, The Proclamation of the Kingdom, The Transfiguration, The Institution of the Eucharist

The Sorrowful Mysteries: The Agony in the Garden, The Scourging at the Pillar, The Crowing with Thorns, The Carrying of the Cross, The Crucifixion and Death of Jesus.

The Glorious Mysteries: The Resurrection, The Ascension, The Descent of the Holy Spirt, The Assumption of Mary, The Crowning of Mary as Queen of Heaven and Earth.

The Apostles Creed
I believe in God, the Father almighty creator of heaven and earth and in Jesus Christ, His only Son, our Lord, who was conceived by the Holy Spirit, born of the Virgin Mary, suffered under Pontius Pilate, was crucified, died, and was buried. He descended into hell.

On the third day he rose again from the dead. He ascended into heaven and is seated at the right hand of God, the Father almighty. He will come again in glory to judge the living and the dead. I believe in the Holy Spirit, the Holy Catholic Church, the communion of saints, the forgiveness of sins, the resurrection of the body, and life everlasting. Amen.

Our Father
Our Father, who art in heaven hallowed be thy name; thy kingdom come; thy will be done on earth as it is in heaven. Give us this day our daily bread and forgive us our trespasses as we forgive those who trespass against us; and lead us not into temptation, but deliver us from evil. Amen.

The Hail Mary
Hail Mary, full of grace. The Lord is with thee. Blessed art thou among women, and blessed is the fruit of thy womb, Jesus. Holy Mary, Mother of God, Pray for us sinners, Now and at the hour of our death. Amen.

The Glory Be
Glory be to the Father, and to the Son, and to the Holy Spirit. As it was in the beginning, is now, and ever shall be, world without end. Amen.

O my Jesus
O my Jesus, forgive us our sins. Save us from the fires of hell. Lead all souls into heaven, especially those in most need of thy mercy. Amen.

Hail Holy Queen
Hail Holy Queen, Mother of Mercy, our Life, our Sweetness, and our Hope. To thee we cry, poor banished children of Eve. To thee we

send up our sighs, mourning and weeping in this vale of tears. Turn then most gracious advocate, thine eyes of mercy toward us, and after this, our exile, show unto us, the blessed fruit of thy womb, Jesus. O clement, O loving, O sweet Virgin Mary. Pray for us O Holy Mother of God, that we may be made worthy of the promises of Christ. Amen.

Final Prayer

Let us pray. O God, whose only begotten Son, by His life, death, and resurrection, has purchased for us the rewards of eternal life, grant, we beseech Thee, that meditating upon these mysteries of the Most Holy Rosary of the Blessed Virgin Mary, we may imitate what they contain and obtain what they promise, through the same Christ Our Lord. Amen.

MORE BOOKS BY ROBERT CANTER

The Shadow Angel: Genesis

Monsters are real. Though most of the world lives in a state of blissful ignorance, there are things that go bump in the night. The only thing that stands between mankind and the monsters that plague the Earth is Daniel Adrian Angeleschu, The Shadow Angel. His soul locked in perpetual servitude, Danny has served as the Vatican's greatest monster hunter for five hundred years. Now his mission brings him to South Bend, Indiana, and it's bound to be an assignment he'll never forget.

The True Story of Mrs. Claus

The whole world knows the legend of Santa Claus, but few people realize that he wouldn't be able to do what he does without the help of his beloved wife. If you don't know the truth about Santa and Mrs. Claus, I'd say it's time you learned.

Printed in the USA
CPSIA information can be obtained
at www.ICGtesting.com
JSHW020820280724
67111JS00001B/27